BLOOD POLITICS

BOOK FOUR OF THE BLOOD DESTINY SERIES

HELEN HARPER

CHAPTER ONE

DARK MIST SNAKED AROUND MY ANKLES, THEN CURLED UPWARDS into the still night air. From somewhere to my left there was a rumbling bellow that sent rippling chills down my spine. Both my hands, slick with damp sweat, clutched onto silver throwing daggers while painful burning heat coursed through my veins.

There was a rustling to my right. I flicked a glance over to the shadowy copse of looming trees, and shifted my weight imperceptibly, ready to meet head on whatever was about to appear. The bellow sounded again, closer this time, but the danger in the small forest was more pressing. The cracking and heaving of falling boughs and branches indicated the imminent arrival of the beast, and a faint green glow sparked up from my hands in anticipation. I side-stepped, trying to gain a better vantage point.

The pain in my shoulder had increased from a dull ache to sharp sear, making it difficult to continue to grip the daggers. I tightened my fingers, and waited, trying to ignore it. The crashing sounds got louder and I could now see the giant oaks leaning and falling as my foe cleared a path for itself. A tinge of cloudy red seeped across my vision and I blinked several times in quick succession, attempting to clear it, then, when that didn't help, shook my head in short, sharp staccato movements. It didn't work.

I cursed inwardly and hunched down slightly, hoping that by making myself smaller, I'd have more of a chance to surprise the creature and gain the advantage. No such luck though. Just before it reached the edge of the tree line, it stopped, the more vertiginous tips of the oaks swaying unnaturally. There was a snort from within the tall dark shapes and my eyes lifted upwards, noting the height of the cloud of exhaled breath. Fuck. This thing was big.

The pair of us stood there in silence for one quiet moment, each facing the other through the veil of night and shadowy trees. A brief thought skittered through my mind, but I pushed it away before it could fully form. Whatever this thing was it was dangerous and I couldn't allow myself to be distracted now.

Then it moved, with more silent grace than I would really have thought possible for a beast of its apparent size, and from the edge of the canopy a shape began to appear. Through the haze of red as yet marring my vision, I still couldn't work out what manner of nastie it truly was, even when one large clawed foot lifted itself out from under the cover of the trees and planted itself onto the dark earth in front of me. Its deadly talons gleamed.

A shot of uncontrollable pain lanced through my shoulder and I cried out involuntarily, dropping the dagger from my left hand. Goddamnit. There was no time to scoop the weapon back up, however, as a second scaly foot joined the first. I looked upwards, slowly, my eyes tracking the rest of the thing's body as it emerged. It was fucking huge – to the point where I had to crane my neck upwards to get a proper look at it. A drop of something landed on my face. Disgusted, thinking it was slimy drool, I reached my now dagger-less hand up to wipe it away. Except it wasn't saliva – it was blood. I looked up again and realised that something was hanging from the creature's mouth. Twisting my head, I tried vainly to work out what it was. The beast, as if trying to please me, helpfully leaned down, allowing me to begin to make out what the blood-sodden shape actually was.

There was a clump of dark material dangling lifelessly from within its jaws, like a bunched up ballgown. Who on earth would be wearing that much in the middle of summer? I squinted further, catching sight of pale skin at the edge, cocking my head to get a better view. Whoever the unfortunate victim was, they were most definitely dead, as even though I couldn't make out their face, their neck was skewed at a horrifyingly unnatural angle.

I jumped slightly as there was another earth-shattering roar from behind. The creature in front shifted its weight, fixing one giant yellow dragon-like eye on me. I leaned forward and prodded the lifeless thing in its mouth, feeling the clammy skin of the dead. My movements disturbed it, however, and it flopped forward towards me. It was a man - his mouth was open in a silent shriek, but his eyes were covered with an unmistakeable caul. Thomas. The agony in my shoulder increased and the cloud of red across my eyes deepened to a vivid scarlet, and I screamed.

* * *

I WOKE, my whole body covered in a sheen of cold sweat, and a sheet wrapped constrictingly round my legs and torso. Lying there for a moment, heart thudding painfully in my chest, I blinked away the hot tears and swallowed hard. Then I pulled myself together and extricated my limbs from the damp cotton, getting out of bed to yank an over-sized t-shirt over my head and pad to the bathroom. I flicked on the light, wincing at its brightness, turned on the tap and scooped up cold water to splash over my face.

I reached over for a towel, patting my skin dry, then stared into the small mirror. I looked pale, with heavy dark rings under my eyes that appeared in stark contrast to the rest of my skin.

Sighing, I ran my fingers through my now almost shoulder-length hair, and tried not to think any more about Thomas. Instead, I curled my nails into my palms and gritted my teeth, and stalked into the kitchen.

My mouth was almost painfully dry so I yanked open the fridge door and pulled out a carton of orange juice, then drank deeply from it, without bothering to get myself a glass. I had virtually drained the entire thing when there was a sudden sharp knock at the door that caused me to swallow the wrong way and start choking and spluttering, juice flying out of my mouth in all directions. I wiped the back of my hand across my face, trying to get the worst of the citrus smears off, then cursed irritably to myself and reached out for a cloth to wipe down the juice spattered fridge. The knocking continued, more insistent now. I ignored it.

Come on, kitten, open up. I know you're in there and you're awake.

I continued dabbing at the dribbles of the juice that had managed to somehow cover half of my small kitchen, and didn't bother to answer the annoying Voice in my head.

Corrigan's fist against my door increased in both tempo and volume, a drumbeat to some silent tune of annoyance that only he knew how to create. I wanted him to go away so I go crawl back to bed and try to get some real sleep.

Mackenzie...

There was a warning note in his Voice now that did nothing more than irritate me. Who did he think he was coming round here in the middle of the night? Surely the bloody Lord Alpha of all the sodding stupid shifters had better things to do with his time?

I heard a door bang in the flat above me. Great, now he'd woken up the neighbours. I'd only moved in four days ago, it was hardly time to start pissing them off just yet.

Fuck off, Corrigan. I am trying to sleep.

No, you're not.

He gave up on knocking and began thumping on the door instead. Jeez. It wouldn't surprise me if someone called the freaking police at this rate. Rolling my eyes in exhausted exasperation, I put down the cloth and walked out the kitchen and towards the front door. I was just reaching for the handle to open it, when there was a loud splintering noise and I jumped backwards while the whole door burst open with a crash. On the doorstep in front, leg only just lowering, stood Corrigan, looking terribly pleased.

I stared at him aghast. "You kicked open my fucking door?"

He grinned at me ferally. "I had to make sure you were alright, kitten. You were screaming in my head." He licked his lips. "It was...disturbing."

Screaming in his head? Oh shit. That meant that I'd reached out and called for him in the throes of my nightmare. Then I thought for a second. "Hold on a minute. I only woke up five minutes ago and you live on the other side of the city." I put my hands on my hips and cocked my head at him. "You might be fast, my Lord, but you're not Superman. What were you doing hanging around this part of town?"

Corrigan had the grace to look at least slightly abashed, but he was saved from answering as there was the unmistakable sound of a door upstairs opening and heavy footsteps walking down the narrow staircase towards us. A moment later a heavy-set man appeared in blue-striped pyjamas appeared, cricket bat gripped in his hands.

He waved it threateningly in Corrigan's direction and spoke gruffly. "What the hell is going on here?"

The Lord Alpha held up both his hands, palms turned outwards. "Nothing to worry about, sir. I'm sorry if I woke you up."

My neighbour glanced down towards me, taking in the destroyed door, then flicked a glance back at Corrigan. "Doesn't look like nothing to me. You upsetting this lady?"

I felt a surge of warmth towards him, and cleared my throat.

5

"Everything's fine. I know this guy. He just, er,..." My voice trailed off. Just what? Kicked in my door because he's a were-panther psycho control freak?

Fortunately, Corrigan's wits were somewhat more sharp than mine at this time of night and he stepped in to rescue me. "My friend, here," he laid heavy emphasis on the word 'friend' so that there was no mistaking his meaning, "has diabetes. When she didn't answer her phone or the door I grew worried that she'd fallen into insulin shock." He smiled disarmingly. "You can't be too careful, you know."

My neighbour looked at me for confirmation, so I nodded mutely, trying not to look pissed off that Corrigan was trying to insinuate that we were in some kind of romantic relationship. The idiot probably thought that he was marking his territory when I'd already made it pretty clear that I didn't need or want him around. Well, I didn't need him at least. And as for the want part, I was sure that would pass soon.

I found my voice. "Honestly, everything's fine. I'm so sorry that we woke you up." I shot a hard look at Corrigan. "It won't happen again. I appreciate you checking though."

The man's grip on the cricket bat relaxed. "Any time, Miss. I'm just upstairs if you need anything. Flat 3D."

I smiled at him as he shot me a meaningful look, then watched as he turned and walked back upstairs. Once I was sure he was safely back inside his own apartment, with the door closed, I looked back at Corrigan and glared.

"Four fucking days!" I hissed. "And already the neighbours think I'm some kind of nocturnal weirdo with crazy friends. Speaking of friends, what the hell was it that you were trying to suggest anyway?"

He shrugged. "Well, we have been on a date already, kitten. You know it's only a matter of time." His chipped emerald eyes gleamed at me with promise lurking in their depths.

My mouth went dry. "Piss off. I told you that I don't need you and that I want to do this alone."

"At least for now."

"Huh?"

"That's what you said," Corrigan replied tolerantly. "You need to do this alone, whatever 'this' is, at least for now."

He was throwing back the words that I'd said to him at the mages' academy after Thomas had been killed by the wraith. And after I'd shifted into the dragon that I now kept having nightmares about. I stared at him, nonplussed.

"I am a patient man, kitten," Corrigan continued. "I can wait until you've come to terms with what you are."

I rubbed my eyes tiredly. It was too fucking late – or too fucking early depending on which way you wanted to look at it – to be dealing with this now. "I am at terms with what I am."

"Sure you are. That's why you're having nightmares." Corrigan's gaze fell onto my now destroyed door. "Come back to the keep with me. You can't stay here now that anyone can waltz in without so much as a by-your-leave."

"Yeah? And whose fucking fault is that?"

Corrigan opened his mouth to speak but he was interrupted by yet another voice. "The keep is a long way off. Don't worry, I will keep watch and make sure that you're not interrupted again."

I looked over, surprised, and realised that leaning against the shadows was a Fae. Corrigan growled.

"Who the hell are you?" I snapped.

The Fae stepped out into the dim light of the corridor. "You can call me Beltran, although really my name is unimportant. Her Majesty has asked me to ensure that you are undisturbed." His violet eyes flicked to Corrigan. "You are disturbing her."

My mouth dropped open. Un-freaking-believable. All I needed now was for a bloody mage to show up and start waving around sparks of magic in my so-called defense and my night would be complete.

"There's a witch waiting outside. I can always exhort her to cast a ward so that nothing may pass over the threshold,"

7

Beltran continued without a trace of apparent emotion in his voice.

I rolled my eyes. Everything was now becoming suddenly clear. This had nothing to do with Corrigan fancying a little midnight flirt or wanting to make sure I was alright after my nightmare. This was about some kind of stupid power play between the faeries, the mages and the shifters, with me as the unwilling prize. Well, they could all just fuck off. Despite my tiredness, flames of exasperated heat were uncoiling themselves within the pit of my stomach.

Corrigan took a step towards the Fae. "Miss Mackenzie does not require your assistance. Do you even know who I am?"

Oh, for Christ's sake. He didn't really just say that, did he?

Beltran took a step towards Corrigan and sneered. "Am I supposed to be scared of a little pussy cat?"

Every sinew of the Lord Alpha's muscular frame stiffened and dark patches of fur began to spring out on his uncovered arms. This had the potential to end very, very badly.

"Okay, boys," I said, stepping between the two of them. "It's the middle of the night. You've already woken up my neighbours once. Let's call it quits so that I can go back to bed."

The pair of them continued to eyeball each other over my head. I raised my voice. "I mean it. You two need to fuck off now because I'm getting annoyed. And you won't like me when I'm angry."

Corrigan muttered something under his breath that I didn't quite catch. I ignored him pointedly. "Leave. Now."

The Fae moved his gaze from Corrigan down to me. Something flickered in his eyes and he bowed. "As you wish." He moved back, melting away into the darkness.

I turned round to face Corrigan. "You too."

He opened his mouth to speak, but I made a face at him. "It's a dangerous day when I'm the calm one, Corrigan. I want to get some uninterrupted sleep and that Fae will be back in a heartbeat if you don't leave too." I looked over at the splintered door frame. "And I think I can take care of myself, don't you?"

"Of that I have no doubt, kitten."

"Then please go," I said quietly.

He sighed, then reached out and brushed away some hair from my face. I tried hard not to flinch at his warm touch. "As you wish. But," his eyes grew hard for a moment, "call me if you need anything."

"Of course." Not a chance, buster.

He stood there for a heartbeat longer, unfathomless emotion in his eyes, before blinking languidly and smoothly stepping past me into the night.

Sweet dreams.

As if. I squeezed myself into my flat, trying to avoid knocking the door that was now hanging off its hinges, then grabbed a wooden chair and propped it carefully against the knob to hold it shut. Cursing the Otherworld in general, I stomped back off to bed.

CHAPTER TWO

IT WAS LATE WHEN I FINALLY AWOKE AGAIN. SUNLIGHT WAS streaming in annoyingly through a gap in the curtains and hitting the side of my face. I groaned slightly to myself, wondering whether the events of the night before had just been a product of my imagination. However, when I finally managed to get myself out of bed and check, it became apparent that unfortunately they'd been real. I stared mournfully at my broken door for a moment, hoping that my new landlord wasn't planning to make any surprise visits to check on his new tenant before I managed to get it fixed.

Possession-less as I virtually was, the flat itself was rather bare. It came supplied with a few basics: a sofa, a bed, a kitchen table and chairs – one of which was currently keeping the front door closed – and very little else. I'd not even had time to stock the cupboards yet, and the absence of coffee was grating on me. I made a mental note to make sure that I managed to leave work in time this evening to buy a proper coffee machine and some of South America's finest, then shrugged on my usual uniform of jeans and a dark t-shirt and picked up my backpack on my way out. At least there was nothing worth stealing inside the flat, I figured ruefully, as I left the door hanging precariously against the frame. Corrigan still had a hell of a lot to answer for though.

The bookshop was a short ten minute walk away, and I knew from my previous strolls back and forth that there was a small coffee shop along the way. I checked my watch and decided that there was time to pick up a triple espresso. Opening day wasn't until next week and, while there was a hell of a lot to still get ready before then, at least being a bit late wouldn't cause too many problems. When I emerged from the shop, one coffee and one foul-smelling herbal tea clutched in my hands, there were prickles against the back of my neck and, without turning round to check, I knew that I was being watched. It was hardly rocket science to work out where I was going though, so I did my best to ignore them and continued forward. If those idiots had nothing better to do than follow me round all day, then that was up to them.

The new, improved, and somewhat displaced, Clava Books was situated along a busy London thoroughfare. I'd suggested to Mrs. Alcoon that we should change the name – after all its namesake, the Clava Cairns, was on the other side of the country – but she'd insisted on keeping it the same. After ensuring that she could never return to Inverness by burning down the original and making everyone think that she'd died inside it, I could hardly argue. We'd been fortunate enough to be able to take over the lease of the new building thanks to some generous compensation from the mages. I had the distinct feeling that it was my good books they were trying to stay in, rather than Mrs. Alcoon's, but she deserved something after her livelihood and home had been ripped out from under her so I'd kept quiet and let her take the money. She was living in the small flat above the shop and, even though we hadn't officially opened yet and therefore had no profits to speak of, there was enough left over to pay me a wage to cover my own expenses.

The bell tinkled as I pushed open the door, announcing my arrival. Mrs. Alcoon's lilting Scottish voice drifted over a greeting to me from behind a towering pile of boxes. "Mackenzie, dear, are you quite alright?"

"Sure, Mrs. Alcoon, I'm fine."

Her head popped up, and her eyes regarded me seriously. "You should see a doctor, you know, dear. That might help you to sleep better."

Mrs. Alcoon wasn't exactly a mage, but she did possess some weak Divination powers that allowed her moments of prescience and insight. Clearly this was one of those moments.

"Honestly, I'm fine," I repeated, reassuring her. I lifted up the tea. "Here, I brought you a drink."

She beamed at me, and stood up so I could pass it over to her. "Oh, you are wonderful. You should really have gotten another cup though as I think we're going to have a helper with us today."

I frowned at her, puzzled.

"The March-Mage called. He's sending over his best librarian to give us a hand with getting ready."

I grinned. "You mean the Arch-Mage?"

She waved a dismissive hand in the air. "Oh, yes, Arch-Mage, sorry. A lot of this Otherworld stuff is very new to me, you know, dear. It's difficult to get all the names right."

Technically speaking, no humans (even those with minor powers) were allowed to know about the Otherworld, and its denizens did a good job of keeping it secret. However, considering that there had been no sensible explanation other than the truth as to why Mrs. Alcoon had lost months of her life in a coma, coupled with the fact that her slight Divination skills had already picked up on my Draco Wyr heritage beforehand, pretending otherwise had seemed pointless. Thankfully, the mages had seemed to agree and I'd had no disagreement about revealing the whole truth to her from any other quarter either.

To be fair to the older lady, she'd dealt with all of the revelations remarkably well. She had known about the existence of the Ministry for years before I'd met her though. I gave her a suspicious look and wondered whether her 'mistake' had been deliberate. She blinked back at me innocently. Hmmm.

A thought struck me. "Hold on, he said his best librarian?"

Mrs. Alcoon sipped her tea. "Yes, dear."

Uh-oh. If that was who I thought it was going to be, then Mrs. Alcoon's mettle was going to be tested more than both either she or I had anticipated. I shrugged mentally. She was made of stern stuff; she'd cope. I flipped open the plastic lid to my coffee and took a large gulp, scalding the sides of my throat, then placed my cup to one side and got to work.

The bookshelves were already in place, and we'd spent the previous week giving the walls a coat of inoffensive cream paint, and the wooden floor a fresh varnish. Now all that really remained was to sort out the stock. I reached over into the nearest box and began pulling out books, ready to put them into order on the shelves. I'd managed to convince Mrs. Alcoon that Gaelic tomes weren't going to draw in much of an audience here in London although she'd vetoed the idea of going mainstream and selling bestsellers. Instead we were touting ourselves as a 'New Age' bookstore. In essence that meant all manner of Otherworld-based books, along with some make-believe human versions. The colourful book on top of the pile proclaimed itself as 'Crystal Wisdom: How to harness the power of gemstones to change YOUR life'. Yeah, that would be a human one then. I started two piles: one fit for normal public consumption that we would place near the front of the store, and one for the more discerning Otherworld customer, that would be somewhat hidden towards the back. I also started my own secretive pile that I hid surreptitiously behind me, ready to stuff into my backpack later. I'd sneaked a couple of vampire books into the purchase order for my own perusal and, while I was sure that Mrs. Alcoon wouldn't have minded me ordering a few books for myself, I was fairly confident that she wouldn't be impressed with my reasons as to why I'd ordered those particular ones. Aubrey and his little vampire friends still had a lot to answer for after their actions at the mage academy that had inadvertently caused the death of my friends. I wasn't about to forget what they'd done and, somehow or other, I was going to make them pay.

Before too long, I was surrounded by books. I rested back on my haunches for a second, looking around. I barely seemed to have made a dent in the boxes that packed the floor space. This was going to take some time. I was just reaching out for the next box, when there was a snap and crackle in the air. Looking up, I noted the purple shimmer, idly wondering to myself if there was a way to prevent the mages from dropping in unannounced whenever they wished. Not that I disliked them or didn't want their custom, but I wasn't really particularly keen on the idea that they could show up whenever and wherever they wanted to. I'd have to do some investigating to find out. There had to be a mystical version of a doorbell that we could somehow install.

"Dear? The air is humming and looking really rather peculiar," called out Mrs. Alcoon from the other side of the store.

"I think that'll be your helpful librarian," I commented.

I hadn't even finished my sentence when a familiar chubby figure came fluttering heavily through the portal. While I, of course, would have been throwing up all over the newly varnished floor, Slim irritatingly appeared none the worse for his travels.

"Fecking hell. Is this it?" the little gargoyle exclaimed.

I flicked a glance over at Mrs. Alcoon, who was blinking rapidly. "Goodness," she murmured.

"Can't fecking believe I've been made to come all this way for a little shop. Fecking humans." Slim wheeled round in the air and fixed a beady eye on me. "Not that you're human, you weird fecker."

"Good to see you too, Slim," I smiled.

As the steely custodian of the library in the mages' academy, Slim clearly knew all about what happened back in February when I'd shifted into a dragon and killed Tryyl, the wraith that had left destruction and devastation in its wake. The Arch-Mage had assured me that he had placed a geas – an oath – on all the witnesses so that my real identity wouldn't go any further. I was somewhat skeptical but could do little about it now. It wasn't as if I could go around threatening the entire Ministry, even if I did apparently have the ability to transform into a fire-breathing beast. I hadn't actually tried to shift again since that terrible day.

The dragon form had so completely taken over my consciousness, and had been so consumed by the blinkered desire for violence, that I was kind of afraid to attempt it. I had discovered that I liked being in control of emotions. I supposed it was rather ironic that it was Thomas, whose death had caused me to lose all that control, who had taught me to feel that way.

Mrs. Alcoon found her voice. "Well, this simply will not do, Mr Slim. It will not do at all."

Uh oh. I watched the older woman warily. Maybe she wasn't going to cope with being confronted by a flying purple gargoyle with a penchant for old books quite as well as I'd thought. She lifted a single finger in his direction.

"Do not move," she stated firmly, then disappeared underneath the counter and began rummaging around in something, before standing back up and brandishing a flowery yellow headscarf. Mrs. Alcoon held it up in front of her face and squinted sideways at Slim. "Yes, this will suit nicely, I think."

Slim's eyes narrowed suspiciously. I watched, thoroughly amused, as she carefully picked her way around the boxes until she was directly in front of him. Then she reached out around his waist and, in one swift motion, tied the scarf around his middle, knotting it at the side and hiding his naked nether regions.

"What the feck are you doing?" screeched Slim, short arms scrabbling down to his side trying to snatch off the offending piece of fabric.

"Mr. Slim," Mrs. Alcoon began in a patient voice, "Mackenzie and I are most grateful to have your assistance and we do hope that you convey that thought to your March-Mage. However, flying around here with your bits hanging out all day long simply will not do." She fixed him with a beaming smile. "It's simply too distracting. I'm sure you understand." She patted him on the shoulder. "Now, can I get you some tea perhaps?"

Slim gaped at her, then stared down at himself. The clash between the yellow of the scarf and his purple skin was really rather extraordinary. I couldn't help myself: a tiny snort escaped me, causing the gargoyle to spin round in the air and snarl.

I tried to look serious, and failed. "It suits you, Slim, it really does. I think yellow is definitely your colour."

"You can fecking shut your trap," he hissed.

"Mr. Slim," repeated Mrs. Alcoon, "would you like some tea?"

He muttered an affirmative reply, not looking at her.

For her part, she smiled at him benignly. "Then I'll be right back." She disappeared off into the small kitchenette at the back of the shop.

As soon as she'd gone, Slim jabbed a stubby finger in my direction. "If you fecking tell anyone else about this, anyone at all..."

I grinned. "My lips are sealed."

He stared at me suspiciously, then grunted unhappy acquiescence. "Well, let's get to work. Sooner I get out of this fecking hell hole and away from that crazy woman the better."

* * *

WITH SLIM'S HELP, the process of unpacking the books and sorting them out became much faster. He had a few choice words about our selection, muttering away to himself whenever he came across a particularly New Age endowed human text, but I had to admit that he knew his stuff and was able to arrange the piles much more efficiently and knowledgeably than I could. It helped, of course, that he didn't get distracted by every third book like I did, and feel compelled to sit down and read a chapter of it. When Mrs. Alcoon brought out his tea, he sniffed at it warily before taking a tiny sip. I stopped what I was doing and watched, waiting for him to spit it back out again, but instead a curious spasm crossed his face and he said nothing else. He ended up drinking the entire thing, causing me no end of surprise. For once, however, I wisely kept my mouth shut.

By the time it was midday, everything was unpacked and in piles around the floor, and I was depositing the flattened cardboard boxes outside, ready to be collected for recycling. I'd managed to drop the vampire books into my backpack without the others noticing, and planned to read through them carefully at my leisure later on. I designated myself to go out and pick up some sandwiches for lunch, hoping that it was safe to leave the pair of them behind on their own. Certainly Slim could hardly go wandering about the streets of London, and I didn't trust that Mrs. Alcoon would manage to bring back anything edible. Hungry as I was, there seemed little other choice.

I turned left out of the shop, thinking that I'd wander down to the small supermarket on the corner and pick up some crusty bread and perhaps a rotisserie chicken if they had any left. As I did so, a tiny movement caught my eye from across the street. I paused mid-step, thinking for a moment, then continued, keeping careful watch on the busy road next to me. I deliberately slowed my steps, making it appear to the entire world as if I were simply out for a relaxed stroll in the daytime sun, and counted down in my head.

I'd timed it perfectly. As soon as I reached the crossroads, the traffic signal changed to green and the stream of cars revved up and continued on their journeys, effectively blocking anyone from crossing over to my side of the street. As soon as that happened, without turning my head, I turned left down the street and away from my watchers, and began to run. I pelted down the pavement, dodging passersby. There was a hairy moment when I almost got entangled with the lead of a small terrier that was tied up to a nearby lamppost and began barking at me, but I managed to leap over it, then twist left again down a small alley that led along the back of all the shops, parallel to the direction I'd just come. The faint smell of urine and rotting rubbish reached my nostrils, reminding me that on my list of things to do was finding some time to clear out the back of the bookshop so that at least we could avoid having any unpleasant whiffs drift in and bother the customers. For now, however, I ignored it and continued to sprint, this time unencumbered by pedestrians, until I reached the end when I turned left again out onto the street and up to the same busy road that I'd originally been on, albeit a few hundred metres back from where I'd started.

Now that I was to the rear of my trackers, I was in a position to find out exactly who it was wasting their time following me around. I still didn't really care whether they were there or not, but I was curious who the might and power of the Otherworld had decided to send to babysit me. The first one was easy to spot, not just because she was frantically searching up the street for me, but because I also knew her. I hadn't been naïve enough to presume that Corrigan himself would spend his entire time following me around, the previous night's encounter notwithstanding, but I still felt the slightest twinge of disappointment that it was Lucy, the honeybadger shifter with the appetite of a horse who I'd first met in Cornwall, and not the Lord Alpha himself. Telling myself that I felt that way just because I'd wanted to prove that I could give Corrigan the slip without even breaking into a sweat, I dismissed her, and looked for the others.

Where Lucy had by now managed to start crossing the road, the other two were still standing on the opposite side, about halfway down the block. It was apparent that the reason they'd not started to come after me was due to the fact that they were starting to come after each other. They were facing each other, clearly squaring off, while the shoppers nearby gave them a wide berth and more than a few nervous glances. I chuckled to myself, and leaned backwards slightly to get a better look. The mage, not anyone I'd previously encountered, had his back to me, but his profession was recognisable thanks to his odd attire. It seemed to be de rigeur that as soon as mages made it out of the academy, they ended up in attention-grabbing clothing that proclaimed their distinct personalities as loudly as possible. Having spent barely a couple of months wearing the constricting mage uniform myself, I didn't blame them. This particular specimen was wearing shocking pink neon jeans and a green t-shirt, with some kind of floppy hat perched on his head. Clearly, staying unobtrusive wasn't high on the mages' list of intentions and I wondered what it said about me that they didn't care that I'd know I was being followed. It seemed likely that it was more about making sure that the shifters and the faeries knew he was there than anything else.

I watched as he reached over to the Fae opposite him and gave him a tiny shove. Apparently Beltran still hadn't been relieved of his duty yet. He leaned in towards the mage and flicked him on the nose. I snickered. Despite my amusement, however, the tension in both their bodies was clear; their mutual hatred was visible even from across the crowded street.

"Quite a show they're putting on," commented a voice next to me, making me jump.

I cursed myself for being so wrapped up in the proceedings that were unfolding between Beltran and the mage that I'd not been paying attention to what was nearby, and glanced over at the owner of the voice, before immediately relaxing. It was a slight, bespectacled chap who I'd never seen before, but who clearly was about as dangerous as a tub of margarine.

"Mmm," I murmured agreement.

"Do you think I should call the police?" he asked, with a slightly anxious tone.

That probably wasn't a good idea. "Oh, I'm sure they'll sort it out themselves," I said reassuringly. "There's no point in escalating the situation further." Or getting the human police wrapped up in affairs of the Otherworld at least.

I continued to watch the pair of them, wondering whether I should intervene and nip their posturing in the bud. Before I could make a decision either way, however, Lucy reappeared next to them. She gesticulated irritably in my direction. I guessed that my scent had finally given me away, and wondered if it would be worth my while getting in touch with Julia to see if she could make me up some masking lotion in case of future encounters. I discarded the idea as pointless almost immediately. Corrigan could contact me whenever he wanted through the Voice, the mages just needed to set up a simple Divination spell if they wanted to find me and, if I allowed a single drop of blood to fall, the Fae – well, Solus anyway - would know exactly where I was. It highlighted how ridiculous the whole notion of them all following me around really was.

Beltran and the mage turned towards me, frowning.

"You know them?" The man beside me asked, with a curious note in his voice.

"Not exactly," I answered, smiling at him politely and hoping he'd continue on his way. Fortunately, he seemed to get the message as he smiled back and nodded, then made to cross the road himself.

Lucy, Beltran and the mage were all staring at me so I gave them a grin and a little wave. None of them looked particularly happy. I shrugged. That was hardly my concern. My stomach rumbled, reminding me why I was outside in the first place. My original curiosity satisfied, I headed back down the street to finally pick up some lunch.

CHAPTER THREE

When I eventually made it back to Clava Books, the bell on the door signalling my return, Mrs. Alcoon and Slim were in the midst of a full throated discussion.

"Dear, the alchemy collection needs to go at the front. "

"Don't fecking call me dear. And you can't put it at the front." Slim put his hands on his flower wrapped hips. "It's not for human consumption. It needs to be kept at the back for the real readers."

Mrs. Alcoon raised her eyebrows. "So humans aren't real readers?"

"You know what I fecking mean," he grumbled loudly. "Those books are dangerous. You can't just let anyone get their hands on them."

"And why not? The number of people, human or otherwise, who genuinely possess the ability to make any kind of use out of these books is miniscule. Anyone who purchases them is doing so out of curiosity, not out of some bizarre need to turn objects into gold."

"Are you fecking mad, woman?" Slim screeched. "Alchemy is not about turning things into gold. It's much more complex than that." His wings flapped, indicating his annoyance. "We should have kept you in fecking stasis when we had the chance."

I cleared my throat before things got out of hand. They both turned and glared at me.

"Mackenzie, dear, you've been gone a terribly long time."

"Sorry," I said with a trace of guilt, realising belatedly that leaving these two on their own really hadn't been the best idea in the world. "I had a couple of things to sort out."

"Well, you should fecking take care of things later, shouldn't you?" snapped Slim.

"Don't talk to her like that."

Slim's wings flapped harder. "I'll talk to her any fecking way I please. I'm doing you two a favour by being here."

"Well, Mr. Slim," said Mrs. Alcoon calmly, "you are free to leave if you wish."

The little gargoyle muttered something under his breath.

"Sorry, dear? I didn't quite catch that."

"Oh, I'll stay," he muttered again. "But only because you'll upset the delicate balance of the Otherworld all on your own if I don't." He rose heavily up into the air from his perch on the counter, and flew through to the kitchenette.

As soon as he was gone, Mrs. Alcoon turned to me. "I really rather like him, Mackenzie dear."

"You could have fooled me," I said disbelievingly, pulling out the bread and fillings that I'd just purchased.

"Oh," she gave a short, dismissive chuckle. "That's just banter. He's really rather cute in fact."

I considered suggesting that she avoided telling Slim that she thought he was 'cute', but decided that would probably mean she would take every opportunity to point it out to him. While this was a side to Mrs. Alcoon that I'd not previously encountered, I did know a fair amount about how friendly banter had the potential to go very wrong. It was probably best not to get involved. She gazed down at the jar of mayonnaise that I'd set out onto the wooden counter.

"He doesn't really live up to his name though, does he?"

Puzzled, I frowned over at her.

"I mean," she said by way of explanation, "he's not very slim."

Mrs. Alcoon picked up the mayonnaise and pushed it underneath the shelf under the till and out of sight. "It'll do him good to avoid fatty foods," she said, nodding solemnly to herself.

Yup. It was definitely a good idea for me to keep my mouth shut.

* * *

SEVERAL HOURS – and several bouts of bickering later – we were pretty much done. The books were all on the shelves and, although there had been several moments of disagreement about where some sections should be placed, we eventually managed to get there, with Mrs. Alcoon marking off all the stock as we did so. I rubbed the edge of my t-shirt sleeve against my forehead, wiping off the layer of sweat and grime, then sank down onto the floor.

"Three days ahead of schedule," Mrs. Alcoon stated proudly.

"Ahem," Slim coughed pointedly.

She beamed at him. "Of course we couldn't have done it without you, Slim dear."

She reached over to where he hovered in the air and gave him a peck on the cheek. I watched in astonishment as he flushed in embarrassed pleasure. Some days I thought I'd never understand people. Or living breathing gargoyles.

"I could come back you know. To help out from time to time after you've opened up properly." He scowled to himself, "But only because you clearly need some fecking proper professional help."

"Why, Mr Slim, that would be lovely. Thank you, dear."

He coughed again then swivelled round to face me. "You should take care," he said gruffly.

I must have looked surprised because he elaborated further.

"A lot of people know what you are and a lot of people want a piece of you. You should choose your friends wisely." He jerked his head back towards Mrs. Alcoon. "She's a good'un - if you can keep her in fecking line."

"Um, thanks," I stuttered slightly, "I think."

He nodded his head and then made for the portal that was already beginning to gleam and shiver in the air, vanishing quickly before our eyes.

"Those portal things are really rather useful, aren't they?" commented Mrs. Alcoon.

I begged to differ, but I stayed silent and just smiled at her.

"He's right, you know," said Mrs. Alcoon. "A lot of dangerous people now know the truth about you, Mackenzie. You can't keep pretending otherwise. The shop is ready and we don't open up until Monday. That leaves five days. Why don't you take some time off and sort yourself out?" She gave me a hard stare. "Get in touch with that fairy fellow who has your book."

I frowned at her. "If Solus had anything to tell me then he'd have been in touch by now."

"From what you told me, he was embarrassed by the way he acted before when he thought you'd been lying. Maybe he's waiting for you to contact him first."

I very much doubted that Solus really ever got embarrassed by anything. But she was right, he still had my book. It was a strange sentient thing that had found me first in Inverness and then afterwards at the mages' academy, and purported to tell the history and secrets of the Draco Wyr. Unfortunately it was written in Fae so I'd tricked Solus into reading it for me so I didn't have to spend months of work on translation. It hadn't worked out very well.

I shrugged. "Yeah, okay. Maybe I'll try that."

"Mackenzie Smith," said Mrs. Alcoon sharply. "You've been prevaricating for months. He knows more about your heritage than you do and it's time you stopped acting as if nothing has happened. You need to, what is it that they say? Mane up?

"Man up," I muttered.

"Man up, then. The Mackenzie Smith I knew up in Inverness wouldn't have let the grass grow so idly under her feet. Get in touch with this Salus fellow…"

"Solus."

"This Solus fellow, and find out what you need to know. Then you'll be free to get on with the rest of your life. Your young man won't wait around forever, you know."

"I have no idea what you mean," I said, grumpily, being deliberately obtuse.

"Mackenzie," Mrs. Alcoon said gently, "don't be an idiot. You're worried about your Draco Wyr side and what might happen if you shift again, and you're worried that your Lord Alpha gentleman will break your heart. And because of those worries, you're not living your life. Sort yourself out before one of those goons out there who's following you around does it for you."

I stared at her in surprise.

"You're not the only one who is aware of their surroundings, dear. Don't think I don't know what's going on. You can't hide from yourself forever."

"I'm scared," I said, in a small voice.

"Of course you're scared. But you're also the bravest person I know. So start showing some of that bravery and sort yourself out."

For a long moment I didn't answer. Then I took a deep breath. "Okay, I can contact Solus and see what he says. You're right. I need to find out what the book says. But the only reason that Corrigan is interested in me is because everyone else is."

"Are you so sure about that?"

"Well," I paused, "that and the fact that he's enjoying the chase. As soon as I give in, if I give in, he'll get bored and move onto something else."

"And if you don't do anything he'll move on eventually anyway, so what have you got to lose?"

Everything, I thought. I wasn't sure I'd be able to cope with the idea of having Corrigan to myself for how ever long that might be, then be forced to watch him move onto pastures new with barely more than an 'it's been fun, kitten'. The man might irritate the hell out of me but being ignored by him would be so very much worse.

I forced a smile onto my face. "I'll get in touch with Solus," I repeated.

Mrs. Alcoon sighed. "Then I suppose that'll have to do for now. I'll be right here if you need any help."

I felt a hard ache of rising tears bottle themselves up in my chest. "Thanks."

"You're my family now, Mackenzie, you know that." She patted me on the hand. "I'll see you back here bright and early on Monday morning, and not before."

I nodded, not trusting my voice any further, then managed a watery smile and picked up my backpack, walking out and leaving the little shop behind.

* * *

I WAS MORE nervous than I cared to admit about contacting Solus again. Deciding I'd wait a couple of hours to get up the courage first, I walked home, dimly aware that I was still being followed but too lost in my thoughts to really care. Just before I reached the steps up to my block of flats, however, I felt a soft tap on my shoulder. I spun round, immediately in defence mode, then relaxed when I saw who it was.

"Tom!" I said, pleased, reaching over to give him a hug.

"Hey, Red," he grinned at me with the ease of an old friend. "You're looking good."

"I thought you were now too important to the Brethren to be given babysitting duty."

He looked slightly embarrassed and shuffled from left to right. "Well, I have something I wanted to give you. That Betsy and I wanted to give you." He reddened slightly and reached back into the inside pocket of his jacket, then pulled out a creamy expensive looking envelope. "Here." He thrust it out to me.

I took it, then looked askance at him. He lifted a shoulder, half-shrugging. "We've set a date."

"Oh, fantastic!" I leaned in to hug him again. "Tom! I'm so happy for the two of you."

He beamed at me, his smile reaching from ear to ear. "You'll come, won't you? To the wedding?"

"Nothing would make me happier. When is it?"

"August 14th. We thought the weather would be nice then." He looked down at the ground for a moment then back up at me. "It's going to be in Cornwall."

Oh. I felt my heart squeeze momentarily at the thought of my old home. "Okay. Um, yes, sure. I can still be there."

He appeared slightly anxious for a second. "Betsy spoke to Anton. He won't cause any trouble. Not now that everyone knows you're not a shifter."

A grimace crossed my face. "It turns out I'm more of a shifter than everyone realised."

Tom looked confused.

"Ignore me," I muttered. As much as a part of my old life that Tom was, and as much as he already knew about me, he clearly had other things going on in his life that didn't need to be complicated by me and my problems. It was good to know at least that Corrigan hadn't gone telling all of his little Brethren minions the truth about my dragon side.

Tom, thankfully, let it go. "Oh, before I forget," he said, digging into his pocket again, "Lord Corrigan asked me to give you this." He held out a key.

I stared at it for a moment, frowning. "What's it for?"

He shrugged. "I dunno, Red, he didn't say." A mischievous look crossed his face. "The key to his heart?"

I thumped him on the arm. "Fuck off."

"He's not really been out with anyone else, you know. Not the whole time that I've been with the Brethren."

"I do log on occasionally to the Othernet, Tom," I scoffed. 'I've seen his string of ladies."

He looked at me earnestly. "That's just for show. More often than not, they're already spoken for. There's not been anyone serious."

Suspicion filled me. "Did he order you to tell me that?"

Tom looked hurt. "No. Just because I'm with the Brethren doesn't mean I can't think for myself, and it doesn't mean I'd manipulate you like that."

"If he compelled you," I pointed out, "you'd do whatever he wanted."

"He's never done that. He's not a bad person, Red."

I sighed. "I know he's not, Tom. He's just another complication that I don't need right now. And I certainly don't need half the world trying to match-make me with him."

Tom widened his eyes and tried to look innocent. "I have no idea what you mean."

I snorted. "Sure you don't."

He grinned at me. "Anyway, look, I've got to go. Maybe we can catch up properly some time. Have a real sparring session like back in the good old days."

"I'd really like that."

"Be seeing you."

He loped off back down the street. I watched him go, a fond expression on my face, until I glanced over and realised that there was both a new Fae and a new mage staring at me suspiciously, as if I'd been cavorting somehow with the enemy. I rolled my eyes at them expressively then turned and headed inside.

CHAPTER FOUR

BEFORE I'D EVEN REACHED MY FRONT DOOR, I'D REALISED WHAT the key was for. The gleaming lacquered red paint virtually screamed at me from the other end of the hallway. I wondered whether the colour had been his choice or not and stared down at the key in my hand, supposing that I should have expected no less. After all, he'd been the one who'd broken the bloody thing down in the first place. It was nice of him to bother fixing it.

Then I shook myself. Who the fuck was I kidding? Corrigan wouldn't have fixed it; he'd just have ordered someone else to do it for him. Much like he'd ordered Tom to come and give me the key. That was what being the head of one of the largest Otherworld organisations meant, I reminded myself. Having far too much power and far too many opportunities to make others do your bidding. I did not need to get myself involved with that any more than I already was. Stupid fucking Brethren.

I unlocked the door and stepped inside, then hissed in further anger. On the kitchen table was a delicate china vase filled with flowers. Their sweet scent filled the small flat. So it wasn't enough that he had to break down my door and then send someone else to fix it, but he also got someone to invade my privacy and enter my living space at the same time. Prick. He had no sense of boundaries. I dropped my backpack in the corner, the books inside thumping loudly against the floor as I did so, and scowled to myself.

There was a sharp knock at the door. I marched over and flung it open, ready to give him a piece of my mind. It wasn't a shifter standing there waiting, however, it was a mage – the one who was now trailing me around.

"What?" I snapped.

I probably should have softened my tone a bit as the poor guy looked absolutely terrified. He bent down and picked up a box then handed it to me. "Here." There was a definite tremor on his voice. "This is from the Arch-Mage. With his compliments."

I stared at him for a moment, then took the box. "Thanks."

The mage turned and virtually ran away back down the corridor. I closed the door, carried the box into the kitchen and unwrapped it. It was a coffee machine. State of the art by the look of it, and with several cartons of rich dark coffee included. I was tempted to throw it back out of the door, even though I'd forgotten to buy coffee on my way home and it would be more than handy to have around.

I shook my head to myself. "You are far too easily bought, Mack."

Sitting down heavily on one of the kitchen chairs, I eyed both the flowers and the coffee machine, wondering what Corrigan and the Arch-Mage thought they were trying to gain. Really, I should return the gifts: I didn't want anyone to think I was a pushover. I reached out and touched the coffee machine. It was far nicer than anything I'd be able to afford myself. But I couldn't accept it. And if I couldn't accept the coffee machine, then I couldn't accept Corrigan's flowers either. The front door was another matter – that had been his fault in the first place. I picked both of them back up and was about to head outside to reluctantly hand them back to my babysitters when there was yet another knock.

"Oh, for fuck's sake," I growled, dropping both the vase and the coffee machine back onto the table and stomping towards the door, flinging it back open.

It was the Fae this time. "Of course," I said, sarcastically. "And what are you bringing?"

He bowed wordlessly and handed me over a small package, then elegantly twisted on his toes and left the same way as the terrified mage had. I sighed deeply, then opened it up. My eyes widened when I saw what it was though. Fuck. I closed my front door yet again and walked slowly back to the kitchen, laying it carefully on the table. I reached out to touch the paper and then snatched my hand back again. Well, I could hardly give the things back now. What the Fae had given me was a perfectly translated version of the Draco Wyr tome that I'd given to Solus – the very text that I'd been on the verge of contacting him about. I couldn't dump it back in the arms of the anonymous Fae outside and then demand that Solus tell me what it was all about. And if I couldn't give the Faes their gift back, then I couldn't give the mages and the shifters theirs back either because they'd scream and shout that I was being unfair. This was freaking ridiculous; I really didn't need to have to deal with the constant one-upmanship.

I rubbed my eyes. I was going to have to sort this out and sit down with all three of them. If they wanted to follow me around then that was their prerogative, but they had to respect my space and had to stop buying me things. I understood that discovering a Draco Wyr in their midst had them all excited, but each and every one of them was going to have to tone it down. I wasn't a toy. I pursed my lips and decided that first thing the next morning I'd contact them all. Enough was enough. Right now, however, I needed to clear my head and give myself some space before the simmer in my veins exploded into real flames. If I stayed here with the Fae text and as much coffee as I could drink in a month, then I'd be up all night reading it. I knew that I might not like what I read either. It could wait another day; instead I was going to go for a run and get some fresh air. The exercise would sort me out for now.

I pulled on my running gear as quickly as I could, then stuffed my shiny new key into my pocket and exited. I had no idea whether my Otherworldly babysitters were geared up for running or not, but it really wasn't my problem. I shrugged to myself. If they could keep up, then bully for them. Without acknowledging their hovering presence on the other side of the street, I started to jog, slowly at first to warm up. One of the major drawbacks of living in a city was the number of roads and traffic lights that I'd be forced to wait for, so it made no sense to start pelting my way along in a sprint. At least there was a sizeable park not too far away.

It took around fifteen minutes to reach the park itself. The sky was already starting to darken, despite the fact that it was now summer and the nights were considerably lighter. It didn't really make much difference to my run, but it might make it harder for my little troupe of followers to keep up. I grinned slightly to myself and began to speed up.

The park was fairly busy: numerous families out enjoying the last of the daylight, groups of kids playing games, and, of course, several joggers on the same track as myself. I did my best to ignore them, not wanting others to set a pace for me, and stayed on the tarmacked path for a while, but with the night drawing in it was becoming too annoying having to keep veering out of the path of those leaving so eventually I gave up and moved onto the grass. I cut round the bend, skirting the large trees then began to run more cross-country. It felt much more peaceful this way and I could almost imagine I was no longer in London, but instead out in the fresh air of the countryside. Keeping my breathing even, I picked up the pace further, and allowed my mind to empty. A couple of rabbits saw me coming and quickly scampered out of my way, dashing into nearby burrows. Other than that, and the distant hum of traffic, I felt as if I was completely alone.

Of course that was until I caught the flicker of green out of the edge of my eye. I frowned. It was too ephemeral and just too *green* to be a jogger. And there was no way that a tree or a bush moved like that. Interested, I headed in the direction of it. A small thought nagged at me that curiosity killed the cat, but, let's face it, I needed something to take my mind off all my other humdrum worries. However, when I reached the area where I'd thought I'd seen the flicker, there was nothing there. I heard some footsteps behind and, slowing to a jog, glanced round my shoulder. The Fae, naturally, was keeping up, although there was no sign of either the shifter or the mage. Either of them could of course draw on their Otherworldliness to produce a better showing, whether by casting a tracking spell or by shifting, but this was a pretty public area and I doubted that they would try it. Whatever might have been lingering in the trees had either been frightened off by my own approach or by the faerie's. It was time to find out.

Without warning, I sped up again, this time using every ounce of energy that I had. I zigzagged to my right, hoping to confuse the Fae behind me. With lightning fast reflexes, there was little I could do to outrun him, but I was fairly confident that I could outsmart him. I'd been regularly using this park since we'd taken the lease over on the bookshop almost three weeks ago, and it wasn't so large that I didn't already know my way about it well. I knew that coming up was a small annex used to house gardener's tools. It wasn't the most pleasant of places and the local youths also tended to use it as a dumping ground for their discarded cans and bottles, but it would serve my purposes. I ran to the side of it, making it appear as if I was going to pass it by without a second glance, and then started to lean over to the right even more, as I knew that both the building and the trees would camouflage my actions. As soon as I thought I was hidden from view, I halted abruptly and wheeled round, stepping quietly towards the tree-lined side of the building, then pressed myself against the brickwork. Either this would work, and I'd be able to head back in the direction that I'd come to see if I could investigate the flicker further, or it wouldn't and I'd just end up looking a bit stupid. Either way, it would make my run even more interesting.

I had made it just in time. The Fae loped past, with an even unbroken gait, and continued down the park and away from me.

I punched the air in momentary exultation and then quickly pulled myself together and ran back the way I'd come, hoping I'd have a chance to find out what the flash of green had been before either the mage or the shifter finally caught up, or the Fae realised what had happened.

When I reached the trees again, I came to a stop and looked around. Shit. There was nothing there. Either it had been my stampeding approach that had scared it off or I had been seeing things. Annoyed with myself, I turned back again to leave.

"Psssst!"

I spun round. What the hell had that been? I looked left and right, but couldn't see a damn thing. If this was going to turn out to be a kid having a laugh I was going to be seriously pissed off. Then I heard it again.

"Psssssssst!"

Dawning realisation hit me, and I slowly lifted my head to look up. My eyes narrowed as I caught sight of something hanging in the branches, cleverly camouflaged by the leafy foliage of summer. Then, all of a sudden, a small, faintly green tinged face emerged, peering down at me.

"We don't have long before they'll be back. I have a message to give you."

My brow crinkled. "You're a dryad."

She looked irritated. "Yes, of course I'm a dryad. What did you expect?"

Well, I supposed it kind of made sense that that's what I'd find in amongst the trees, but dryads were notoriously shy. This one clearly not so much.

I ignored her question. "What's the message?"

"Go five hundred steps due east from the Vale of Heath sign tomorrow night after twelve. Speak with Atlanteia."

"Who?" I was damned if I was going to go wandering around somewhere I didn't know in the middle of the night without knowing who I was supposed to meet, or why.

"Atlanteia."

"Yes, I got that part, but who's she?"

The dryad looked away from me and down the path. "They're coming. Make sure you are alone tomorrow."

"Okay, but…"

She vanished. My eyes searched the branches for any sign of her at all; it was as if she'd never even been there in the first place. A dryad initiating contact? That had to be a first.

I felt, rather than heard, the presence of the Fae back behind me. Without turning, I pointed randomly up at a tree. "Would you believe that I think there might actually be a red squirrel up there?"

I glanced backwards. The Fae stared at me silently, ignoring the heavy pounding of feet as first the shifter, then the mage appeared.

I shrugged. "Not a nature lover then."

He continued to stare at me. Bloody hell, give me Solus any day over this silent bugger. Speaking of…

"Can you tell Solus that I want to talk to him at his earliest convenience?"

The Fae blinked.

I sighed. "Lord Sol Apollinarius? Can you tell him?"

He jerked his chin up ever so slightly in acknowledgment. It would have to do. I could, of course, contact the Summer Queen herself. In fact, I had no doubt that she'd take my call, so to speak, but she was rather scary. I also still owed her a visit in Tir-na-Nog itself, one of the promises Solus had extracted from me long ago for his help, and I didn't really want reminding of it. At least I knew that on my home turf I could handle Solus. I looked over at the mage and the shifter consideringly, then decided I'd get in touch with their respective organisations on my own. At the rate it had taken these two to catch up to me, I could be waiting till next week if I left it up to them. Now that I had a good reason to make them stop trailing around after me like they were the Secret Service, I wanted it done as quickly as was humanly – or, even better, Otherworldly -possible. I flashed a smile at them all, and then turned and headed for home, wondering what on earth I'd done to merit attention from the tree nymphs.

* * *

AFTER JUMPING IN THE SHOWER, then sitting back down at my kitchen table in a pair of comfy clean pyjamas, annoying gifts pushed to one side, I mulled over who to speak to first. I was obviously going to have to wait to see if Solus showed up, assuming that his silent Fae buddy had the power of speech at all of course and actually managed to convey my message. It would be easy to get in touch with Corrigan, as all I had to do was to initiate the Voice with him. I checked the time and realised that it was getting rather late. I decided to try the Arch-Mage first.

One of the few modcons in my new little flat was a telephone. This was a fairly new experience for me as I didn't tend to use the phone often. However, the landlord had insisted and had even gone so far as to ensure it was connected in my name. I lifted the receiver, and was about to start dialing when I realised stupidly that I didn't have the number for the Ministry. I could hardly call up inquiries either. I imagined the conversation in my head. It would go something like me asking the operator for the number of the most powerful wizard in town and her calling the men in white coats in return. If I wandered outside and asked the mage sentry I was pretty sure that I could get hold of the right phone number, but I'd either have to pull on some clothes first or display the fact that the sole terrifying Draco Wyr in existence was wearing a pink Hello Kitty two set. Nope, that wasn't going to happen. I pursed my lips, then stood up and padded into the living room instead and plonked myself down on the sofa, flipping open my laptop.

I'd been too busy finding somewhere to stay and helping Mrs. Alcoon set up the shop to log onto the Othernet recently. Feeling the tug of curiosity as to what was going on in the world, I cast my eye over the headline pages. For the first couple of weeks after I'd left the mages' academy, I'd been terrified that some Otherworldly gossip columnist would proclaim the events that had resulted in Brock and Thomas' deaths to the world, along with my so-called secret identity. As time had gone by, however, and there was nothing to speak of other than a couple of stories detailing the event as a 'tragic accident', I'd begun to relax somewhat. Despite the passage of time, I remained nervous every time I logged on, and was immensely relieved that there was still nothing further. The last thing I needed was even more people finding out what I really was. Rather than screaming headlines about dragons, there was something to do with a magical explosion up in Birmingham, that the Ministry had been forced to act quickly to cover up before the local police got too interested, and an unpleasant story about some desecrated Otherworld graves in Paris. I proudly resisted the temptation to click onto the society pages to check out the photos of Corrigan and his various dates to do some investigation into whether Tom was right about them, and instead typed in a query for the Ministry's phone number instead.

Several answers appeared quickly on my screen, and I scrolled down until I found one that looked like it might be right, then picked the phone back up and jabbed the numbers in.

The phone rang several times before someone picked up. "Charter College," answered a bored voice.

"Um, hi," I said. "This is Mack Smith, I'd like to talk to…,"

The phone clicked. I started for a moment, staring at the receiver, then a familiar baritone voice filled the line.

"Mackenzie," echoed the overly warm tones of the Arch-Mage. "How are you? Did you receive my little gift?"

I thought about the gleaming coffee machine on my kitchen table. "Er, yes. Thanks."

"I knew you had a penchant for coffee from the time you spent with us, so I thought you'd appreciate it."

"Yeah, don't fucking do that again though."

There was a moment of silence. Then, "I beg your pardon?"

"Look, I appreciate that you're trying to be nice and all, but let's not forget that you're the people who effectively tortured me then forced me to go back to school. That didn't exactly turn out so well for any of us."

The Arch-Mage coughed. "Mackenzie, I can only apologise if you feel any antagonism towards us for past events. Let me make it up to you."

"Cut the bullshit," I said, firmly. "What you should have said is that I deserved to be beaten up by your goons because I broke into your headquarters. And that sending me to the academy was the best way to help me understand my powers. That if you'd known the full truth then things would have been different."

"Well, I, yes, that's what…"

"Get a grip. You're playing all nice now because you want to have me in your back pocket. Well, buying me things isn't going to achieve that. Neither is following me around all fucking day long either."

Thankfully for my sanity, the Arch-Mage reverted to his former self and a note of haughtiness exerted itself through the phone. "We're hardly going to let the shifters and the faeries follow you around and know what you're doing, when we don't."

"Oh, don't worry, I'll be having words with them too. But I need you to back off. I like you, and I like the Ministry, and I will help you out if you need me to. For now, quit pissing around and give me some peace."

"Fine," said the Arch-Mage stiffly.

"Thank you." I could afford to be gracious now that I had

what I wanted. "I read about what happened in Birmingham with the explosion. Is everything alright?"

"We believe the situation was contained."

"I'm glad to hear that." I wanted to ask him what had happened to the Palladium too, the small ancient wooden statue that had caused so many problems a few months before. I was a bit of afraid of the answer though, and rather worried that, despite my exhortations to the opposite, the Arch-Mage would offer to give it to me as a present. I didn't want that chunk of wood anywhere near me ever again. I chickened out.

"Well then, I'm sure I'll be speaking to you soon."

"I do hope so, Miss Mackenzie." The Arch-Mage hung up.

I wondered how annoyed he was with me, then put the phone down and decided he'd just have to deal with it. One down. Two to go.

Next up was Corrigan. I took a deep breath and told myself firmly that it was important to retain the same modicum of business-like conversation that I'd had with the Arch-Mage. Easy.

Corrigan? Are you available right now? There. That was an appropriately perfunctory opening.

There was a moment of silence before he answered back in my head. *Kitten, for you I'm always available.*

Fuck. The way he'd purred the last word made my imagination go to places that I didn't need it to. Stay focused, Mack. *I need you to back off.*

Whatever do you mean?

I appreciate that you fixed my door.

Did you like the colour? I thought it would suit you.

It's great, I shot back flatly. *But enough. You can't just let the pack wander into my flat whenever they want to. It's my flat. And you can't give me flowers. And you can't follow me around any more.*

He didn't immediately reply. There was a knock on my front door, a rap that seemed to be beating out some kind of tune. I walked out and opened it up, and took in Solus standing just on the edge of the threshold wearing some kind of black as night kilt, with a crisp white shirt unbuttoned virtually to his stomach.

For goodness' sake. I beckoned him inside without saying anything. A lazy smile crossed his features and he opened his mouth to speak, but I shushed him and pointed him towards the kitchen table. He shrugged and wandered over, pulling out a chair then flipping out the back of his kilt with a flourish to sit down.

Corrigan? Are you still there?

His reply was dangerously quiet. *You didn't like the flowers?*

It's not that I didn't like them. It's that you forced the mages and the faeries into thinking that they had to give me gifts too. I'm not about to prostitute myself out to the highest bidder.

I don't care what they do. I only care what you do.

Well, what I do is enjoy going about my daily life without constantly being interrupted.

Like you've just been interrupted by that faerie?

That explained the long drawn out silence then. The shifter that was watching had clearly informed Corrigan about my visitor.

This is exactly what I'm talking about. You can't track my every single movement. I need some privacy, Corrigan. And, for your information, he's here so that I can tell him exactly the same thing that I'm telling you.

To not give you flowers?

I sighed in exasperation. *To give me some peace and stop following me around or giving me expensive presents.*

I could sense waves of silent menace emanating from him. *What did he give you?*

Again with the privacy invasion. I'm not saying I'm going to ignore you, Corrigan, I just need some space. Not just from you but from everyone.

And what if something attacks you because they know that you're a dragon and they have decided that your head would look good on their wall?

Technically, my Lord Alpha, I'm not a dragon – I'm a Draco Wyr. Plus, I think I've proven that I can look after myself.

I waited for a moment, crossing my fingers. Solus noticed the gesture and raised his eyebrows in mocking amusement. I glared at him.

Fine, kitten. I will do as you wish if you grant me but one boon.

Name it, I answered rashly without thinking.

Dinner. Saturday night. I will come and pick you up. He then immediately broke off the connection, before I could protest otherwise. Outfuckingstanding.

"His Lord Furriness, I presume?" drawled Solus.

I nodded, distracted, then sat down on a chair opposite the Fae.

"You really need to get him out of your system, dragonlette. Just fuck him and be done with it." He watched my reaction carefully.

I made sure not to give him any satisfaction by reacting and kept my face pointedly blank. "Thanks for coming, Solus."

He bared his teeth at me in the semblance of a smile, then stretched out like a cat and put his hands behind his head. "How could I say no? Then I'd have missed the opportunity to see you so glamorously attired."

I scowled at him. He smirked back, then continued, "I had rather been hoping you'd be in touch before now. But beggars cannot be choosers and I am here now to do your bidding."

"Then tell your Queen to leave me alone."

He quirked up a single perfectly plucked eyebrow. "Dragonlette, one does not simply tell the Summer Queen of the entire Seelie Fae what to do. I had presumed that you were smarter than that."

"I'm sure you can find a way to re-phrase it more politely, Solus. But I need some privacy and I need you, the mages and the shifters to stop following me around."

Solus brushed some imaginary dust off his shoulder. "Really? And why now all of a sudden does this bother you?

You've been perfectly content up till now to let us hang around."

"Well, now I'm settled in. I'm not going anywhere, and you know where I am. So I'd like some peace and quiet."

He sniffed. "I see. Does this have anything to do with these objects?" He waved a hand over the table and its contents, a faint sneer on face. "Flowers? And coffee?"

"And one translated Fae book."

"If you don't want it dragonlette, I will happily take it back."

"You know I want it."

Solus leaned forward. "Have you read it yet?"

"No."

He seemed disappointed. "Ah, well. Perhaps when you do, you'll get in touch with me again. There are a few things that I may be able to help you with." He nodded his head towards my shoulder. "How's the mark?"

"It hurts sometimes, Solus," I said, telling the truth. "Usually in my dreams. I don't know why."

He stood up and walked round to me, placing his right hand onto where the scar was hidden beneath the soft cotton fabric of my pyjama top.

"What are you doing?" I asked suspiciously.

"Shhh," he said softly.

The warmth of Solus' hand quickly turned to a cold burn and I winced.

"Shit! Solus, that hurts."

"I told you to be quiet, dragonlette."

I grimaced and squirmed slightly, but stayed in place. Solus damn well better know what he's doing, I thought uncharitably. His cold touch seared through my top and skin, biting into my flesh underneath. I gritted my teeth until he finally pulled away.

"There. It shouldn't bother you quite so much now."

I moved my shoulder around in a semi-circle, first one way then the other. It did feel a bit different. I sent the Fae a quick look of gratitude.

He grinned at me, white teeth flashing. "Now, dragonlette, I need you to tell me the truth."

I gazed up at him, askance.

"What do you think of my sporran?" He gestured down towards his crotch.

I punched out, aiming for his stomach, but he just laughed and danced away.

"Idiot," I muttered.

"I'm glad you finally got in touch, my little fiery one. I will arrange for the tail to be removed and inform her Majesty in my own manner."

"Thanks, Solus."

He pointed down at the collection of translated Fae papers. "And read those. You will find them enlightening."

I nodded. Then he snapped his fingers, which I was sure was more for effect than because he needed to, and vanished.

CHAPTER FIVE

By the time I awoke the next day, it was already mid-morning. I had been tempted the previous night to take Solus' advice and read through the Fae translation, but my eyelids had already been starting to droop and sleep had seemed to be by far the best course of action. Fortunately it had been dream-less.

Now, wide awake and with a steaming cup of black coffee in front of me, the pristine white pages were shouting out at me. If I was honest with myself, I was absolutely terrified about what secrets it might reveal.

Not too many months ago, I'd been desperate to discover more about myself and my weird blood; since shifting into a dragon I wasn't convinced that I needed to know the truth any longer. What I'd not told anyone, and what I barely allowed myself to consider even in my most alone moments, was that during those seconds when I had became more monster than human, all semblance of rational thought had completely fled me.

I was used to having my bloodfire take over my thoughts and actions, of course, but I'd always still managed to remain inherently myself somewhere inside. When I'd transformed, consumed by the rage and pain of seeing both Brock and Thomas massacred in front of me, there had been nothing left of me

44

inside. Not one scrap. All that I'd been was a mass of unthinking death and devastation. A tiny part of me dreaded to think what I might have done if someone else had gotten in between my dragon form and Tryyl.

I inhaled deeply. Solus had naturally read it, and he was still sticking around. Being a typically arrogant Fae, he no doubt believed in his absolute invincibility against all odds, but surely even he would be sensible enough to steer clear of me if I was all that dangerous, I rationalised to myself. And, by knowing more about what my true nature was really like, I'd have a better chance of guarding against anything terrible happening. Of course I was glad that I'd managed to kill the wraith as well.

"You didn't actually hurt anyone innocent, Mack," I told myself aloud. Not that it meant I still wouldn't though.

I inhaled deeply, sucking calming breath into my lungs. Okay. I knew I was going to eventually read the bloody thing no matter what, so why not get it out of the way? I made to put the coffee cup down on the table top and realised that flickers of anxious green flame were licking around my fingers. Not helpful. Closing my eyes for a moment and practising some of the meditative techniques that my old anger management counsellor had taught me, I forced myself to settle down. When I checked back, the flames were gone.

I pulled the papers over to me, then turned to the first page. I'd already managed to translate the first chapter on my own back when the original had been in my possession, very slowly deciphering each and every word with the help of a bilingual dictionary. I couldn't be entirely sure that I'd managed to be accurate, however, so I started by re-reading what I already knew.

It turned out my original efforts had been fairly spot on. Other than a few odd words here and there, and clumsy wording, I'd worked out all of the main points. At some point in the very distant past, a remarkably foolish mage had attempted to experiment on a real, honest to goodness bona fide dragon, by transforming it into human form. Said dragon had not appreciated her efforts and, as well as eventually killing her and numerous other humans who got in his way, he also spent a lot of time shagging the local maidens and getting several of them pregnant. Before too long, however, a sturdy warrior by the name of Bolox had been smart enough to try and kill the dragon. His shoulder had been maimed in the ensuing fight and, while his efforts had ultimately proved successful, the scars on his shoulder never disappeared. Ever since that point, all progeny of the dragon had the same scars visible on their own shoulders, in some mystical transferable version of a knot-in-string reminder that whenever they came across any descendants of Bolox it was their duty to slaughter them instantly. The scar thing didn't really seem particularly logical, but I guessed that neither did being stupid enough – or magically endowed enough – to transform a dragon into human form.

Something tugged at my memory. One of the first things I'd been required to do when I'd started at the mages' academy was to read, understand and memorise their complicated legal system. I was sure that one of the unbreakable rules had been that it was expressly forbidden for anyone to ever attempt to change the true nature of a living creature through magical means. Now that I thought about it in the context of my great-great-great-and-so-on-grand-daddy, it made perfect sense.

I flicked over to the next chapter, which traced the lineage of that original dragon down through the centuries. Many of the original women who'd been unfortunate enough to have caught the eye of first ever Draco Wyr had died in childbirth, their babies along with them. Enough had survived, however, to continue the line, albeit diluting the wyrm blood as they went along. The anonymous author of the book speculated that many important figures throughout history could claim to be of the Draco Wyr suggesting, although not offering much in the way of proof, that people like Boadicea, Julius Caesar and Genghis Khan all benefited from the power of their blood and heritage. The people they slaughtered didn't benefit much from it, I thought, not that I didn't admire some of what they'd achieved.

The second chapter ended with the author surmising that the reason the Draco Wyr had virtually died out by the turn of the nineteenth century was that their combative nature and dwindling powers caused the majority of the species to involve themselves in too many situations that resulted in their deaths at a young age. There was also the implication that many of them had been hunted down and bled dry, due to various Otherworld creatures desiring the power of Draco Wyr blood for themselves. I thought of Iabartu and nodded to myself. It didn't appear that much had changed in the last two hundred or so years.

Pushing the papers aside, I wandered into my little bathroom and leaned against the sink, staring at my reflection in the mirror. Clearly, in terms of the whole nature versus nurture debate, nature was winning as far as I was concerned. My innate temper did indeed lead me into many situations which I would be wiser to avoid. Of course I doubted that many of my ancestors had enjoyed the option of anger management counseling. Perhaps being able to avail myself of such things meant that I'd be more successful at life than my forebears. It occurred to me that I should probably make an appointment to continue with the sessions. Anything that would help me stay in control, even if only minutely, could only be a good thing.

With that thought in my head, I decided to leave the rest of the book for now and see what else I could procure to help myself. I picked up my backpack, first extricating the vampire books from it and placing them in a corner to be read carefully at a later date, and headed outside. Once I was out on the pavement, I glanced carefully up and down the street. It was filled with shoppers, few of them paying me any attention. It appeared that my pleas the night before had been heeded as I couldn't see anyone, Otherworlder or otherwise, keen to follow me around. Excellent.

Instead of turning left towards Clava Books as I normally

HELEN HARPER

would, I headed right. There were still a few hours before the shops would start to close so my little excursion would let me kill two birds with one stone. Before too long I was standing outside a small store bracketed by earthy coloured signage. Mrs. Alcoon and Julia would be proud of me.

I didn't think I'd ever entered a homeopathic shop up till now. The restorative powers of herbal remedies had hardly escaped me, however, so I wandered up and down the shelves until I found something that I thought might work: a small bottle filled with a viscous liquid and a label that proclaimed itself as 'Temper-Soothe'. I picked it up and read the label.

There was a long list of ingredients, but the main ones seemed to be Passiflora Incarnata and Skullcap. I grimaced. Neither sounded particularly appealing but my knowledge of all things herbal was not exactly extensive. I considered calling Julia to see whether she thought this would be the right fit, but then decided against it. It would probably just worry her. And, after all, I was only taking the remedy as a preventative measure, much like vitamins. I paid for it at the counter, ignoring the slightly raised eyebrows of the shop assistant, then headed back outside again, this time flagging down a taxi.

"Where to, Miss?" asked the driver, the twang of Cockney apparent in his accent.

I gave him the address, then sat back and watched the world go by. Some days I wasn't sure if I'd ever get used to living in such a large city. It certainly didn't help my powers of spatial awareness. Out in the countryside, I found it relatively easy to work out my position and how to get to where I needed to go – here it was much harder. As I wasn't completely confident that I'd be able to find my next destination, and I didn't want the taxi driver to use his famed black cab Knowledge to help, I had directed him to Alcazon, the swanky restaurant frequented by the more well to do inhabitants of the Otherworld. From there, I'd be able to re-trace my previous steps to get to Balud's weapon shop. There was no way my budget would stretch to being able to afford to eat at the restaurant – my one and only previous visit had been with Solus and he'd been paying. I'd just have to keep my fingers crossed that I had enough spare cash to buy myself something sharp at the shop. It wasn't that I thought that my pending nocturnal visit to meet a dryad was going to be dangerous, just that it didn't hurt to be prepared. The irony of buying a herbal remedy to stop me from attacking someone needlessly in a rage in the same afternoon as procuring weapons that would help me in such an attack wasn't lost on me. They were both for protection, I told myself firmly, just different kinds of protection, that's all.

Before too long, the driver pulled up across from Alcazon, and I reached into my backpack to get out some cash. I was just handing it over, however, when something caught my eye and I suddenly drew back.

"Everything all right?" the taxi driver inquired solicitously.

My eyes were fixed across the street. "Er, fine, just…just wait a minute, can you?"

He shrugged, and sat back in his seat. My attention remained focused on the couple who had just emerged from round the corner. It was impossible to miss Corrigan. He strode along the street as if it belonged to him, black hair glinting in the afternoon sun, and white v-necked t-shirt moulded to his chest so that every taut badass shapeshifter muscle was revealed. The dark-haired woman at his side, and on whose back he was currently placing a protective hand, was clearly a shifter too. I didn't recognise her but I hadn't grown up in a pack without being able to pick one out at a hundred paces. Whoever she was, she somehow managed to pull off looking both dainty and powerful at the same time. The hackles on my skin rose as I watched the pair of them, and I felt the familiar surge of heat fire up in the pit of my belly then ripple through my blood. I quickly sat on my hands in case inadvertent green fire decided to sprout up. I wasn't quite sure how I'd explain that to the taxi driver.

I knew that what I was feeling was jealousy and I knew that I

49

had no right to that emotion. But it still didn't stop it from flooding every molecule of my body. So much for there not really being anyone in his life. It just confirmed for me that he was only hanging around me now because he thought he could use the fact that I was a Draco Wyr to his advantage, just like the Faes and the mages did. The woman seemed to sense my stare because at one point she glanced straight over in my direction. I sank down into my seat and hoped that she'd not seen me. It seemed to have worked as she turned back again without breaking her stride. I waited until the pair of them had disappeared inside the gleaming glass-fronted building, then yanked out a hand and dug into my backpack, pulling out the Temper-Soothe. I twisted the cap off then chugged down several gulps. He could do what he wanted, I told myself. I had no right to be angry at him because I had no claim on him. But that didn't mean that I couldn't feel the bloodfire ripping through my system anyway.

The taxi driver eyed me sympathetically in his rear view mirror.

"Boyfriend?" he asked.

"Not exactly," I said sighing, before handing over what I owed him, along with more of a tip than I'd originally intended. "Thanks."

"That's okay. I'm sure he's not worth it anyway, sweetheart."

I really wished that he hadn't tacked on that endearment, as it caused the fire to flare up inside me even more. I took another swig of the herbal medicine and forced a smile on my face, gritting my teeth as he drove off, then stomped off down the street towards the troll's store.

* * *

MY MOOD DIDN'T SEEM to have improved much by the time I arrived in front of Balud's shabby door. I'd all but drained the Temper-Soothe. Shitty stuff. It tasted nasty and hadn't done a damn thing. Next time I'd know to avoid the homeopathic crap and go straight for hard drugs instead. I lifted up the door knocker and slammed it down hard several times, feeling it vibrate against the wood as it did so.

After what seemed like an eternity, the door eventually creaked open, and Balud's dark beady eyes were blinking up at me. I pasted on a smile.

"Hi! Remember me?"

He stared silently at me. Okay, then. I tried to remember what Solus has said when we'd visited before. Maybe there was some kind of protocol involved that I was missing.

"I'm here to buy some weapons," I folded my arms and tried to look as serious and forbidding as possible. "If I can afford them."

The troll's nose wrinkled ever so slightly. Oops. Probably shouldn't have said that part.

"Not that I don't have money," I added in hastily. "I have lots of money. I could buy many things if I wanted to. Although when I say afford, I mean it in an, er, existential fashion. Being able to afford it," I sketched imaginary quotation marks around those words, "depends on whether the quality matches the price."

Balud's nose wrinkled further. Fuck. Now I'd just managed to insult the potential value of his merchandise. I sighed. "That didn't come out right. Look, I was here before with a friend of mine," I wasn't going to stoop so low as to name drop Solus just yet, "and he helped me buy a couple of daggers. They were great. Or they would have been great if the people I was trying to use them against hadn't taken them off me as soon as they saw them anyway. I'm looking for something similar now. Please?"

He stared me for another long moment then finally spoke. "You talk too much." He turned and headed inside, leaving the door open so I could follow. Thank goodness. Although he'd been a bit bloody politer when I'd been with Solus, it was oddly refreshing to have someone who wasn't trying desperately to suck up to me.

The interior hadn't changed one iota from when I'd last been there. I followed Balud down the dingy passageway and into the same room that I recognised from before, with the dirty plastic chairs that remained equally unchanged. The troll waggled his large ears at me and then trotted off. I looked down at the seating arrangements for a moment and decided to stand, figuring that my life would be a whole lot more pleasant if I didn't pick up any nasty Otherworld bugs. Before too long Balud returned, tray of gleaming weaponry in hand. At least he showed more respect to his wares than he did to his surroundings.

I picked up a couple of daggers and tested them. They were perfectly balanced and sharpened to lethal points. I hefted one then another in my hands, feeling immense satisfaction at having some decent protection again at last within my reach. Yes, I didn't necessarily need weapons to be able to fight; Thomas' tutelage had shown me just how possible it was to fight bare-fisted successfully and, yes, I had my green fire which could prove equally lethal. If push came to shove I could also transform into a dragon again, although as I'd already pointed out several times to myself, that wasn't a route I particularly ever wanted to have to go down again. Despite all these things, the familiar feeling of safety that holding daggers again gave me was heartening. Sometimes the old ways were the best. The fact that they were silver, and therefore even more potentially lethal to shifters, was equally satisfying. I imagined myself hurling one through the air at Corrigan. Given my current mood, it was a rather nice idea.

"How much are these?"

Balud fixed me with a baleful glance then named his price. I choked, then laid them back down carefully in the tray. Damnit. Didn't he know there was a recession on?

"Do you have anything, er, cheaper?"

"These are the cheapest." He swept his eyes over me from head to eye with a disdainful glance.

I smarted. Okay, I wasn't wearing Armani and didn't reek of

money like maybe Solus had, but I was still a customer. A customer who couldn't afford to pay for anything, but still…

I tried to not to let the stench of desperation emanate from me too obviously. "Do you maybe have a payment plan?"

The answering look of disgust in the troll's face was enough. I sighed heavily. So much for my grandiose ideas. I figured I could maybe drop by a kitchen shop and pick up some more utilitarian knives there. They would hardly be ideal, but they'd have to do.

I opened my mouth to thank Balud for his time, but he interrupted me. "You want daggers and you have no money. I want help. Do me one favour and I will let you have these." He gestured down at the two weapons that I'd favoured.

I looked at him suspiciously. Agreeing to do a favour for someone in the Otherworld was never ever a smart move. And while I might not always be its most intelligent inhabitant, I wasn't completely without my wits.

"What kind of favour?"

He barked out a laugh. "Nothing too onerous, little girl. I'm a troll, not a Fae. I have a competitor on the other side of the city. Her name is Wold and she is undercutting all my prices and driving away some of my best customers."

I felt a flicker of guilty hope inside me. Maybe I could find out where this Wold was and get some decent daggers from her instead. If the little troll was going to continue to call me 'little girl' then I had little compunction about going to his competitors.

Balud continued. "I don't trust her. Particularly because, as far as I can tell, she is just a front. There is no way that a Batibat runs a successful business."

"A what?"

He looked annoyed at being interrupted. I put my hands up in placation. "Okay, sorry, I'll look up Batibat on my own."

"I'll give you these and you will find out who is behind Wold's shop. This will be our payment plan."

"And what if I take them and then don't manage to find out who Wold's backer is?"

The troll looked amused. "Then I will take my knives back. With interest."

I didn't really want to find out what interest the little shopkeeper would be after. I had no doubt that he had many tools at his disposal to make good on such a threat. He wouldn't be running a successful Otherworld business otherwise. And yet, what he was asking really didn't sound that hard at all. A little bit of digging and a little bit of watching, and I was pretty confident I could get an answer for him. Having Balud as a sort of friend might, in retrospect, be a better idea for my future prospects than anything else I could currently think of.

I nodded to him decisively. "Okay then. Is there a time frame?"

He shrugged. "A week sounds reasonable."

That indeed sounded very reasonable. I wondered if there was something about the Batibat species that I clearly didn't know about and that was going to make this a more complicated task than it appeared on the surface. I guessed I'd find out sooner or later.

"It's a deal." I spat on my hand and held it out to the troll. He did the same, grasping mine in his.

"I will see you back here in seven days time then, Miss Smith."

I stared at him, suddenly startled.

He gave a short chuckle. "I deal with dangerous customers. Do you really think I wouldn't take the time to find out who they are first?"

That made sense. This was one canny troll though. I'd have to watch my step around him. I picked up the daggers and then realised stupidly that I had nowhere to put them other than inside my backpack where they'd be difficult to reach in a hurry.

Balud snorted, and threw me some kind of leather strapped device. "Here. On the house. I wouldn't want you to lose these weapons as quickly as you lost the previous ones. It attaches round your back so that a short sleeved t-shirt can still conceal them. It's much more effective than arm braces." He arched an eyebrow at me.

Arm braces being what I would normally use. There was definitely more to this troll that met the eye. Before I could make any more comments on his astuteness, however, Balud bowed to me.

"I will give you some privacy to put it on and then you can show yourself out. It's been a pleasure doing business."

"Likewise," I murmured, watching as he turned and plodded heavily away, then closed the door and quickly stripped off my t-shirt in order to get myself properly kitted up.

CHAPTER SIX

A few hours later, I stepped off the train at Hampstead Heath station. The weight of the daggers against my back felt comforting. I had practised pulling them out several times, and now had it down to one sharp swift movement that would serve me well if this dryad, unlikely as it was, decided to turn on me. My head was a bit foggy and, as I walked through the darkened park, I felt somewhat sluggish. I'd been trying hard not to think about Corrigan and his latest date but annoying recurring images of the pair of them kept flashing through my mind. I was a fucking idiot.

The night air was cool and I could only hope that it would sharpen my senses up somewhat. I mulled over the possible reasons as to why a dryad would be interested in having a chat with me. Years ago, when I'd lived in Cornwall with the Pack, I'd patiently tracked one down in a bid to find out more about their species. It had taken a very long time to build up enough trust between myself and that dryad for her to even talk to me, and she'd never have become confident enough to seek me out. Not that finding me would have been that easy for her, of course.

Dryads were somewhat tied to their tree habitats, finding it painful to be any distance away from them. The mages had seemed somewhat oblivious to this fact, using them to practise Kinesthetic spells on with their students. I had tried to encourage them to stop it, knowing how traumatic it was for the dryads, but had ended up leaving the academy before I'd had much success. It was theoretically possible that was the reason why Atlanteia was trying to talk to me. Maybe she thought I had enough clout with the mages to make them cease such practices altogether. It wasn't clear how she could possibly know that I had been trying to help them in the first place of course though.

I'd printed out a small map to take with me. Hampstead Heath was a vast area, covering almost 800 acres of land. Although pockets here and there were developed, and the influences of humans were apparent all over the place with its pools and paths, it nonetheless retained a wonderfully wild element to it, with gorgeous trees and plants lining virtually every aspect. I was aware that certain areas of the Heath were used for 'cruising' for random sexual encounters, but I was pretty sure that I wouldn't be anywhere near those sections. Still, I took a long looping route round towards the Vale of Heath, the small village that the dryad had directed me to.

Despite my less than direct wanderings, I arrived at the edge of the village in good time. The moon, although not yet full, was high in the sky and the night was clear. I sucked the clean air deep into my lungs. There was an uncomfortable feeling in the pit of my stomach, a sort of oily nausea that didn't appear to be going away. If I didn't know better I'd have thought that it was shaky butterflies of nervousness. Yet there was no reason to be feeling that way. I shook my head, trying to clear away the clouds that still lurked there, and hoped that I wasn't coming down with some kind of summer bug. Between this meeting and the promise I'd made to Balud, the last thing I needed was to start feeling ill.

I began heading east, following the tree nymph's instructions, and counting out my steps. Remaining wary of my surroundings, I paused at irregular intervals to double check that I wasn't being followed. Everything, fortunately, seemed clear. When I finally reached a count of five hundred, I stopped and hunkered down, preparing to wait for the mysterious appearance of Atlanteia. I didn't have too wait too long. Just as my eyelids were drooping heavily shut, the effort of keeping them open proving to be just a little too much, a voice drifted down towards me from one of the ancient trees.

"You are tired?" It was melodious and light but held a note of doubt.

I pulled myself to my feet, muscles tensed and hands by my sides, ready to yank out Balud's daggers should the need arise. "No, er, yes, a bit. I think I've caught some little bug that's all."

The wispy figure of a dryad appeared in front of me. She had long flowing hair and slightly green stained lips. The moonlight danced lightly over her pale skin and she sniffed at me delicately. "You have ingested sculletaria. In large quantities. Is it possible you have been poisoned?"

I blinked at her, feeling defensive flickers of heat flare up. Poisoned? What the hell? Then it occurred to me what she was referring to and I started to relax again slightly. "You mean skullcap, don't you?" I shrugged. "I had some earlier on today. I was trying to avoid, um, what I mean is, I needed a herbal remedy to help combat, er, negative feelings of... stress. I have quite a stressful life. You know, being contacted by Otherworld people all the time."

Slick, Mack. Real slick.

She flicked back her hair languorously and peered at me. "It's not wise to take skullcap in large quantities."

"Yeah, it doesn't taste very good either," I commented wryly. "Anyway, enough about me. I take it you are Atlanteia?"

The dryad lifted an imaginary skirt and curtsied. "And you are Mackenzie Smith."

"Please, call me Mack. And tell me what I'm doing here in the middle of the night."

I hadn't meant to sound quite so sharp, but I was pissed off with myself for not realising that the TemperSoothe that I gulped down earlier would have caused me to feel this unwell. Atlanteia, fortunately, appeared unfazed.

"It has reached our notice that you have been a friend to the dryads of late."

Ah hah, so I was right then. "You mean with the mages."

She inclined her head. "They are desisting from their torture of our more vulnerable citizens."

"They weren't really trying to torture you," I stated, feeling the need to at least give the mages some fair representation. "They didn't realise, I think, that what they were doing was harmful. I'm glad they've stopped though."

"Regardless, it was your intervention that created this outcome. We are most appreciative."

I felt uncomfortable. I hadn't really done all that much. "Um, thanks. It wasn't that big a deal to be honest."

"It was to us," the dryad said softly. "That is why I am contacting you now. We need help and we think that we can trust you to provide it."

I did my best not to let my surprise show and thought briefly of Alex, my old mage buddy. Trying to help him out a few months ago hadn't worked out all that well. I might not be the dryads' best choice, despite Atlanteia's belief to the contrary. My thoughts must have been more transparent than I realised, however.

"You are concerned," the dryad stated.

"If you're in trouble, then there are probably other people who can help you better than I can," I said honestly, "as flattered as I am that you would think of me."

"We don't trust those people. Gold might encourage their intentions otherwise but we have no need of money and therefore have none to give."

I thought of Corrigan. As much as it galled me to consider it, he would probably agree to help them out without any monetary compensation in return. It would suit his ego to be seen to be

HELEN HARPER

friendly with other members of the Otherworld and at least he'd have the might of the Pack behind him to help.

"I can put in a good word for you with the Brethren. If they give you their word, then they won't break it."

"We don't want the shifters. Not the kind of shifters you mean, anyway." Atlanteia's gaze turned hard.

Fucking hell. "You know what I am," I said, irritated that yet another group of people were aware of my so-called secret.

She shrugged elegantly. "We see many things. The trees whisper secrets to us. They like to gossip."

"You're fucking kidding me." I had a sudden vision of a circle of oaks tattling to each other about the foibles of the world, swaying in some bizarre version of Chinese whispers.

"The evergreens are the worst," Atlanteia said, as if reading my thoughts. "Something to do with never resting thoroughly no matter what the season is."

Bloody hell. I'd never feel comfortable in a forest again.

"I still don't think I am the best person to help you out," I said firmly.

"We do," the dryad placed a pale hand on the aspen next to her. "The trees do."

"Well far be it for me to argue with a piece of wood," I said sarcastically.

Atlanteia's gaze turned disapproving. "We will help you in return."

"It's not that I need something in return, it's that I might not be the best person to help you in the first place. Things don't always work out that well when I'm around."

"We have faith in your abilities. Besides," she flicked her hand casually across the night air, "you don't know what it is we are asking yet."

I folded my arms and exhaled heavily. "Okay, what is it?"

"Will you aid us?"

"If I can. " I said, relenting. "But you have to tell me what it is you need help with first."

Shadows crossed her face. "Very well. We have a small community near Shrewsbury at a place called Haughmond Hill. Dryads have lived there peacefully for hundreds of years."

"But?" I prodded.

"But," Atlanteia sighed, "in recent years the woods lost their protected status as the planting of some non-indigenous trees drove out the wildlife. And despite the area's heritage and history, even for the humans, there is a developer who is aiming to convert the land into a holiday home park."

"And cut down a lot of trees in the process?" I guessed.

She nodded solemnly. "We don't understand how he is getting around the local council. On previous occasions such as these we have managed to discourage such developments through what little power we have. And despite the humans' rampaging need to destroy the world that they live in, they have for the most part left our small enclaves alone. This time nothing we do is working." She pushed back the green hair that fell in an elegant wave against her face. "We're not like other species, Mackenzie. Mystical forces bind each of us together, like invisible roots. Our sisters are in pain and, confined here in London as I am, makes it impossible for me to help them on my own."

"Invisible roots?" This was getting weirder and weirder.

"It's complicated."

I stared at her. Apparently too complicated for her to bother explaining it to me in any more detail. Whatever. I guessed it wasn't really important. "What makes you think I'll be able to stop this?"

"There are many human activists who we have used in the past to aid our cause. This time, for reasons unknown, we are unable to rouse them into action. However, someone with your potential power, and knowledge of the human world, could do so. Encourage those groups to fight for us. " She smiled humourlessly. "Not literally fight, of course. We are not keen on violence."

"And that's it?" It all seemed just a little bit too easy.

"That's it." Something flickered in the dryad's eyes. I had the sneaking suspicion that there was more to this than she was telling me. However, it seemed to be a difficult proposition to refuse. Get some long-haired hippy types to protest against the building of a holiday camp? Not only did it sound do-able, it also didn't require any fire-breathing or fire-fighting on my part. The potential of anyone actually getting hurt – or worse – in the process was miniscule.

I pursed my lips and nodded thoughtfully. "Okay then. I'll help you out."

"Time is a factor. The development is due to start clearing the land on Monday."

"Monday? For fuck's sake! You could have given me a little more time to work with. That's four sodding days away!"

"We had been hoping that things would not progress this far so quickly."

"I'll bet," I said sarcastically, tiny flames of anticipation zipping along my veins at the very short time scale I had to work with. "Fine. If that's the time I have, then that's what it'll have to be. I'll travel to Shrewsbury first thing in the morning." I still had Balud's little problem to sort out too, but I thought I had a way around that.

A slow smile spread across Atlanteia's face. "We won't forget this, Mackenzie."

"It's Mack," I repeated. Before the words had left my mouth however, the dryad had melted away back into the safety of whichever nearby tree she had sprung from. Alrighty then.

"See you," I called out softly, and rather pointedly.

Nothing answered back other than the quiet rustle of leaves as a light breeze ran through them. I shrugged to myself and turned away, heading back towards the village. I wasn't quite sure what I'd been expecting of her, but it certainly hadn't been a plea for help. I had to admit rather selfishly that it felt good to be needed. The trees were casting elongated shadows across the path, making me wonder exactly how many dryads there were inhabiting this park and whether Atlanteia was their de facto leader. The politics of tree nymphs were not something I'd ever previously considered. Or indeed the politics of trees either. I chewed my bottom lip and cast a wary eye up at the branches overhead.

"So," I said aloud, my voice sounding strange in the relative silence of my surroundings, "if you lot gossip so much and see so much, do you know who really killed JFK?"

The trees didn't answer. Maybe they couldn't communicate across continents and didn't know.

"Is Lord Lucan still alive?"

There was an unremarkable lack of response. My head was starting to feel woozy again so I looked back down to the path, trying to make sure that I didn't trip on any low lying plants or roots as I walked.

"First sign of madness, Mack," I told myself. Although that probably wasn't accurate. The first sign of madness was no doubt overdosing on a fucking herbal remedy.

I was still musing over my innate stupidity when, without warning, an arm grabbed me from behind, latching itself around my neck. Instant heat sparked up within the pit of my intestines and I kicked out backwards with as much force as I could muster.

My reactions must have been dulled, however, and my movements slow, as my attacker easily dodged it, and began to squeeze harder until I was fighting for breath. Fuck. I forced myself to stay calm and not panic.

Whoever was behind me was tight up against my back, making it difficult to effectively manoeuvre. Thinking quickly, I used my left hand to clutch at the suffocating hold around my neck, then lashed out with my right to where I assumed my attacker's head was, slamming my palm upwards in a bid to connect with their nose. As expected, my hand was blocked with ease, but as soon as I felt the answering smack, I wrenched my left hand upwards and behind, getting purchase on the hilt of one of Balud's daggers that was strapped back to my back and managing to slide it out, twisting the blade as I did so in order to slash whoever was brave enough to think they could take me on. There was a hiss of pain as my plan worked, and the chokehold loosened, allowing me to pull myself quickly out from under it and spin to meet them head on.

My eyes narrowed when I realised who I was facing. I probably should have found the time to at least flick through one of those vampire books.

"What the fuck do you think you're doing, Aubrey?"

His blood red eyes stared at me, unblinkingly, and he laughed without humour. "I'm looking for a pet. I thought maybe a hamster would do."

I tightened my grip on the dagger, judging where it would be best to throw it. As a vampire I knew I would find it nigh on impossible to kill the prick, short of staking him or ripping his head off, but I was confident I'd be able to do him some damage at the very least. Sure, I'd ripped off Tryyl's head when I'd been in dragon form, but that was a route I wasn't prepared to go down unless I really had to. Not that I was even convinced that I'd be able to shift at will; I hadn't ever tried. Still, without looking, I was happily aware that my familiar green fire had already sparked up at my fingertips. Maybe I could barbecue the bastard.

I kept talking, trying to distract him. "You know I'm not actually a werehamster, right?"

"No shit," Aubrey drawled, without a trace of tension in his voice. "Even if I hadn't already whetted my lips on a drop of your blood, the fact that you've had the beasts, the wizards and the faeries watching you would suggest that there's more to you than meets the eye." He bared his teeth. "I knew if I was patient enough they'd eventually disappear though.'

I decided that I could probably aim the dagger straight at his jugular. That would incapacitate him long enough for me to then light him up with fire.

"So that's what this is about? You want a drink?"

He ran his tongue around the edge of his very sharp and very white teeth. "I've been able to think of little else since that morsel I had of you back in February. Now I'm going to have a lot more."

The obvious hunger in his low voice sent a shiver down my spine. I'd have to kill him now. What a shame.

I opened my mouth as if to retort further, then let the dagger fly, too quickly for him to react. Unfortunately, with my senses dulled as they were by the overdose of TemperSoothe, my aim was off by just a fraction. It was enough though to miss his throat entirely. I flicked my wrist instead, in order to send out a stream of lethal flame towards him, and then watched, my stomach dropping, as the fire fizzled out in a cloud of smoke. Oh shit. A wave of lightheadedness spun through me and, for one single heartbeat, I stared at Aubrey while he stared at me. Then I spun round and ran.

When I wanted to, I could sprint as fast as any human. I knew that the bloodsucker would be faster than me eventually though, so I'd just have to reach the safety of the village before he caught up. My heart was pounding in my mouth and adrenaline was burning through my system. I'd just have to hope that it burnt through the lingering traces of the skullcap pretty fucking quickly too. There were few trees around now – not that either they or the dryads would be much use against the might of Aubrey. I was on my own. Long grass whipped against my calves as I forced myself to go full pelt. The lights of the Vale of Heath flickered into view and I put my head down and gave it everything I had, faint relief sinking through me at the impending safety that the potential human witnesses could offer.

It might be the dead of night but it was just possible that someone was awake. Even Aubrey in his current mode of absolute predator wouldn't risk being seen by someone.

The letters on the sign proclaiming the village entrance became visible just as I heard a whooshing sound right behind me and Aubrey careened into my back, knocking me painfully to the ground. The breath was slammed out of my lungs and, just when I was about to twist and find some way to defend myself properly, sharp pain lanced through my neck as he sank his teeth in. I struggled against him, but it was all in vain as the dizziness in my head increased and nausea rose up in my stomach. I kicked out and tried to yell, but it was too late and my cry was swallowed up. With nothing else left to try, I opened up the Voice connection in my head, managing to force out Corrigan's name. My vision, however, was already dimming around the edges, and I faded away into an ever spiralling darkness.

CHAPTER SEVEN

When I woke up, I knew without opening my eyes that I was where I shouldn't be. There was a lingering smell of familiar spicy citrus in the air, not strong enough that its owner was present, but enough of it to suggest that he'd definitely been in the vicinity. My neck, at the spot where Aubrey's teeth had latched on, throbbed dully. It was a good sign; it meant I was still alive. Oddly, I felt more embarrassed than annoyed that I'd allowed the red-eyed wanker to get the better of me. Still, it just added one more tally to the list of my grievances against the bloodsuckers. I'd make sure that eventually Aubrey in particular paid back tenfold what he'd doled out. Right now, however, I had other priorities.

I slowly lifted up one eyelid and took a peek, just to be sure. I was in a huge bed, smothered by a soft duvet, and in the centre of a large mahogany panelled room. I'd been here before. I pushed myself up onto my elbows to get a better look and confirm my suspicions. Fuck it. I was in Corrigan's own bedroom. No doubt he'd be off gloating somewhere at the fact that he'd had to come galloping in and rescue me from the clutches of the evil vampire. I'd never live it down. Scowling, I sat up properly, then looked down at myself. Bloody hell. I was wearing some kind of frothy pink lace concoction that was as far removed from the muted plain t-shirt I'd had on when I'd originally left home as it was possible to get. My eyes narrowed. Had he undressed me?

I heard the muffled sound of voices from the other side of the door, and the clink of some china. Standing up quickly, and wrapping myself in the duvet like a giant marshmallow, I prepared to tell him exactly what I thought of him. Saving my sorry skin did not give him carte blanche to take off my fucking clothes.

I opened my mouth to tell him in no uncertain terms exactly what I thought, then snapped it shut again when I realised who it actually was bustling into the room.

"Hey, Mack."

I beamed at Betsy, letting the duvet drop, and rushed over for a hug, mindful of the tray she was carrying.

"I'm so happy to see you, Bets," I exclaimed. "I can't believe you and Tom have finally gotten around to setting a date."

She blushed slightly and grinned at me. "I know! Can you believe it? I told him that having the ceremony in Cornwall would be a bad idea but he insisted. He wants Julia to be able to be there without being made to travel. And it'll be lovely to be back at the old place again." She grimaced for a moment. "I just wish it meant that we didn't have to invite Anton too."

I dismissed that and smiled at her. For a moment we both stood there like idiots, grinning at each other with the unspoken memories of times gone by. Although I'd always been closer to Tom, Betsy and I had been friends for a long time. In fact, she'd been the first person who I'd ever told about my bloodfire. The best friends are the ones who you can be away from for months or even years, but then when you meet up again it's like you just saw them that morning.

She nodded towards my neck. "What the hell happened anyway? Lord Corrigan had the whole keep up at three o'clock in the morning out hunting for you. It wasn't until the mages got some kind of tracking spell out that we found you." She frowned at me. "How many of the bloodsuckers were there?"

I coughed. It wouldn't do my badass reputation much good if I told her there had just been one. "Er, forget about that and tell me how the fuck I ended up wearing this thing?"

Betsy glanced down at my frilly night dress and giggled. "Suits you. Pink is really your colour."

"Fuck off."

She laughed again, and put down the tray on the edge of the bed. "It belongs to one of the shifters who's here from time to time."

Would that be a dark-haired shifter who enjoyed the company of Corrigan from time to time too? I thought about asking Betsy but, given her proclivity for gossip, decided it might not be such a good idea if I wanted to keep my pointless jealousy to myself.

Fortunately she didn't seem to notice my inner turmoil and gestured down at the food instead. "Here, you should eat something. I got you some good coffee too."

My stomach growled, and I grabbed a roll and started nibbling away at the edges. "It's great to see you, Betsy, it really is, but I need to get my clothes and get out of here. I've got a hundred and one things to do."

Betsy stared at me. "You can't go."

I stopped chewing. "Oh yes I can."

"Mack, Lord Corrigan gave strict instructions that you were to be kept under guard at all times. He was all for storming straight round to the vamps in fact, but this old wizard guy convinced him that it would be better to wait till you came round to find out what actually happened and who it was."

I figured that the 'old wizard guy' was the Arch-mage. Brilliant. As if I wasn't being pestered enough by the lot of them already.

"So where is his Lord Furriness now then?"

"He stayed with you until it was clear that you were going to be alright then he left to go up north." She wrinkled her nose.

"There's been a lot of bother with a group of rogues recently. He's gone to try and sort it out."

Score one to me. It would be a hell of a lot easier to get out of here if Corrigan wasn't hanging around.

"And the Arch-mage?"

Betsy looked confused.

"The old wizard guy?"

Her expression cleared. "Oh, him. I think he's downstairs talking to Staines."

I chewed my tongue and thought for a minute, then looked over at my old friend. I hated to do this, but I didn't have much choice. I really did have things to do. "You know, Betsy, you're right. I should stay. In fact, I'm actually starting to feel a bit ill again. Maybe I should lie down for a few more hours."

She looked worried, which made me hate myself. "Are you okay? Should I go and get someone to have a look at you?"

"No, no, honestly, I'm alright. I think I just need to rest."

"Mack, are you sure?"

I nodded firmly. "Thanks for the food and the coffee though."

The concern didn't leave her eyes, but she patted me on my shoulder. "I'll come back in an hour and check on you."

I sat down on the edge of Corrigan's massive bed and watched her go. As soon as she had closed the door behind her, I reached over and gulped down a mouthful of some hot coffee, then rushed over to the window and yanked open the heavy brocade curtains. She'd no doubt tell Corrigan if he inquired that I wasn't feeling well, so he'd hopefully lay off contacting me through his Voice to give me enough time to make my escape. Judging by the bright light outside it was already afternoon, and I had places to be. I knew from my previous unwilling visit here that this room was high up and that there wasn't a fire escape.

That didn't mean that I was trapped, however. My head was clear, proving that the effects of the TemperSoothe had gone from my system, and that I'd not lost so much blood that I was in any danger. Adrenalised bloodfire flared up in my belly and ran through my veins until I could feel my fingertips tingling with the heat of it. It would keep me sharp enough.

"Focus the fire," I whispered to myself, and undid the latch on the window, and leaned out.

I was a long way up. Months ago, when Solus had blithely transported me here for kicks, Corrigan had said that he was on the fifteenth floor. Looking out, that appeared to be about right.

It was okay though, heights didn't really bother me. I glanced around the window, realising that I was fortunate that the Brethren's keep was an old building with plenty of ornate stone carvings built in, then swung out. My bare toes found purchase in a smooth weather-beaten groove, and my fingers pinched painfully onto the edge of the window frame. I felt vulnerable in the stupid pink nightie, and the vaguely intelligent part of me recognised that this was potentially a very stupid thing to be doing. After all, just scant hours previously I'd been full of bravado that I could kick Aubrey's arse, and look where that had gotten me. One slip and Mackenzie Smith, the fearful and terrifying Draco Wyr, would be a smear of strawberry jam on the pavement.

But I was also strong. I had no more freaking herbal shit swimming around inside of me. And if I could just reach out and grab the drain pipe that was affixed to the side of the fort then I could simply shimmy all the way down to the ground. It was clearly an old design and I knew that it would be made of stern stuff. Certainly stern enough to carry my weight anyway. I held my breath and let go with one hand then stretched over. My fingertips just scraped it. There was nothing for it but to jump. I closed my eyes and leapt, my hands fixing around its cool metal curves just in time. I exhaled and then began to inch my way down.

It was painful, and a couple of times I had to carefully release one hand and grip on tightly with the other so I could stretch out my fingers to rid myself of cramp, but I made good progress and after less than ten minutes I was already halfway down. At one point I passed by a genuine stone gargoyle that looked so remarkably like Slim that a loud guffaw escaped me. It had heavy eyebrows, and pointed ears placed on either side of its prominently chubby cheekbones. I gave the statue a quick smile, then a slight breeze picked up and the pink monstrosity began to whip around my thighs. At least I was still wearing underwear.

I continued my descent, easing myself down the drainpipe bit by bit. I wondered how difficult it would be climb up it and storm the Brethren's defences. Not that I'd want to, of course, but you'd think that it would be something that the shifters would have considered. Next time I spoke to Corrigan, if he wasn't too pissed off with me to listen, I'd point out the weakness to him. That would be fun.

I was starting to shiver by the time I finally made it to the bottom and planted my feet firmly back onto the ground with a sigh of relief. Now all I had to do was see if I could get a taxi to take me home. I had some money stuffed into a drawer back in my flat that would cover the fare. It was regrettable that I had to leave behind my backpack – and my one remaining dagger from Balud that I had yet to even bloody pay for. Having to spend hours arguing my way out of the keep had just seemed too tiresome though. I could retrieve my things later. I turned round to face the road.

"Spiderman would be proud," drawled Solus. "I'm not sure your costume matches up to his, however." He was standing on the edge of the pavement, eyeing me curiously.

A flicker of irritated bloodfire rose deep within my veins. "Have you just stood there and watched me spend twenty minutes clambering down?"

"I wasn't just standing." He waved a brown bag in my face. "I was eating lunch at the same time. And enjoying the view." He winked at me with a salacious leer.

"Picnicking on the side of the road doesn't seem to be your style, Solus." I glanced anxiously up and down the pavement, nervous that some shifters would appear. I was also trying not to be too irked that the bloody Fae in front of me hadn't decided to help me get down. I concentrated on pushing the ember of heat back down again.

"It's not." He flicked his hair back and sniffed rather imperiously. "However when I was told that my good friend had been attacked by vampires, I had no time to do much more than rush here to make sure you were alright." He patted his flat stomach. "But I have to eat."

"Why aren't you inside with the others?"

A sheen of angry dark purple flashed across his eyes, although it was gone so quickly I almost thought I'd imagined it. "The shifters and the mages didn't see fit to invite us to the party. I expect the only reason the witches are there is because your muscle-bound Lord couldn't find you without their help. I'd have found you quicker than they could have."

I watched him curiously. "Is your nose out of joint because they didn't come to you?"

"If you had but whispered my name then I'd have been there by your side, dragonlette. I am hurt that you didn't think of me."

"I guess I didn't have time to bargain for what you'd want in return. And my fucking name is Mack." I didn't have time for this. Unfortunately there was still no sign of any taxis. I moved away, trying to put some distance between myself and the keep.

Solus strolled along beside me, hand covering his heart in mock pain. "I am wounded that you would think I would do such a thing."

"Are you kidding me? Every time I've asked you for help you've needed something in return. That's fine, Solus, I'm happy with that arrangement. But don't be pissed off because just once I went to someone else. Anyway, I thought you could track me through my blood and knew when it was being spilled."

"Only if it hits the ground, dragonlette. Your new vampire friends clearly weren't messy enough eaters to let that happen."

I grunted. Whatever. A black cab was trundling along the

road so I raised my hand out to flag it down, but there was already someone inside. Bugger it.

"So who were they?" Solus continued.

I sighed. "Who were what?"

"The vampires. Which ones attacked you? The Summer Queen is unhappy at their actions and has promised vengeance."

"I don't need the Summer Queen to stand up for me. I am perfectly capable of doing so on my own." I crossed the road at the traffic lights so I could turn left onto a busier street where there might be more passing traffic. A car honked at me. Unfortunately it was just some idiot pointing out that I'd walked outside without bothering to get dressed. Fuck off. I was getting annoyed now.

"Mack."

Something in Solus' voice made me stop and look at him.

"We are friends in as much as I am ever friends with anyone. And those undead wankers tried to mess with you. My friend. So I am going to mess with them. Tell me which ones it was who did this."

Jeez. I blinked at the Fae in surprise.

"What?" he said. "Do you think that just because I'm a Fae I can't feel a bit of loyalty towards someone?"

"No," I said, although that was pretty close to the mark. "I just didn't expect you to take it so personally. And it's okay. I will deal with him later."

"Him? You mean there was only one?" The disbelief in Solus' voice was vaguely ego-boosting and vaguely embarrassing all at the same time.

"I meant them," I muttered, unwilling right now to tell him that there had just been one sole vamp who had truly kicked my arse. It was becoming ridiculous that I was getting more embarrassed at myself than angry at Aubrey.

"Look, Solus," I said, "you understand the concept of promises, right?"

The Fae nodded at me.

"Well, then I've made a couple of promises that need to be fulfilled pretty fucking quickly. I need to get to Shrewsbury and I need to help out a certain troll shopkeeper at the same time. I don't need my friends getting all worked up about the vampires on my behalf because I can sort them out myself later. So I have to get home, get some clothes and get a move on. If you can help me with that, then I would really appreciate it. If you can't then get out of my fucking way."

"I can help you with that," he said quietly.

"Great."

"Shall I transport you home and then to Shrewbury?"

"No, just home will be fine. I'll catch the train."

A faint look of disgust crossed Solus' face.

"I need the travel time to do a bit of research," I said by way of explanation. I also didn't want to spend any more time throwing up thanks to supernatural travel than was absolutely necessary.

"I see. I assume that due to the manner in which you exited the Brethren's walls their furry Lord doesn't know what you're doing?"

"That would be correct," I said primly.

Another car drove past, horn blaring as its occupants caught sight of me. Some guy leaned out and wolf whistled. Solus didn't look at them, but he jerked his wrist and there was a loud bang as the rear tyre burst and the car skidded off to the side, slamming into the side of a nearby building. I smirked.

"Well in that case I can still have a little fun." His eyes danced mischievously. "Hold on tight, dragonlette."

I clutched onto his arm and took a deep breath. The air flickered for a moment and then I was standing inside my flat, alone, bile rising in my throat. I did my best to force it down, then hurried into the bedroom to pull on some clothes and pick up some bits and pieces. Thank goodness for the Fae. At least they had some uses. And I didn't want to admit to myself just how touched I felt by Solus' anger on my behalf.

With my trusty backpack still back at the keep, I had to make do with a plastic bag. Figuring I probably still had a bit of time before my disappearance from the keep was noted, I threw in a change of clothes and my laptop, then spent a heartbeat looking down at the Fae translation. I decided I wouldn't risk losing it, so I shoved in the larger of the vampire books instead, along with a small washbag containing a few essentials.

A hammering on the door made me jump. Fuck. I'd thought I'd have more time before either the mages or the shifters caught up to me. I wondered if that meant that they had my flat under surveillance again. Well, they couldn't stop me from going to Shrewsbury. I'd promised Atlanteia that I'd help her out and that was what I was going to do. I'd already lost more time than I'd intended by spending most of the day sleeping in Corrigan's bed. My own problems would just have to wait for now.

I stalked over to the door decisively and wrenched it open. Instead of who I was expecting, however, there was the hunched over figure of a man, leaning against the wall and clutching his stomach. What the fuck?

I peered at him. "Er, can I help you?"

He looked up, his brown eyes meeting mine. There was something remarkably familiar about him, but I couldn't quite work out who he was or where I'd seen him before. Regardless of his identity, there was a seething hatred emanating from every pore of his body - and it was directed entirely at me.

"You did this," he spat.

Um, what? I stared at him, utterly confused.

"You fucking did this," he repeated. "What did you do?"

"Sorry, I don't know who you are." And get off my bloody porch, I thought irritably, I'm in a hurry.

He pushed himself off the wall and reached out, snatching the collar of my t-shirt in his fist. I was more surprised than alarmed but, when he brought his face up to mine, I could feel the colour draining out of my cheeks as I finally recognised him. Bloody hell, it was Aubrey.

CHAPTER EIGHT

I STARED AT HIM, SHOCK AND DISBELIEF MINGLING IN MY VEINS. "Your eyes. They're not red. And your skin, it looks…" my voice trailed off. It looked fucking healthy. Like a human's.

I reached out and gently prodded his cheek, then drew it back quickly. "It's warm."

"It's daylight. I walked here in the fucking sun. I've not done that since 1851." Aubrey let go of my t-shirt and sank backwards, virtually tripping clumsily over his own feet. "You did this," he howled. "You tricked me. As soon as I'd finished drinking, the cramps started. And now," he gestured hopelessly down at himself, "now I'm human."

I began to laugh. I couldn't help myself. It started off as a sort of muffled wheeze, then built up until I was gasping for breath and tears were starting to run down my cheeks. "Oh my God. You thought that you were going to kill me and instead I've ended up killing you."

His dark brown eyes narrowed at me in pure malevolence, which just made me laugh all the harder.

"Do you have any idea how much fucking pain I'm in? It hurts everywhere. I'm one hundred and eighty three years old and I have never felt pain like this before. And I'm so weak. It's like the strength has been completely sapped from me. What did you do?"

"Hey," I said, still full of mirth, "you brought this on yourself. I did nothing. I'm purely an innocent bystander."

"I tasted your blood before. Nothing happened. What did you do?" he repeated with an agonised shout.

"Well, I guess you just didn't drink enough last time. Let's be fair, it was barely a lick. How much did you take last night? How much does it take to kill someone?" I congratulated myself on staying calm and not taking this opportunity to beat the shit out of him.

"I wasn't trying to kill you. I just wanted some blood. You're still alive aren't you?"

"And now so are you. Welcome to the land of the living, Aubrey." I picked up my bag and made to move round him. "Now, if you'll excuse me, I have a prior appointment to keep."

He straightened up, although I could tell it was an effort for him to do so. "Oh no, you can't go anywhere. You are going to undo whatever is it that you've done and change me back." Inexplicably, a tear rolled down his cheek.

I looked at him implacably. "I can't do that. I don't have the power to turn people into vampires, Aubrey. You'll just need to deal with this on your own."

He stretched to grab onto my t-shirt again, but I easily moved out of his reach. "Not so big and strong now, are you? This fucking serves you right," I hissed. " If it wasn't for you and your antics with the Palladium then my friends would still be alive. I'm not about to forget what you did, you wanker."

"All I did was give it back! I didn't fucking kill anyone." A second tear joined the first. He made no move to wipe either one away. It appeared that human Aubrey was struggling to keep hold of his emotions. It made a change from the cold-hearted bastard who I'd previously met. Whatever. His sudden transformation into human form negated the need for me to search him out to get my revenge for what he'd done both at the academy and at Hampstead Heath. I was done.

I turned round and shut my door, making sure it was properly locked. My key was still in my backpack so I'd have no way of getting back inside again without first retrieving it from the keep. I figured that I'd worry about that when I returned to London. Sending a beaming smile towards the now former master of the undead, I side-stepped past him and walked out

"You're not going anywhere without me," he screeched from behind me.

"Try and stop me then," I shot over my shoulder, casually.

He lunged towards me and, yet again, I easily dodged his grasp. Sinking down onto his knees, he covered his face with his hands and began to sob. I felt the faintest twinge of sympathy inside me, just a tiny flicker, and crouched down next to him.

"Aubrey, you need to get over this. You will get over this. You were dead, and now you're not. You get the chance to start again and hardly anyone ever gets that. Embrace it."

He pulled his hands away from his face and stared at me. "You're a fucking idiot. Do you have any idea how much power I have as a vampire? How much influence? I don't want to be a human, they're just pathetic. Those petty emotions and small-minded ideas. They're just animals." His tears were running unhampered now.

The flicker of sympathy I had inside me died an explosive death, and I stood back up. "And now that's you. Enjoy," I said coldly.

I turned on my heel and walked out. Clearly he was as much of an unpleasant human as he was vampire. I guessed it was mildly interesting to note that being a prick didn't necessarily come with being a bloodsucker, that it was much more innate than that. I shrugged. At least it meant he was no longer my problem.

I was halfway down the street on my way to the Tube when the inevitable happened.

Where the fuck are you? Corrigan enunciated every word, reverberating them around my skull.

Hi honey.

Mack, I swear to God, if you don't tell me where you are so I can come and get you, then I will hunt you down and kill you myself.

Ooooh, he was calling me Mack. For once he was being serious. I calmed myself down and tried to put myself in his shoes. *Corrigan, I am eternally grateful that you came and helped me out. I really am. But I've got things to do – I couldn't just hang around the keep.*

He snarled. *And what if the vampires try and attack you again?*

They won't.

How do you know that, Mack?

I just do.

No, you don't. I'm sending two shifters round to you now. They will be with you round the clock to ensure that nothing like this happens again. What the hell were you doing in Hampstead Heath in the middle of the night anyway?

Something inside me snapped. *It's none of your fucking business what I was doing. And you can send round the whole of the sodding Brethren if you want. I'm not there. I told you, I've got things to do. Now stop treating me like a child and piss off back to your little shifter girlfriend so I can get some peace.*

Silence rebounded back at me. For a moment I thought he'd taken the hint and broken the connection, but then he spoke again, with an underlying purr apparent in his Voice. *You're jealous.*

No, I'm not. The lie was so obvious it made me cringe.

I don't have any shifter girlfriends, kitten. I don't have any girlfriends. The reason being that I'm waiting around for you to come to your senses.

Come to my senses? Because the only sensible thing to do is to date you? I cannot believe your arrogance. Leave me the fuck alone.

You really do have the most atrocious language. I wonder what it would take to get you stop swearing so much. His Voice was calmer now, but somehow that made him sound all the more dangerous.

Corrigan, I began.

He interrupted. *If I pushed you up against the wall, let's say the wall of my bedroom that you're now becoming intimately familiar with, and then started at your neck, kissing that smooth skin from the edge of your collarbone then up, all the way up to your lips, and had one hand in your hair while the other unbuttoned your shirt, would you stay quiet then?*

My mouth went completely dry. A booty call was absolutely the last thing I'd expected.

What? Corrigan continued, taunting me softly. *Cat got your tongue?*

I tried to gather my wits. *I don't have any shirts, I only wear t-shirts.*

The words were out before I managed to think twice about them. I groaned inwardly. That was it? Really? The wittiest reply I could come up was that I didn't having fucking buttons? I tried to dissemble further. *This is a completely inappropriate conversation, my Lord.*

I've told you not to call me that. But I tell you what, act as if I really am your Lord and do what I say. Go back home so I can make sure that you are properly protected.

Oh, sneaky. Well, it wasn't going to work even if all my thoughts and emotions were all in a sudden muddle. I drew myself up and slammed my hand against a nearby lamppost, gaining a shocked look from a nervous passerby. *I have told you, I don't need your protection.*

I heard him sigh in my head. *You have got a posse of vampires after your blood, Mack. You need to put your ego aside and stop acting like a suicidal maniac.*

I gave up. *It's not a posse, Corrigan, it's just one, okay? One fucking vampire.*

You let one vampire get the better of you? His Voice dripped with disbelief.

The shame. *Let's just say that I wasn't feeling very well, alright? And he won't be a problem any more.*

Is he dead?

Not exactly.

He roared in my head, a sudden psychotic shifter turnabout. *Then for fuck's sake stop thinking that you're invincible.*

I winced at the explosion. *I don't think that. He really is not going to bother me again.*

I felt a tap on my shoulder and turned round. Human Aubrey was standing there with a weak grin on his face. Bloody hell. *I have to go now, Corrigan.*

Mackenzie...

You should get someone to check out the exterior of the keep. If I can climb down the outside, someone else can sure as hell climb up. It's a weak point in your defences.

He snarled in my head. *You fucking climbed down the keep? From the fifteenth floor?*

Bye Corrigan. I broke off the connection then fixed my attention on Aubrey.

"What do you want?"

"I don't have anywhere else to go," he whined.

"And that's my problem how?" I twisted away from him and walked down the steps to the train station.

He trotted beside me. "Please. Let me come with you. I won't be any bother. But I can't stay in London in case the others find out that I'm not a vampire anymore." He clutched at my arm. "They'll rip me apart and feast on my innards if they find out I'm suddenly a human. And I mean that literally. I know what I said before about humans was stupid. I'm sorry. I'm so sorry. Maybe you can teach me how to be a better person. Now that I'm human I need someone's help. I don't know how to act or what to do. I might do something stupid and someone innocent will end up getting hurt." There was a puppy dog note of hope in his voice. What a crock of shit.

"God, you're pathetic," I muttered.

"So can I come?"

"Of course, " I said sarcastically, "stay by my side and never leave it again. I'm not sure I could cope with the desperate knowledge that you are suffering."

I wrenched my arm away and began to walk the last few steps to the station. He ran after me. Ignoring the few people around me, I took a swing at him, connecting with the side of his head. He fell down, grabbing my ankle as he landed heavily onto the pavement.

"Let go," I hissed in anger.

His hand released me. I half-turned to leave him behind and he got up onto his knees and clasped his hands together.

"No," he bawled loudly, "you have to let me come with you." He started crying again.

I felt eyes on me from across the street and glanced over to see a uniformed policeman watching us closely. Great. He probably thought I was abusing the idiot. The last thing I needed right now would be for him to get involved.

I turned my head to Aubrey and gave him my death stare. "It's a free country - do whatever you want. Just don't get in my fucking way."

A tiny smile crept across his face. "Really? I can't believe it. You're amazing, just amazing." He leaned forward, still on his knees and hugged my legs.

I bent down. "Get the fuck up. Stop crying. If you're going to come then you need to stop drawing attention to yourself."

"Yes, yes," he nodded vigorously. "Whatever you say. Are we catching a train? Can we stop at the kiosk first? I need to get some aspirin, I really am in a lot of pain here."

"Don't push your luck."

"Okay, okay." He nodded again as I rolled my eyes. I was definitely going to regret this.

* * *

I COMPLETELY IGNORED AUBREY, going so far as to buy myself just one return ticket to Shrewsbury when we arrived at the main terminal at Piccadilly, and leaving him to sort one out for himself on his own. I'd spent so much time dealing first with getting out of the keep, then with Aubrey and Corrigan, that there was only one more train left to catch that day if I wanted to get there before the next morning. Even that still meant having to change at Birmingham. There was barely enough time to grab my change from the ticket machine and run to the platform before the train pulled away. Somehow or other though, Aubrey managed to keep up because when I sank down into the seat on the half empty carriage, he was still right beside me. I wasn't completely sure why I was bothering to let him continue to hang around, but at least he gave me something else to mull over other than Corrigan's very disturbing words. I decided firmly that I had too much to do to spend time thinking about what he'd said. That's why it was so annoying that it kept popping back into my head. Especially with the images along to match.

Eventually, I couldn't stand the clamour of my own thoughts any longer and I glanced over at the ex-vampire. He was staring down at his fingernails in fascination. Weirdo.

"Do you have a phone?"

"Huh?" he looked up stupidly, still half lost in reverie.

"I said, do you have a phone?"

He looked momentarily taken aback, and then bobbed his head and dug into his coat pocket, handing over a sleek black mobile.

"Thanks," I muttered, and began to jab at the keys. "Aubrey, you do realise that you have fourteen missed calls?"

He grunted. "It's the others. I was supposed to be at a meeting this morning to see what we could do to further undermine the Ministry."

I looked up and stared at him. "You do know that I'm friends with the mages, right?"

He grunted again and went back to examining his fingernails. "They used to be blood red."

I was confused. "The mages?"

"My nails. Not surface blood red, but the shade of deep arterial gorgeousness." There was a wistful edge to his voice that made my stomach turn.

Disgusted, I turned back to the phone and punched in Alex's number. We'd been in touch off and on since the terrible events at the academy back in February, but our chats had retained an awkward quality to them. Nonetheless, I felt that he owed me and could help with my Balud situation. Unsurprisingly, his ringtone was the Beach Boys, although he picked before they were barely into the chorus.

"Hey," he answered lazily. "I don't know who you are, dude. How'd you get this number?"

"It's me, Alex, I'm using someone else's phone."

"Mack Attack! How's it hanging?"

"Given that my anatomy doesn't work that way, I guess not great. Are you free to talk right now?"

"Sure, yeah. What's the problem?" The muffled background noise faded as he clearly moved away to somewhere more private.

"I need you to do me a favour. It's nothing dangerous," I said, hastily, before he could begin his usual feeble protestations, "I just need you to keep an eye out on a shop for me."

I filled him in on the info that Balud had provided about his competitor.

"Sheesh, dude. I dunno. What if the Batibat thing sees me?"

"Then act like you're nervous about going into her shop and buying something. All you need to do is to keep track of who goes in and out of the shop so I can work out who is really behind the whole operation. It'll be boring, but not hard, or dangerous."

"So that you can pay him for the weapons that you've already managed to lose?"

"I've only lost one. I know perfectly well where the other one is."

"And how is Lord Shifty keeping these days?"

I squirmed and prevaricated. "He's fine. Can you do it, Alex?"

"'Course, Mack Attack. Shall I call you on this number?"

"Nah, that might not work. The phone's owner may not be with me for long." Aubrey shot me a baleful look as I said that. I scowled at him, and stood up, squeezing past his knees to get away from him and move into the next carriage. "Listen, Alex, there's something else too. Apparently the vamps were meeting this morning to see what they could do to weaken the mages. I don't know what they were planning or why, although I can try to find out. I thought maybe you should know though. So you can tell the Arch-Mage."

"Yeah, except he's kind of been ignoring me lately. I don't think he's happy about the way things turned out, you know, before. I did hear that you were attacked by a group of vampires though. Is that what this is about?"

"Uh, not really. Do you think you can get in touch with him anyway?"

"I'll try. It's not much to go on though."

"I know. I will see what else I can wheedle out."

"Are you okay? I didn't ask before because I figured that you're the Mack Attack, you know, that you're good no matter what a bunch of bloodsuckers do to you. But you're not under any compulsion or anything now are you?"

"That stuff doesn't work on me."

His answering question was filled with doubt. "So how did you let the vampires beat you then? Why didn't you just shift?"

"First of all, there was only one, and he didn't beat me because I'm still here and I'm still standing. Believe me, I think he's come out worse off. Or at least he thinks he has." I knew I was being cryptic but I was getting irritated at having to continually point out that I'd been bested by one measly vamp. "Second of all, I don't want to shift. I don't know what will happen if I do. I think it's safer if I just stay me."

"And get your blood drained in the process?" Alex sounded about the same as Corrigan had, an angry protective edge to his voice. Prickly heat tingled at my toes.

"I'm fine."

"Yeah, but…"

"I said I'm fine."

"Okay, dude, chillax. Look, I'll head over to the shop now and find somewhere nearby to hunker down and watch it. I can email you with the details of who I see going in."

"That would be perfect Alex, thank you."

"Any time, Mack Attack."

"It's Mack," I responded automatically.

"Sure thing," he chuckled, then hung up.

I turned off the phone and stood there for a moment staring at it. It was getting really annoying that everyone was being so prissy with my safety. I knew that they all meant well and I guessed that it was nice that they cared. It was better than those dark days right after I'd left the keep and I'd been so completely alone. But, for goodness' sake, I was capable of making my own decisions and looking after myself. I'd managed this sodding far without having half the Otherworld standing over me as if I was some kind of fragile flower. The worst of it was that I knew the mages would cast a Divination spell and find me in Shrewsbury virtually the second I arrived. Then I'd have them all hovering around there too.

I cursed under my breath, then stomped back to where Aubrey was sitting, and tossed his phone back into his lap.

"Problems?" he asked, looking up at me with a sudden malicious gleam in his eye that reminded of me of the predatory vampire he used to be, instead of the whiny human he'd become.

"No," I snapped. Fortunately I was saved from having to respond further as a trolley came trundling past, offering brightly wrapped biscuits, limp looking sandwiches and coffee. I ordered myself a cup, Aubrey following my lead and doing the same. After the girl had taken her change and pushed further on, I took a small sip and winced. It was bloody awful coffee.

"Oh my God," breathed Aubrey.

"Let me guess, you've never tasted British Rail's finest before?"

He cradled the small plastic cup lovingly in his hands. "This is delicious. It's so deep and rich and earthy. Is this what coffee tastes like?"

I peered at him. He didn't seem to be being sarcastic. "You've never had coffee before?"

"Of course, I've had coffee before, but it never tasted like this before."

"You mean like it's made of dishwater?"

He looked at me as if I was crazy. "It's amazing." The expression on his face was one of stunned wonder.

"You, Aubrey, have never lived." Then I realised that wasn't far off from the truth. "Maybe that's at least one thing you can take from now being a human. You have new improved tastebuds."

He took another sip of the coffee, his eyes wide with child-like wonder. "Miss Smith, you may be right."

Miss Smith? Seriously? "Call me Mack."

"Okay. Whatever you say, Mack." He took another drink, savouring it slowly in his mouth before swallowing, and turned to me. "So come on, then. Tell me what you did that made me human."

As if. He might not technically be a vampire anymore but you didn't undo almost two centuries of being part of one of the most untrustworthy groups of the Otherworld in less than a day. The last thing I was going to do was to tell him that I was a Draco Wyr who possessed blood that not only lit up my insides as if they were on fire and enabled me to shift, but also apparently had healing qualities that extended so far as to cure vampirism. Not a single theory in any of the vamp lore books that I'd read back at the academy had whispered the vaguest hint that such blood existed, even if they'd propagated all sorts of other rumours as to how a cure might be achieved. That thought, however, provided me with an easy escape route.

I shrugged. "Well, I took this herbal remedy a few hours before I was at the Heath. I think you're only supposed to take a small sip but I guess I kind of overdosed. I was feeling really woozy before you showed up and I'm sure it was down to that."

Aubrey's eyes widened fractionally. "What was it?"

"It's called TemperSoothe."

He snorted.

"Hey," I said, protesting, "I have some anger issues, okay? I've been going to anger management counselling. It's just difficult to keep up with the sessions sometimes. I thought it might help. Anyway, it's got skullcap and Passiflora Incarnata in it."

He nodded slowly. "So you think that this Temper stuff is what turned me."

No. My weird blood did. "Who knows?"

His jaw tightened and I could see him thinking. "So if you've got anger issues, then you've drunk it before, right? That's why your blood tasted strange the first time around."

"Mmm," I murmured non-committedly.

"Where did you get it from?"

I told him the name of the shop. "I don't think drinking more of it is going to turn you back, Aubrey."

"No, but I could use it against my enemies. I could make them be human too." His hand curled into a fist and he thumped it against his knee. "It'll be fantastic. I can pulverize them into dust. I can make them feel the agonising pain that I now feel."

"Is it really so bad? You've already discovered that you have the power to appreciate the taste of something other than blood. Now you can do more. Meet a girl, a real girl. Have normal sex. Have children. Grow old." I ticked off the list on my fingers.

He spluttered. "We're not living in a teen vampire romance! I'm one hundred and eighty three years old. That means that every single living person seems like a child to me. You all possess the maturity of toddlers as far as I'm concerned. I've seen two world wars, the industrial revolution, and the death of the slave trade. I used to drink with the fucking Bloomsbury group! What kind of possible relationship could I have with a human whose most important life experience has been the launch of Facebook?" His voice was rising, and a few of the other passengers were starting to look round.

"Okay, okay, I'm sorry I brought it up," I said soothingly. "Why don't you get some rest and see if you can have a little nap. It'll relax you."

Aubrey's eyes narrowed suspiciously. "Then you'll just get off at the next station so you don't have to be with me anymore."

"I can't," I said patiently, "this is the last train and I have to get to Shrewsbury." I reached down into the plastic bag at my feet and pulled out my laptop, tapping it. "Besides, I've got work I need to do."

He watched me for a moment, as if I was suddenly about to push past him and leap off the train just to get away from him, then finally relaxed. "Okay. Is that what humans do?"

I nodded.

"Okay." He leaned his head back and closed his eyes.

Thank fuck.

CHAPTER NINE

It didn't take long for Aubrey to start gently snoring. It was no wonder. I figured he'd probably not slept since he'd bitten me the night before. Not to mention the now depleted rush of adrenaline I imagined he'd had to deal with from the physical and emotional trauma of his transformation. It made my life easier. While I decided that maybe I didn't really mind if he tagged along for a bit – because perhaps I could potentially help him with the whole human thing rather than letting him roam the streets on his own like a ticking time bomb – I didn't trust one red blood cell in his entire body. And that meant that even though I could hardly hide where I was going, there was no reason for me to divulge the reasons as to why. Atlanteia hadn't explicitly told me to keep schtum, but the lengths she, and probably all the other dryads, had gone to in order to make sure that nobody else knew about her request did suggest that she wanted it kept a secret. If Corrigan or Alex or Solus or someone of that ilk could help, then I had no compunction about telling them if I thought it would help the dryads' cause. I wasn't bound to stay quiet. But I certainly wasn't going to start blabbing to a vamp, ex or otherwise.

For a charge, that admittedly had me cursing, I was able to get a wifi connection. It was unusual for me to stick to normal human channels and not jump immediately onto the Othernet, but that wouldn't serve my purposes right now as it was the humans who I needed to galvanise into action. It didn't take me more than a few minutes before I found what I was looking for.

There was a group set up not too far away from Shrewsbury currently protesting against a road being built to improve links between two towns outlying Cardiff. They were clearly fighting a losing battle. The protests had been ongoing for around nine months, as had the local council, who had already cleared the planned route and were laying the groundwork for the next stage. All the approvals had gone ahead and it was patently just a matter of time before the road was completed. The main objection, apart from the felling of a considerably number of trees (which were surely dryad-less), was that bats had been sighted in the area. Sadly for the anti-road campaigners, it was one single report of one small colony (or cloud, as I learnt the collective noun often was) of bats in one small farm. It didn't even appear particularly credible.

I cast a glance down the sleeping Aubrey. With bats as a clear winning choice to encourage others onto my side, he might prove to be more useful than I could have imagined. I was pretty confident that all the old legends about vamps shifting into bats were a waste of time, but I bet that Aubrey still knew a fair few things about the creatures.

The website was careful not to mention any protestors by name, focusing instead on the 'government lackeys', 'council bullshitters' and 'pro-road scum', but there was a handy generic email link at the bottom of the page. I dug inside myself, allowing my bloodfire to well up in empathetic antagonism, then fired off a lengthy and passionate email regarding the tragic situation of the imaginary bats of Haughmond Hill. I felt slightly guilty at the lie, but it was not as if the fact of the development was a lie, more that there probably weren't any bats. I couldn't know that for sure though. There might be some there. Hoping that I'd hit the right note with the campaigners, I then continued searching, finding four other nearby groups and three other websites where I was also able to post various messages under different pseudonyms about the immediate need to halt this 'catastrophic' development. I knew that it wouldn't be that easy to get the environmentalists on my side; if it was then the dryads could probably have sorted it out themselves. They might not have their own wifi access in their tree habitats, but they obviously weren't without their own resources. Besides, Atlanteia had already said that their usual efforts weren't working. I doubted she'd have been so concerned if there wasn't something, if not supernatural, then at the very least nefarious, also involved. However it got the ball rolling at least and gave me a few ideas as to how these protest groups operated.

With that accomplished, I logged onto my own email to check to see whether Alex had sent in any updates yet. There was nothing. It was probably too soon. I hoped that he was at the very least outside the shop by now. Its mysterious owner who had Balud so concerned was going to be more likely to show up now that night had fallen, much like many Otherworlders would, if he really was trying to keep his identity a secret. The cover of darkness could hide a multitude of sins.

I was tempted to venture onto the Othernet, just to see whether or not there happened to be any pap photos of Corrigan with the dark haired shifter who I'd spotted him with before. He'd said she wasn't his girlfriend – or at least that he didn't have a girlfriend anyway – but that didn't mean I didn't still want to know exactly who she was. However, an announcement came over the tannoy that we were pulling into Birmingham, so I snapped the laptop shut and roughly prodded Aubrey awake instead. He was grumpy and appeared to have somehow lost the power to form coherent sentences, but he managed to disembark and stumble along beside me towards the next platform so we could change trains. As soon as he sat down again, he fell instantly back asleep, his head lolling dangerously towards my shoulder and a small trickle of drool making its way down his chin.

I watched him for a few minutes before pushing him back upright again to prevent him from using me as pillow. He jerked his head away from me with a phlegmy snort, but then almost immediately started drooping towards my apparently comfortable shoulder yet again. I rolled my eyes, and tried to inch away from him. It didn't work. Eventually, giving up, I left him alone, ignoring the heavy weight of his head as it landed yet again on top of me. It was a losing battle anyway. I reached back down into my plastic bag and pulled out the vampire book I'd brought along and flipped through the pages. Thanks to Aubrey's inadvertent transformation I no longer need to exact any sort of revenge on the vamps. It didn't hurt to know as much about them as I possibly could of course. Unfortunately, the most it seemed to say about curing vampirism was that it was impossible. That was clearly a falsehood so I probably couldn't trust anything the book said at all.

I leaned back in my seat, ignoring Aubrey's muttered protestations as my movements jolted his head and pondered the entire situation. One of the things that Iabartu, the demi-goddess who had set my exile from the pack into motion, had said about my blood was that it could be used to control others. I wondered whether I could make Aubrey to do what I wanted him to now. I flicked him a quick glance. That didn't seem to be the case so far. I couldn't even prevent him from falling asleep on top of me. I frowned as my thoughts drifted further. According to legend, Draco Wyr blood also had potential healing properties, although I hadn't ever tested that theory, despite coming close when Corrigan had red fever, normally fatal to shifters. I chewed my bottom lip. If my blood cured Aubrey, so to speak, could it cure cancer too? How about AIDS? If I'd given some to Julia when she was attacked back in Cornwall would her leg have been able to re-attach itself? What about if I gave her some now? It had to have some pretty fucking strong healing power if it could eliminate whatever it was that made Aubrey an undead being of the night. Bloody hell. Did that mean it could bring people back from the dead? Images of John, Thomas and Brock flitted rapidly through my head, one after the other.

No. It wouldn't be right; as much as I wished they were still alive and as much as I regretted the circumstances of all their deaths, even trying to bring them back, regardless of success, would surely upset the balance of nature. I wasn't prepared to give myself the power of life and death. Nobody should be allowed that kind of strength. It might be worth testing out the curative element, however. That didn't seem quite so *wrong*.

I was still mulling over the possibilities when we pulled into Shrewsbury. I shook Aubrey awake, then got off the train with him trailing in my wake. The station was well lit, with a row of taxis waiting outside. We clambered into one, directing the driver to the outskirts of the town. I didn't want to broadcast our destination quite just yet, so told him to drop us off at a farmhouse I'd spotted on the map beforehand that wasn't too far away. Aubrey stayed quiet.

I looked over at him, thoughtfully. "Aubrey, touch your nose with your index finger."

He seemed confused, but did what I asked. I raised my eyebrows. Maybe I *could* control him.

"Is this some other human thing?" he inquired "Like the tastebuds?"

I jerked my head at the taxi driver in the front, silently warning Aubrey to watch what he said. Okay, perhaps I couldn't control him. He'd probably just followed my instructions because he thought it was a new and exciting human experience. I frowned. There was still something about that which bothered me though.

I waited until we'd been deposited in front of the dark and silent farmhouse, with the driver already disappearing off into the distance, before I spoke again.

HELEN HARPER

"You were human once. You must have been, what, thirty when you originally became a vamp?"

His mouth turned in disgust. "Please. Twenty-nine."

"So you know what stuff tastes like. You know that touching your sodding nose isn't some human thing."

"You don't get it," he said patiently, "once you are turned, everything else prior to that fades into complete insignificance. I can barely remember my life before then. Once you are attuned to the susurration of blood, to the iron rich succulent density of it, nothing else is important." He licked his lips.

My stomach turned. "How many people have you killed?"

"I take it by people, you mean humans?"

I nodded.

"Not that many. Most deaths are by accident really. The average person has ten pints of blood in their system and can lose up to four pints of that before any real damage is done." He shot me a sly look. "How would you feel if you drank four pints of beer? Would you be satisfied?"

"I guess," I said doubtfully. I'd drunk more than that more than once in the past.

"It's possible to drink more. Nobody needs to, but sometimes we do." He shrugged. "It's not a great idea to leave bodies all the over place though. Especially with the availability of modern post-mortems. We try and avoid it."

"But you have killed people?" I prodded.

"Haven't you?"

"No!"

"You've killed Otherworld creatures."

"Yes, but…" my voice fell away.

"They're not human."

"No," I protested. "It's got nothing to do with the fact that they're not human, it's to do with the fact that when I kill them they are trying to kill me. Or someone else. It's about protection. I'm not a fucking psychopath."

"You already told me you had anger management issues," he

pointed out. "I think that might make you more of a potential homicidal maniac than me."

"I have fucking emotions. I feel guilt and remorse and pain and pity. Bloodsuckers don't."

He cocked his head slightly in agreement. "You're right. I must admit that having feelings again is proving to be somewhat difficult." Aubrey blinked, his eyes suddenly welling up. "I miss it so much. Not having to think so much or worry so much. I don't know how you do this all the time. It's so difficult, Mack." He sniffed loudly then wiped his nose on his sleeve.

Jeez. Soulless Aubrey might have been a prick, but this version had the potential to be even more annoying. He wasn't wrong about the emotions part though. In the past few hours he'd covered a hell a lot of them – and all were at the extreme end of the scale. It was like he was some stereotypically over the top pre-menstrual teenager. I shook my head.

"Come on then."

"Where are we going?"

"You'll see."

"You're so wonderful letting me come with you, Mack. Just so…"

I jabbed him in the chest. "Shut the fuck up."

His mouth snapped closed and he blinked in acknowledgement. That was bloody better.

* * *

IT WAS ABOUT three miles to Haughmond Hill from where we were, first along the tarmacked road and then a right turn up a trail. Now that I was away from the city and back out in the countryside, the pathetic figure of Aubrey at my heels notwithstanding, I felt my soul lighten. In this kind of environment I was much more at home. It was easier to track noises and register the presence of others; in the city with all the constant noise it was virtually impossible. Right now, I knew that the only people in the vicinity were Aubrey and myself. Here, I was in control. There would be no sneaking up on me from behind, no sudden creatures appearing above me without my knowledge, no Otherworld inhabitants getting the jump on me...

I let out a pained cry as Aubrey inadvertently stepped on my heel, the edge of his shoe biting sharply into the flesh of my ankle. I spun round and glared at him.

"Idiot."

His eyes filled with tears again.

"Oh, don't bloody start that again. Although the least you could do is apologise."

He stared at me mutely.

"Well?" I put my hands on my hips, feeling slightly like some old school headmistress waggling her finger at a recalcitrant child.

Aubrey opened his mouth and then closed it again.

My eyes narrowed. "Are you fucking sulking?"

He still didn't answer. Hold on a minute. I thought back to the last words I'd said to him and considered. "Okay, you can speak if you want to."

"Oh, thank goodness," he wailed. "I'm so terribly sorry, Mack, I didn't mean to hurt you. It's just it's dark and I'm not used to this kind of place. The path is all bumpy and there are things on it like roots and shit. I used to have no problem with that. Vampires have got great night vision," he added mournfully.

Everything was suddenly becoming clear. I'd been right the first time around. I peered at him. "What else have I told you to do?"

"You said that I have to call you Mack and that I must never leave you no matter what."

"What? I didn't say that!"

"Yes, you did," he stated seriously. "You said I had to stay by your side and never leave you again."

"I was being fucking sarcastic!"

He shrugged.

Sweet Jesus. He'd better bloody hope that I was going to be able to supersede that instruction or I'd probably end up ripping his head from his body. I watched him curiously. He didn't appear to be unhappy. It was a strange sensation, knowing that I could compel someone to do whatever I instructed. I wondered if it was permanent or whether it would wear off as my blood left Aubrey's system. It had to be as a result of the amount that he'd taken from me. He'd had a taste months before and clearly hadn't been following my orders then as he'd done the exact opposite to what I'd wanted him to. That went for Anton also, who'd tasted my blood when we'd fought for Corrigan and the rest of the Brethren back in Cornwall. Just that tiny lick had made Anton practically addicted to my blood however. I hoped that meant that Aubrey wasn't now the same because, even without him being a vamp, the quantity that he'd drunk could create a need in him that would outweigh almost any other desire.

"Are you hungry?" I asked carefully.

He thought for a moment before answering. "No."

I eyed him. "Okay then. " I turned back round and continued heading up the hill, now very aware of him at my back. "Actually, Aubrey, you take the lead."

He nodded agreement and then moved in front of me. "I don't know where to go though."

"That's alright. Just keep going straight and I'll tell you where to go. Don't say anything until I tell you to either. I need to listen out in case there's anything out here." And I didn't want to have to listen to him either.

He complied, continuing up the trail as I followed. It was a rather broad flat hill so the slope was easy to navigate. We picked our way up, somewhat slower now that Aubrey was leading, but making steady progress nonetheless. I tried not to worry too much about what he might end up doing and instead listened out hopefully for any bats. Unfortunately I couldn't hear or see any.

Still, before too long, we emerged out at a decent sized carpark.
I knew from my research that towards the east and slightly behind us were the ruins of an old abbey, and that just up ahead was a quarry. This meant that the area Atlanteia was worried about had to be more to the west, where there were areas of dense trees. There were several clearly marked and well labelled paths to follow so, choosing the one that would allow us to cover the largest area, I crooked my finger at Aubrey, gesturing in the direction I wanted to head, and we began to veer left.

I wasn't entirely sure what I was expecting to find. Obviously the development hadn't started yet and it was the middle of the night so there was no-one around to question. I was hoping that the dryads who lived here would make themselves known so that I could ask them a few questions. It was possible that Aubrey's presence might scare them away of course. As tempting as it was to leave him behind in the car park, in the event that there was something out there he might come in handy. His supernatural vamp strength had no doubt abandoned him, but he had to have some lingering traces of ability that would prove useful.

We spent thirty minutes or so wandering along, the moon high in the night sky and the stars sharp and clear, before I noticed it. One of the lessons I'd had back at the academy had been in the art of Illusion. The cackling mage who'd been my tutor had found it funny to use her art to hide from me the very building in which the lessons were meant to be held. I'd found it immensely irritating at the time, but it was proving its worth in terms of learning as I now realised that even in the darkness there was something odd flickering at the edge of my vision, alerting me to the fact that some kind of magic had been woven here to conceal something. Feeling immensely satisfied that I'd noticed it, while wondering how on earth mages could be involved in this, I tapped Aubrey on the shoulder, quietly telling him to wait, then backtracked, keeping the flicker within my periphery vision.

When I was sure I knew where to look, I stopped. The

glimmer was right in front of me, indicating that something wasn't quite right. Slowly, and oh so very carefully, I bent down and picked up a twig, poking at it. There was a quiet whoosh, as if a gust of wind had suddenly announced itself into the silent night air, and then the spell unravelled before my eyes. I heard a gasp from Aubrey further up the path and my mouth dropped open in horror as I registered what had suddenly been revealed.

CHAPTER TEN

The area uncovered by the unmasking of the spell was perhaps only about ten metres squared. The ground was empty and black, as if it had been scorched by fire, and in its centre stood a large tree, completely absent of leaves or any other sign of life. Its branches had a grey brittle appearance, highlighting that it was as completely devoid of life as the earth and the pale figure of the dryad hanging from it. She appeared to be bound there by her wrists, in a pose eerily reminiscent of a crucifixion.

I tried to take a step forward, as if to see whether I could still rescue the tragic tree nymph, despite the fact that her shrunken flesh made it clear that she had been there for some time. However there was some kind of invisible barrier in my way, preventing me from moving into the dead space. I pushed forward with every ounce of strength that I could muster, but it was clear that I wouldn't be able to break through by sheer physical power alone.

Aubrey moved silently to my side and stared up at the dryad's body.

"Any ideas?" I asked.

He glanced at me mutely. Oh yeah. "You can speak."

"It's so elegant," he breathed. "This is a masterpiece."

I couldn't help myself. Reaching over, I slapped him hard across the cheek and gave him a disgusted look.

"Owwww!" He clutched his face with his hands, the wounded expression in his eyes clear even through the darkness. "You don't have to resort to violence. What did I do?"

I didn't know why I'd ever thought that vamps were smart. I supposed that I'd assumed that living for so long afforded enough life experience to understand at least some of the nuances of polite society. Clearly I'd been completely wrong.

"One minute you are like a puppy dog at my feet, begging to be brought along and gushing at how wonderful I am," I spat at him, "not to mention the constant fucking tears, and the next you're making some kind of sicko comment like that. She's dead, Aubrey. She died a horrible death and you're talking about her as if she's a piece of fucking art."

"I was a vampire for a long time, and I was a bloody good vampire too. We're undead, Mack. I might not kill many people these days but death really is what I know, and I know that whoever did that," he jerked his head towards the tree, "did it very deliberately and very carefully. Look at the way she's strung up. You say I'm talking about her as if she's a work of art, well, that's artfully done. Bodies are heavy, and not all that easy to manipulate into different positions. She's hanging there, from those dead branches, by her wrists. There's nothing holding her up; she's been arranged that way." His voice began to rise suddenly. "You're acting as if I'm more than evil than whoever did that. Bitch!"

I guessed that angry Aubrey was suddenly making a return. The guy was like Jack the Ripper, a Disney princess and Niagara Falls all combined into one. I felt a flicker of bloodfire. "Go round the back and see if you can get through that way," I told him. "Keep trying to find a weak spot."

He snarled at me in rage but, good little servant that he was, his feet were already moving him away before he could finish. He circled round the edge of the blackened patch and began throwing himself at the edges of the barrier, over and over again. I watched him for a moment, part of me hoping that he'd do himself some permanent damage, and then turned my attention back to the tree.

I thought about Aubrey's words and examined the way the dryad had been displayed. He had been kind of right, actually. She was definitely positioned as if to gain maximum effect from a viewing audience. And yet, whoever had done this had then hidden her from sight. What was the point in creating a piece of 'art', and then never letting anyone see it? I fervently hoped it wasn't part of some sick master plan by some nasty Otherworld monster. Atlanteia hadn't so much as breathed that any dryads had already died as a result of the upcoming development.

Unfortunately I now very much doubted that the planned tree clearance had anything to do with some luxury holiday homes. Not unless the target market was psychotic serial killers anyway.

There was a thump from the other side. Aubrey had managed to trip over something and was lying sprawled on the ground. I smirked humourlessly, and then returned my thoughts to the matter in hand. My blood had a helpful habit of being able to open various mystical locks. I really wanted to use it now to get through to the dryad to cut her down at the very least. But I didn't want to trigger any supernatural alarms in the process. As much as she deserved a dignified death, I would probably serve the nymph, or her friends and family anyway, better by concealing not only my own presence, but also my knowledge of her presence.

I stared at her sadly. "I'll come back for you," I whispered. "I promise."

Leaving Aubrey where he was, I continued further on up the path. Surely one of the other dryads who lived here had to have seen something? If those trees were as capable of communicating as Atlanteia had suggested, then the whole bloody forest probably knew what had happened. All I needed to do was to find someone to fucking tell me. Anger and heat were swirling around inside me – at Aubrey for his utter lack of tact and decency, at whoever had done that to the dryad, and at Atlanteia for not telling me that there was some kind of bizarre tree murderer on the loose in the first place. At the very least, if she'd told the truth, I'd have arrived somewhat better prepared.

I stalked up through the trees, then looked right and cut across, leaving the path behind. When I reached a small clearing, I stopped and looked up.

"Come on," I cried out. "You got me here. Show yourselves and tell me what happened."

Somewhere in the distance, an owl hooted. There was no other sound.

Pissed off, I tried again. "Your friend has been slaughtered by some kind of monster. I imagine that's the real reason why I'm here. But if you want me to try and stop whatever did that, you're going to have to help me out a bit and tell me what you know."

I stood and waited. Again, there was nothing. I clenched my jaw and called their bluff.

"Fine, then. If you can't help me, then I can't help you." I turned round. "I'm leaving. You can keep the ex-bloodsucker if you want. That's the best I can do."

I stomped out of the clearing. I'd barely taken more than a couple of steps, however, when a quiet voice floated towards me.

"Don't."

If the woods hadn't been so quiet, I'd never have heard her. "Pardon?" I asked politely, albeit rather loudly.

"Don't leave."

"You're going to have to do better than that. Show yourself so we can have a proper talk, face to face, and I might stay." I wasn't enjoying this conversation very much; playing hardball with an introverted dryad was not exactly my idea of fun. I didn't think I had much choice, however.

"I would rather not. We are not like our city cousins, Mackenzie. We are not so bold."

That figured. Both Atlanteia and the dryad who'd first found me in the park had shown considerably more confidence than I'd come to expect from my previous encounters with dryads in the countryside. Perhaps the pollution emboldened them. Whatever.

"That's not my problem. Atlanteia asked me to come here and help put a stop to a building development. Not deal with a slaughtered dryad."

For a long moment there was no response. Then the voice softly spoke again. "So she's dead?"

Empathy filled me. I closed my eyes briefly. "Yeah. She's dead."

When I opened my eyes again, there was a pale figure in front of me, long fingers gripping the slender girth of a young tree. Silent sad tears of green trickled down her cheeks.

"I'm sorry," I said, ineffectually.

She dropped her head, barely able to even look at me. "We thought…we thought she might still be alright."

I didn't answer, instead waiting for the dryad to pick herself back up again. I hoped it wouldn't be too long, then immediately hated myself for that thought. She flicked pained eyes up at me, and then back down to the ground again.

"We don't know what happened."

I had to strain to hear her. "But you knew she was gone?" I asked gently.

"Yes. We heard her scream. It was…unpleasant."

That was probably the understatement of the fucking year. "What about the trees?"

"They did not see. They spoke of a strange shape, nothing more."

Outstanding. What good did all-seeing trees do if they didn't actually see anything? I gritted my teeth. "When was this?"

"About two weeks ago."

She didn't like expanding on her answers much. "Okay. So does it have anything to do with the development?"

"We think so."

I sighed. "You're going to have to help me out a little bit here. Give me some more information."

The dryad swallowed nervously. "We had managed to contact the local humans. They were coming. We had heard that people in power were on our side. Then Mereia disappeared and everything stopped. As if they'd forgotten the development ever existed. The number of visitors has also decreased. We have not seen this before. So few people in this wood. The animals and birds sense it also. They are quiet. There is an unnatural feeling."

That was an improvement. "Thank you."

She inclined her head gently.

"Why didn't Atlanteia tell me any of this?"

"We know you are afraid of what you are."

Great. Was there anything that the sodding Otherworld inhabitants didn't already know? Apart from useful information about the murdering bastard who had slaughtered an innocent friend of theirs, of course. You'd think they'd pay more attention to what was trying to kill them instead of what was trying to protect them. I gazed askance at the nymph, in full defensive mode and feeling the hackles on the back of my neck rise up. "So?"

"We thought that if there was a chance you had to fight, you would not come. We need you."

"So you thought it would be better for me to walk in here completely unprepared?"

"Atlanteia did not lie."

"Yeah, yeah. She didn't tell the whole truth either though did she?" I looked away from the quivering nymph for a moment, still annoyed but unwilling to scare her off with a snarky attitude. "I'm not going to change." Realising I wasn't being completely clear, I elaborated. "I mean, if you think that I'll transform into a dragon to save the day, then it's not going to happen. I'm not going to do that again."

"It is enough that you are here. We have faith in you." A sad smile lit her features. "We would not have asked you otherwise."

"You know I have someone with me."

She nodded.

"And I might need to get some others to come and help too."

A heartbeat later she nodded again.

"And you cannot tell anyone that you know what I am. Not you, not Atlanteia, not any dryad ever. I don't know exactly who those trees talk to, but they can't tell anyone either."

The dryad didn't pause this time. "You have my word."

"Okay, I'll see what I can do. There are no promises though. I have no idea what we're up against. Something that can not only use supernatural power, but also manipulate the human world is something that is powerful. It might be one entity or it might be many working together. Can you tell me whether there was anything you noticed about Mereia before she was taken? Anything different about her?"

I jerked my head to my left as I heard a muffled yell off in the distance which sounded like Aubrey. He'd probably fallen over again. I switched my gaze back to the dryad, but she'd gone. "Hello?"

Damn it, I didn't get her name.

"Are you still there?"

Nothing. I tutted in quiet irritation. Given how shy that nymph had appeared I'd probably done well to get as much out of her as I did. I'd just have to hope that they weren't keeping anything else back from me. Making a mental note never to entirely trust any dryad, I headed back to rejoin the path and find out what was going on with El Nutso.

* * *

WHEN I ARRIVED BACK at the warded area, I couldn't make out Aubrey's shape anywhere. Cursing under my breath, and trying to peer through the darkness, I began to wander round the barrier, keeping my footsteps as light as possible and my senses alert. Either the compulsion that my blood had placed him under had dissipated, or he'd been attacked by whatever had created the foul display in the first place. After having Aubrey get the jump on me at Hampstead Heath there was absolutely no way I was going to let anything else do the same. Stupid herbal mixtures aside, I had a reputation to maintain.

I was about halfway around when I spotted him. He was lying flat on his back at the far corner. From where I was, he seemed to be completely immobile and I couldn't make out whether he was still breathing or not. I pressed my fingertips together to keep the green fire down. As handy as it was in a fight, its glow might just alert any potential boogie monster to my presence. Instead of heading straight for him, I side-stepped to my right, avoiding the few fallen twigs and branches on the ground. If he had indeed been attacked, and hadn't just idiotically managed to knock himself out, then it stood to reason that whatever had gotten him was now hiding nearby, waiting for any companions to rush to his aid. Fortunately, while I might not be prepared to kill him myself anymore, I didn't actually really give that much of a shit if anyone else bothered to do so. At this particular point in time I was far more concerned with my own self-preservation.

I quickly scanned the blackened inner area, trying to avoid looking too closely again at the dead nymph, but there was nothing there. If anything was waiting in the wings ready to pounce, then it was on the outside. I felt a flicker of regret that I didn't have Balud's daggers with me anymore and then pushed it away. Wishing otherwise wouldn't change anything. I had to focus on the here and now.

I took a step forward and paused, listening. There was nothing. My eyes searched through the dark shapes of the living trees and watched the shadows on the ground for any suggestions of movement. Still there was no sign of anything. I took another step before waiting again. A cloud drifted across the moon, darkening the environment even further. I was fortunate that by now dawn couldn't be far away. If there was anything waiting, then it would be easier to see when the sun rose. I debated my options then decided to take the high road, reaching out for the closest tree and swinging myself up onto its lower branches, then digging my feet into the rough bark to gain an effective foothold so I could climb higher.

There was a sudden groan and I froze, eyes flicking left and right. It sounded again and I realised that it was Aubrey himself making the noise. Guess he wasn't dead after all then. I watched as he sat up, one hand rubbing at his forehead, and the other ripping out tufts of nearby grass.

"Fuck!" he shouted. He thumped the ground. "Fuck!" He picked himself and launched headfirst at the barrier, literally bouncing back off it and falling back down onto the ground.

I rolled my eyes. Really? I hadn't told him to try and knock himself unconscious, just that he should check for weaknesses in the ward. Before he did it again, I dropped down from the tree and walked casually over to him. Not that I cared if he hurt himself, but there was no way that I was going to carry his sorry arse back down the path again if he managed to pass out completely.

When I reached him, he groaned again, but didn't get up. I kicked his feet.

"Hey, butthead, was that wholly necessary?"

He muttered something inaudible. I leaned over him. "What was that?"

"Fat woman. Hideous. Naked. Hit me. Sat on me."

Outstanding. Now he had a concussion and was bloody hallucinating. "We're in a wood, not a stripper joint in Soho. Don't see any naked women around here, Aubrey. I think maybe you've hit your head."

He sat up and stared at me through the gloom. "Didn't."

"Did. I saw you do just that about two minutes ago in fact."

"Didn't."

I put my hands on my hips. I was not going to get into this. "Stand the fuck up. We're going to get out of here and see if we can make it to the nearest village before sunup. I'm hungry and I need a coffee."

He held his hand out in the air, pointing it towards me in a gesture obviously designed to encourage me to help him to his feet.

"Aubrey," I said, keeping my voice deliberately quiet, "let's get one thing straight, you neurotic nutcase. I don't care about you. My friends died as a direct result of your actions. Just because you're not a freaking bloodsucker any more, does not mean that I suddenly like you or am in any way inclined to help you. Pick yourself up and stop acting like a child."

His bottom lip started to quiver. I lifted a warning finger. "Do not, whatever you do, start to cry."

He pulled himself together and stood up, although he was still pouting. I raised my eyebrows and he smoothed his features over, although I could tell it was an effort. I turned away from him, but had the sudden feeling that he was sticking his tongue out at me from behind my back. Without looking at him, I motioned at him to move to the front again and lead the way back down. I really did not need this - the sooner I ditched him, the better.

CHAPTER ELEVEN

By the time we reached the nearest village, a small place called Uffington, the sun was most definitely up. Aubrey continually attempted to shield himself from its gentle rays, darting from one side of the road to the other depending on where the most shade was to be had. He kept muttering away to himself. Occasionally I caught the odd word, which seemed to be focused around burning and pain. At one point, as he sprinted for a half derelict bus shelter to cower for half a minute, I called out that the sun was doing his pasty white vamp skin good, and extolled the virtues of vitamin D, but he paid me little attention. At least he'd given up on the hallucination of being squatted on by some obese naked lady though. The images running through my head had not been entirely conducive to keeping a straight face every time I looked at him.

Fortunately, the pretty little village seemed to cater for early risers and we came across a small coffee shop that was already open for business. The gratitude on Aubrey's face that we were finally getting out of the sunlight was momentarily diverting, even if I didn't quite have the heart to tell him that it wasn't even 8am yet and the sun was only going to get stronger. Once inside we sat ourselves down at a small linen covered table towards the back. It suited Aubrey as it was about as far away from the wide window and the golden slanting rays as he could possibly get; it suited me as it meant I had a perfect vantage point in case anyone or anything passed by. Whatever it was that had decided that brutally slaughtering one of the most passive creatures of the Otherworld was a good idea had used the ward for a reason. It was definitely coming back, and I was going to be ready for it when it did.

A beaming cottage loaf of a woman bustled over. "What'll be, duckies?"

Duckies? She had to be kidding me. I had to bite back the urge to quack nonsensically at her and instead ordered the full breakfast and two pots of coffee. I was bloody starving, and if I didn't get some decent caffeine down me soon I reckoned I was liable to do something I'd end up regretting. Aubrey pointlessly asked for a plate of nothing but black pudding.. Once the woman had wandered back into the kitchen I gave him a glare that would have withered a lesser creature.

"What?" He exclaimed, a tad too loudly for my liking. The waitress might not be in the room, but that didn't mean she wouldn't be able to hear him. "It's made of blood. It's about the only bloody blood I'm going to ever be able to get to eat again." He started to snigger. "Bloody blood." He snorted. "Did you see what I did there?"

I stared at him, completely unamused. He punched me on the arm. "Come on, Mack, lighten up. I know my joke sucked but it doesn't need to create any bad blood between us." He sniggered again.

Oh joy of abundant joys. I looked out of the window instead, and gritted my teeth. Thirty seconds away from the sun and he was already acting like an idiot again. I was tempted to call out to the woman and see whether she'd let me move a table and chair outside onto the sunny pavement. Perhaps then I might get some peace. Unfortunately, just as I thought that, a flicker of movement on the other side of the road caught my eye, and four figures moved into sight. I scowled as I recognised them. Beltran the Fae, Lucy the shifter, and two mages I'd seen lurking around the Arch-Mage on a previous occasion. No doubt one of the mages had cast the Divination spell to locate me, while the other was more adept at Protection and followed behind, faerie and shifter in their wake. I'd known that it wasn't going to be long before they caught up to me, but I'd kind of been hoping that I'd have at least a day. The two mages stood together, directly opposite the coffee shop front door, with Lucy a few metres away on one side, and Beltran the same on the other. They didn't look as if they were getting on along very well. All three of them were standing stiffly and awkwardly, mouths shut in grim lines and arms folded. In this small village they looked about as unobtrusive as a sodding fire breathing dragon would.

Aubrey's eyes followed my gaze. When he saw who was out there he moved faster than I would have thought possible, ducking his head under the table and curling into a small ball. Okay then.

The woman walked back in, carrying two steaming plates of food. She clocked Aubrey immediately. To be fair, it wasn't hard to do. His arse was jutting out from under the table cloth in a most peculiar fashion. Shooting him a bemused look, she edged over and put the plates down. I looked at her and she looked at me. Then I shrugged as if to say 'what can you do?' She nodded slowly.

"So, er, where's your friend gone?"

"He's popped out to the little boy's room," I answered, slowly, raising my eyebrows at her.

"Hmm, well, I hope he comes back before his food gets cold." She said this last part loudly and pointedly.

I forced my lips to curve up in a smile and replied in the same manner. "Yes. It would be foolish of him if he were to miss all this lovely black pudding. Tell me, is it true that it's made of blood?"

There was a distinct moan from under the table.

Her eyes darted underneath and then met mine again. "Why, yes. It's really rather delicious though, you should try some."

"Well, there's a whole plate here. I could always try some of my, erm, companion's. I'm sure he'd never notice if any was missing."

There was a sudden thump and the gleaming cutlery on the table jumped and clattered. Aubrey's head had clearly just connected with the underside of the wood. The waitress put her hand over her mouth and choked back what was apparently threatening to be quite a guffaw.

"I'll just go back to the kitchen now," she said, rather obviously, moving backwards while keeping a perhaps too attentive eye on Aubrey's backside.

I leaned back in my chair as she left. This was suddenly proving a more entertaining breakfast than I could have possibly envisaged. I reached over and took a sip of my coffee. It was a darn sight better than the muck I'd had on the train. I closed my eyes momentarily in simple happiness as the woman left us in peace. What she thought was going on, I had absolutely no idea. I guessed I just had to be grateful that she wasn't going to pry too closely into the reasons why Aubrey had decided to lurk under one of her pretty tables.

A hand grabbed my ankle. "Mack," he hissed.

I ignored him and took another sip, watching my trackers who were still standing stiffly on the other side of the street and idly wondering whether it would be worth my while to try and give them the slip.

The hand tightened. "Mack!" Aubrey repeated.

"Mmm?" I eventually answered.

"Pass me my plate. I can eat from under here."

"Well," I drawled, "I could do that. But won't our little group outside wonder why I'm chucking an entire plate of food under the table? I'll have you know that I am generally thought of as having rather good table manners." I grinned to myself. This was just too much fun.

HELEN HARPER

"Mack," he whined, "I'm hungry."

"So stop acting like a weirdo and come out."

"I can't." There was a plaintive note in his voice.

I began to dig into my breakfast, spearing a bite of bacon and chewing loudly. "Why not?"

"I'm a master fucking vampire that's why not."

"I hate to break it to you, Aubrey, but you're not a vamp any longer. Now you're just a strange little man who is hiding rather ineffectively under a table." I took another bite, and deliberately moaned in pleasure. "This food is really very good, you know. You should try some."

Aubrey groaned. "Mack...,"

"Mmmm?" From across the road I watched as Beltran edged closer to the mages to try to get a better vantage point. The one nearest him shot him a filthy look and turned towards him, saying something that, by the expression on his face, wasn't particularly nice.

"I can't let anyone know what's happened! I've got a reputation to maintain." Aubrey's fingers were beginning to dig uncomfortably into my skin.

"Aubrey," I said, sighing, "sooner or later everyone is going to find out. It's a done deal. You're human."

"Not if I can find someone to turn me back again."

Now Lucy appeared to be getting involved. Her arms were tight by her sides as if she was afraid that she might launch into fisticuffs at any moment. The other mage was facing her, a snarl across his dark features.

"For that to happen," I responded mildly, "you need to find someone to turn you back. A vamp. That means you need to tell someone that you're no longer a creature of the night. Then everyone will know your secret anyway."

"There are a few I can trust," he huffed. "I just have to find a way to contact them without anyone else finding out."

The mage on the right was reaching out towards Beltran with an extended index finger, pointing at him rudely. Lucy's body

116

language radiated the threat of potential violence in the way that only a shifter could.

"What if you find out that being a human isn't so bad?"

"I don't want to be a fucking human! I'm a vampire! Other vampires are afraid of me. You were afraid of me! Now you treat me no better than an animal. Give me some food!"

"You didn't say the magic word."

The mage next to Beltran had taken the rather foolish step of jabbing him in the chest with his finger.

"Mack…" Aubrey was starting to sound desperate.

"You do realise that I could just compel you to come out?"

"You wouldn't do that." His voice drifted up towards me confidently.

"And why not? You got my friends killed, Aubrey, why should I care what happens to you?"

A car drove past the posturing Otherworlders. I noted white faces staring at them. That probably wasn't good.

"Because you're nice."

"No, I'm not."

Aubrey sniffed loudly and gulped. "I'm so hungry. I've never felt a sensation like this before. How long does it take for starvation to set in for humans? I'm already feeling weak." His grasp around my ankle loosened. "See? I can barely even use my hands any more. I'm getting fainter by the second. I don't think I'll ever be able to stand up again. So dizzy…"

I watched in growing alarm as both mages clenched their fists, a sure sign that they were about to raise up some Protection magic. Lucy's tanned skin was starting to darken, and Beltran was murmuring something to himself. Okay, this had gone far enough. I yanked my leg away from the rest of Aubrey's grip and pushed the chair back.

"Mack? What are you doing?"

I rolled my eyes, and picked up his plate of black pudding, practically throwing it down towards him. "There. If you think

I'm treating you like an animal then stay there and eat like an animal. I'll be back shortly."

I stood up and marched over to the café door, flinging it open. My so-called trackers on the other side of the street paid me absolutely no attention whatsoever. It'd serve them right if they had to go and explain to all their respective lords and masters why a monster had suddenly appeared and killed me on the spot while they were kicking metaphorical sand in each other's faces. I stomped over the road and put my hands on my hips, facing all four of them.

"What the fuck are the lot of you doing?"

As one, they all turned towards me, suddenly guilty expressions on all of their faces.

I continued. "Do you see where you are? This is a village! You don't think that someone is going to notice you lot about to get into some kind of stupid brawl?" I pointed to the mages. "You are about to use magic to attack. It's broad daylight! How fucking thick are you? Do you want to spend the rest of the day going around and casting memory spells on this entire place so they forget that they saw blue freaking flame spouting from your fingers?"

Both mages stared at me, like schoolboys caught in the act of leaving a frog on their teacher's chair. Lucy was looking a bit too smug. I flicked my eyes over to her.

"And you! You were about to fucking shift! In the middle of the street, no less. I wonder how your Mighty Lord Corrigan would react to that?" Her face went pale and she looked down at the ground.

I turned my attention to Beltran and jabbed a finger in his direction. "Don't think that you're any better than the rest of them either. You were obviously about to try something too. The whole lot of you should be ashamed of yourselves." I scowled at each and every one of them in disapproval.

The Fae recovered first. "Perhaps, Miss Mackenzie, if you didn't make it quite so hard for us to keep track of you, then we would be feeling less stressed and less inclined to do something all of us might regret."

"So this is my fault? The four of you almost exposing the secrets of the entire fucking Otherworld to a village of humans is because I decided I wanted to get away for a few days?"

Lucy chimed in. "To be fair, Mack, you're not making our lives very easy."

I spluttered. "Easy? What do you think it's like for me having idiots like you follow me round all the time?" I gazed at them all in exasperation. "My life does not belong to your fucking supernatural organisations, no matter what you might think."

The mage on the right stepped forward. When I glared at him, he swallowed and stepped back, but cleared his throat and found his voice. "We're just doing our jobs. We've been told not to let you out of our sight. Less than two days ago you almost died thanks to a bunch of bloodsuckers. If that happens again then our lives won't be worth living."

I folded my arms. "Well, I'm sorry if my death could potentially inconvenience you. But your antics out here are fucking inconveniencing every single member of the Otherworld. Besides which, the vamps are not going to bother me again."

Lucy's eyes widened. "Did you kill them all?"

I stared at her. "No. You know why? Because there was only one."

They gaped at me.

A furrow creased Beltran's brow. "But I thought…"

"That I was a great almighty being of power who lets nothing stand in my way? Well, everyone has off days. Besides, said vampire is currently cowering under a table in there." I pointed back towards the café.

Lucy drew herself up. "I will destroy him."

I moved in front of her. "No, you fucking will not."

"Lord Corrigan…"

"Screw Lord Corrigan. You know why?" And it's not because

he makes me go weak at the knees and literally want to fulfill those crude words, I added to myself.

A gleam lit the mages' eyes. "Why?" They asked together, eagerly.

"Because that vamp over there is no longer a vamp."

Even Beltran looked shocked at that. He opened his mouth to speak and then shut it again with a snap.

I glared at them all. "But you can't tell anyone. He is having some readjustment issues and needs some time. All you need to know is that I am in no danger." Not from vampires anyway. From trying to help out a bunch of tree nymphs, then perhaps the opposite was true. Which gave me a sudden idea. I pursed my lips. "So, this is what is going to happen. I will not run away. You will not do something earth-shatteringly stupid like give away all your identities because you're a bit pissed off at each other."

I received petulantly sullen looks from them all. I sighed. "I can't have four people trailing me round all the time. Not here where any strangers already stick out like sore thumbs. Lucy, you can stay with me."

A smile spread across her face and the other three began to protest.

"That's giving favouritism to the fucking shifters yet again!" spat one of the mages.

Lucy turned to him. "Well she did grow up with us, you prat," she shot back in return. "She's virtually family."

"Enough!" I shouted. "Lucy will stay with me because the rest of you can help me with something else. Then you can all toddle back to your little organisations and tell everyone what a grand job you did getting into the good books of the Draco Wyr." I pointed at the mages. "A couple of miles away from here is an area called Haughmond Hill. There's a warded area that's been concealed by magic. Inside is a crucified dryad." Both of them blinked. "I need you to find out what you can about the ward. Will breaking it trigger off any alarms? Who might have cast it in the first place? That kind of thing. I will be back there later this afternoon and I will see you then."

The pair of them grumbled. "How do we know that you're not just trying to get rid of us?"

"Frankly, I am trying to get rid of you. But I give you my word that I will see you there later. And I do need to know as much about it as possible. You know that if you need to find me all you have to do is set up one tiny Divination spell. It's not like you can't track me down if you want to."

They looked at each other for a moment, then at me. They nodded slowly. "Okay then."

"What are your names?" I asked.

"Larkin," muttered the one on the right. He pointed at his companion. "He's Max."

"Well, Larkin and Max, off you go then."

They didn't move. I stared at them warningly.

"What about him?" Max jerked his head towards Beltran who was eyeing me with an appraising air.

"He's going to go to Cardiff and persuade some environmental activists that they need to pack up sticks and head here to save the trees of Haughmond Hill. If anyone can encourage a bunch of people to come and save the natural world, then it's got to be a faerie."

The Fae watched me impassively for a moment, and I thought he was going to flat out refuse, but then he eventually nodded. A flicker of relief ran through me.

"What are you going to do?" Lucy asked.

"I'm going to finish my fucking breakfast. You can stay out here and look busy."

She looked faintly sad for a moment. Remembering her voracious appetite from our previous encounter in Cornwall, I felt a twinge of guilt but I firmly pushed it away. It wasn't my job to entertain her stomach or my fault that she had elected to follow me around.

I gestured at them all. "Well?"

There was a frozen silent heartbeat then, thank goodness, they all nodded and moved off, apart from Lucy who took a step back and bowed her head. I watched their departures for a brief moment and then turned and went back across the road and into the café.

CHAPTER TWELVE

Aubrey was still under the table when I re-entered. There was an empty plate on top of the linen table cloth, however, signifying exactly what he'd been doing while I'd been attempting to avert World War Three. I moved back to my original seat, and picked up my knife and fork to begin eating again. Unfortunately, my food had cooled considerably in my absence. Something else to blame those idiots for, I thought sourly.

"Mack," hissed Aubrey. "Where were you? What happened?"

I ignored him, and instead continued to chew. I'd been interrupted enough as it was. I was going to enjoy the rest of my meal without letting anyone else disturb me. Aubrey continued to mutter at me from underneath the table, but I let him continue without bothering to answer. I noted from across the road that Lucy had pulled out a mobile phone and was fiddling away with it, her eyes intent on the screen in a manner that any technologically astute teenager would be proud of. At least she was taking the hint and trying to look less out of place. A couple of clatters sounded from where I presumed the kitchen was, but I let the sounds wash over me and instead poured myself more coffee. Life wasn't so bad after all.

Eventually, when I was done, I leaned down, picking up the

edge of the tablecloth, and peered at Aubrey. He looked abjectly miserable, scrunched up into some bizarrely uncomfortable foetal-like position. There were some remaining crumbs of black pudding around his mouth. He was clearly a messier human eater than he had been vamp. When he saw me looking at him, he pouted.

"You were ignoring me," he stated plaintively.

"Imagine that. Get out from under there, Aubrey. You're making a fool of yourself."

"Are they still there?"

"One of them is. It doesn't matter though," I said casually, "I told them what you are."

"What?" he shrieked, lifting up his head and banging it yet again on the underside of the table.

"You heard me." I pulled myself back up.

Aubrey crawled out backwards, and then sat back on his haunches and glared at me.

"You betrayed me!"

I shrugged and put my coffee cup down. He lunged abruptly towards me, fingers curled into claws. I grabbed him by the throat and held his snarling face away, trying to avoid the remnants of black pudding tinged saliva that were spraying out in my direction. He choked and spluttered.

"Let's get one thing straight, oh master vampire," I said sarcastically, "you are here on sufferance. If you want to leave, then you are more than welcome to do so. I rescind my previous instruction. If you want to stay, then you need to goddamn well start behaving yourself. I know for a fact that there's a were-honey badger across the road who will quite happily rip you from limb to limb, whether you're human or otherwise. I am becoming mightily sick of all this emotional bullshit. Get your shit together or get out."

His eyes bulged, glaring at me even through the pain, then he finally blinked in agreement and I let him go. He collapsed onto the floor.

"You're a mean bitch," he choked out.

"Oh yeah? Well, ten minutes ago you were telling me how nice I was."

"I lied," he spat.

"There's the door," I stated calmly, pointing.

He put on a grumpy expression. "It's too sunny outside."

"Suit yourself." I pulled out my laptop and opened it up. It was time to get to work.

A creak signalled the return of the waitress. She raised her eyebrows slightly at the sight of Aubrey on the floor, and flicked a concerned glance at me.

"I'm sorry about my companion," I said. "He's going to sit on his chair now and behave."

Aubrey scrambled up with a groan, no doubt still under compulsion, and sat down on his original chair. I raised my eyebrows at him. He looked away and scowled.

"I'm sorry," he muttered.

"I don't think she quite heard that."

His eyes sent daggers towards me, but he turned to face the waitress and spoke up. "I'm sorry." He cleared his throat. "I suffer from panic attacks from time to time. It won't happen again."

"Oh, that's alright, hen," she clucked, "I understand." She patently didn't, of course, but the pair of us remained safely silent as she cleared away the table.

"Can I get wifi here?" I asked, hopefully. "And maybe another pot of coffee?"

"Of course." She reached into a pocket in her apron and pulled out a small strip of paper, handing it over to me. "Here's the password. I'll just put some more coffee on to brew."

I smiled gratefully, watching as she headed back out again, then turned my attention to the laptop, opening up the internet so I could get to my email.

I could feel Aubrey bristling beside me. "What the fuck is wrong with you now?" I murmured, without looking at him.

"She called me hen," he said disgustedly. "As if I'm a piece of poultry. If I wasn't human, I'd..." his voice trailed off.

"You'd what?"

"Nothing," he muttered, subsiding.

I looked over at him thoughtfully. He was tracing something onto the table top, eyes downward. Was that how I sounded when I got pissed off? All whiny and self-centred? He felt my eyes on him and flicked me an upwards glance. I looked away, logging on instead. I was not going to start comparing myself to an ex-undead Otherworld nastie. I had enough inner turmoil to deal with as it was.

Thankfully, there was a message from Alex to divert my attention. I opened it up, scanning its contents, then frowned, my stomach suddenly dropping and a churn of bloodfire flaring up.

I held my hand out to Aubrey, palm outwards. "Phone," I demanded, rudely.

"Huh?"

"Give me your fucking phone," I repeated.

"Well, there's no need to be so ill-mannered," he snapped. Fortunately for him, he dug into his pocket and handed it over.

I dialled Alex's number and waited for him to pick up.

"Mack Attack? Is that you?"

"Yeah," I answered without preamble. "I just read your email. Tell me in more detail what you saw."

"Dude, you have no idea. You didn't tell me what the shop assistant was going to be like, I mean, jeez, it's enough to give a grown mage nightmares."

"Alex, just tell me."

"Okay, okay, dude, don't get your knickers in a twist. So I was watching all night to see who went in and out. Like I said in the email there was a steady stream of people. A couple of vamps, some shady looking characters, a few who were clearly using masking spells to hide what they really were, I think I even spotted a couple of mages. Then I saw her, the Batibat, when she went to see somebody off. It was just for a split second but, damn. Not only does she look as if she's in serious need of a personal trainer, she is also as freaking naked as the day she was born. That image is going to be seared into my brain for the rest of my natural life. I know you shouldn't judge people by their appearances, but, man, that's one unpleasant looking lady."

I flicked a glance over at Aubrey, to check to see whether he could hear Alex's feedback, but he wasn't paying the slightest bit of attention. He'd gone back to examining his fingernails again, picking away at a small hangnail, then watching in astonishment as a tiny bead of blood formed at the edge.

"Is this the first time you've seen a Batibat, Alex?"

"Dude, I'd never even heard of one till you told me about her the other day. I wish I'd still never heard of one."

I could almost feel his shudder from across the airwaves. I was coming close to shuddering myself. I didn't like coincidences.

"Has there been any sign of the owner?"

"Not that I can see. How long do I need to stay here? I could do with a shower after all that."

"I need you to stay there until you can work out who's really in charge, Alex."

"Mack Attack, you know I'll do what I can to help you. Just," he paused for a moment, "eurgh."

"Hang in there, killer," I said drily, then rang off.

I drummed my fingers on the tabletop. This was not good. Not good at all. I barely noticed the waitress wandering back in with another pot of coffee. A couple of other customers walked in and sat down at a nearby table, chattering away to each other.

I stiffened noticeably for a second, however a quick glance proved that they were clearly just two locals – and human locals at that. Picking up the phone again, I dialled the number for the bookshop, hoping that I'd catch Mrs. Alcoon around.

The voice that answered was definitely familiar – and definitely not the elderly Scottish woman.

"Clava Books," it stated gruffly.

"Slim?" I asked doubtfully.

"Oh, it's you. What do you fecking want?"

I paused for a moment. Could I trust him? He was definitely in the mages' pocket. I had to wonder whether he was still hanging around the bookstore even though it was all ready for the grand opening on Monday because he thought he might be able to keep tabs on me. That seemed kind of stupid though. I already had two mages pretty much here with me to find out what I was up to. The Arch-Mage didn't need to give up the academy's librarian to do the same when I was no longer anywhere near London. I shrugged to myself. Okay then.

"I need some help."

"Why am I not fecking surprised?"

"You can always put Mrs. Alcoon on if it's too much for you. Is she even there?" I asked suspiciously.

"She's in the back. Making tea. What do you want?" The little gargoyle sighed heavily at the apparent trauma of being forced to talk to me.

"I need you to look through the books and find out whatever you can about Batibats. They're...,"

"Nocturnal Indonesian tree spirits. Yeah, yeah, I fecking know," he grumbled.

I started. Tree spirits? "You mean like dryads?"

He snorted. "Hardly. Batibats are daemons that reside in trees. They're completely responsible for bangunot, you know."

"Er, no, I don't. What's bangunot?"

"Nasty fecking disease. Usually affects young men. They die unexpectedly and immediately in the middle of the night. Apparently you can beat it by wiggling your toes because it snaps your heart back to its fecking natural rhythm before cardiac arrest. Don't you fecking know anything?"

"Apparently not. Can you find a picture of one and email it to me?" I rattled off my address.

"S'pose," he grunted, grudgingly. "Can I go now?"

"Just one more thing. Why are you there?"

"Huh?"

"Why are you still at the bookshop?"

"You got a fecking problem with me helping out a bit?"

"No. It's just weird, that's all. Are you behaving yourself?"

He made a spitting sound and hung up. Okaydokey. I hoped I'd not pissed him off so much that he wouldn't send me what I needed, but fortunately my laptop pinged a few moments later with the arrival of a new email. I opened it up and stared at the image. Yeah, pretty hideous and very naked. I moved the laptop round to Aubrey. He paid me no attention whatsoever so I thumped him on the arm. He recoiled and growled at me. I motioned down at the computer and watched as his eyes widened when he saw what was on the screen.

"That's the thing that attacked me! It sat on me! See? See? You thought I was lying."

My heart sank a little further. "I didn't think you were lying, Aubrey, I just thought you'd hit your head a little too hard, that's all."

I chewed the inside of my cheek. It couldn't be the same Batibat in London as who'd attacked Aubrey; that just didn't make any sense. But there was no way in hell that the two weren't connected. It just so happened that Balud needed help beating a little extra competition from a Batibat at the same time that the dryads needed help avoiding some kind of whole-scale massacre that also involved a Batibat? A creature that I'd never even heard of until a couple of days ago? No, sirree, there was no way that these two things weren't somehow linked. The fact that Batibats were apparently also tree dwellers did not lessen my worry. At least now I knew what it was I had to do next.

I jerked my head over at Aubrey. "Come on. I'm going to pay up and then we're going to get going."

"Get going where?"

"Back to Haughmond Hill."

"What? No, no, no, no, no, no, no. I'm not going back there."

I lifted a shoulder, carelessly. "Okay, then stay here."

"No, no, no, no, no, no. You can't leave me. No." Panic filled his eyes and he shook his head emphatically from side to side.

"It's your choice." I stood up and pulled out my wallet from my now rather bedraggled looking plastic bag, replacing the laptop back inside it. Smiling at the waitress, I beckoned her over and paid the bill, leaving a rather hefty tip. After all, she'd performed rather admirably in the wake of Aubrey's antics.

"Thank you," she murmured. "Please do come again." The look in her eyes suggested that even with the tip included, she'd prefer it if we never darkened her door again. I didn't blame her.

I walked out, leaving Aubrey to decide for himself whether to tag along or not. I couldn't really have cared less either way. He followed at my heels, however, crying out in overly melodramatic pain once we hit the sunny pavement.

"So you're coming then?"

"You compelled me to stay with you, remember?" he said sourly, continuing to try to shield himself from the sun with his arm.

"I cancelled that. You can leave if you want to."

"Maybe it didn't work. Maybe because you told me to stay with you, and never leave no matter what, your initial compulsion can't be cancelled."

"You didn't come with me when I left you up beside the ward on the hill," I pointed out.

"Because you'd not gone far away then. How the fuck should I know how it works anyway? You're the one who's doing this to me, not the other way around. Perhaps you'll be stuck with me for life." There was a malicious tone to his voice.

Heavens forbid. I opened my mouth to tell him exactly what I thought of that idea when he suddenly clutched my arm.

"Look!"

Alarmed, my eyes followed his finger, my body already tensing for a fight. But I couldn't work out what he was pointing at.

"What? What do you see that I don't?"

"Are you stupid? There's a charity shop. I can buy some clothes to cover myself up from that fucking sun."

I must have been the first person in the history of compulsion to allow my subject to call me stupid and be this bloody annoying. I shot him an irritated glance. "It's not really hurting you, you know. It's all in your head."

"Like fat naked creatures of the Otherworld sitting on me are all in my head too?" he inquired.

I sighed, giving up. "Fine. But you've got five minutes and that's it."

He beamed a grateful smile at me, and then trotted across the road. Lucy came up behind me as I watched him go.

"He's a vampire?" she asked doubtfully.

"He was a vampire," I corrected. "And a pretty fucking scary one at that."

"How in the hell did he turn human? I've never heard of a cure for vampirism before."

I shrugged. "Beats me. I think something he ate just didn't agree with him." I gave her a serious look. "He doesn't know what I am, and he can't know what I am. He might be human now, but he still thinks like a vamp and can't be trusted."

"Right," she said slowly, "except I don't know what you are either."

I gave her a startled look. "Corrigan didn't tell you?"

She snorted. "As far as our Lord Alpha is concerned, any gossip about you is off limits. He sent three werecats to scut duty for a month because he caught them talking about why he was so interested in you when you're not a shifter." She glanced at me, curiosity clearly eating her up. "I don't suppose you'd like to elaborate?"

I tried hard not to feel too happy that he wasn't broadcasting my heritage to the world. "He's interested in me only because the mages and the Fae are interested in me. It's nothing personal," I said dismissively.

"Right," she said sarcastically, "because the Brethren Lord gives a shit about what a bunch of wizards and faeries do."

"You guys are all part of the same world. You'd think that you'd learn to play nice."

"You're living in a dream world if you think we're all ever going to get along, Mack."

"A bit of idealism never hurt anyone," I retorted.

"Without a bit of realism, you'll end up getting killed," she said quietly.

I had nothing to say to that. The rivalry between the different groups had me baffled, but, other than Mrs. Alcoon, I trusted pretty much no-one so I could hardly argue. All the others had too much of their own vested interests at heart for me to not be realistic about what they wanted from me. I couldn't even really trust Tom and Betsy, my old childhood friends who I'd known for years, because as members of the Brethren and the Pack their ultimate loyalty would always lie with Corrigan. Alex, for all his laid-back attitude, would spring to orders if the Arch-Mage gave them. And Solus was a Fae. Even without the potential threat of the Summer Queen in Tir-na-Nog hovering around, his very nature meant he couldn't be fully trusted. It all struck me as rather pathetic and made me feel incredibly sad.

"Your vampire doesn't look particularly scary at all," commented Lucy, breaking me out of my reverie.

I looked over at Aubrey emerging from the shop. Good grief. He was wearing a large brimmed purple hat of the sort that wouldn't look out of a place on the mother of a bride on her big day. He'd added a long dark trench coat and a pair of stripy woollen gloves. He jogged over to the pair of us, tilting the brim of his hat up so he could give Lucy an appropriately suspicious look. She gave him back as good as she got.

I sighed. "Come on then children. Let's go."

CHAPTER THIRTEEN

BY THE TIME THE THREE OF US REACHED HAUGHMOND HILL AGAIN, the sun was high in the sky and midday was fast approaching. At least I knew from Slim's information that the Batibat was nocturnal and therefore wouldn't be likely to be making a voluntary appearance. With any luck, however, I'd still be able to track down her hiding place and find out just what in the hell was really going on.

Larkin and Max, the two mages, were sitting down on the ground, close to the warded off area. When they saw us approaching, they both scrambled to their feet.

"We didn't think you'd be here so quickly," exclaimed Max, with a note of guilt in his voice that he'd been caught virtually napping.

"Are you complaining about my presence now?" I asked.

Larkin held up his hands. "No, no, definitely not. It's great you're here." He gave his companion a warning glance. I felt oddly good that I had them snapping to attention when I arrived. Maybe I could give myself some kind of moniker to encourage further deference. Arch-Dragon? Lady Alpha? Fire Queen? I chuckled to myself at the absurdity of the idea, then looked round and realised that everyone was staring at me strangely. I pulled myself together and got down to business.

"Right," I said, "what have you found out then?"

"It's a really strong ward," stated Larkin seriously. "Not like anything I've ever seen before."

Max nodded in agreement. "It's definitely not of Ministry origins. It's bound by something very dark indeed. And that dryad is most definitely dead."

I shot him a look. "That much I already knew."

Lucy was staring in horror at the dryad's hanging body. "Oh my God," she whispered. She turned away and began to retch. Aubrey rolled his eyes at the apparent weak appreciation the shifter had for such 'art'. I ignored him and focused on the mages.

"Can you tell what will happen if we break the ward?"

"You can't," Max said firmly.

I was irritated. "Can't what?"

"Break the ward."

I sighed deeply. "Let's imagine that I can. What would happen?"

He appeared completely nonplussed. "I, er, have no idea."

"Well, fucking find out," I snapped. I turned my attention to Larkin. "Are you the Divination guy?"

When he didn't immediately answer, I clicked my fingers impatiently in front of his face. "Divination? Are you the guy?"

"Um, yes." He ran a nervous hand through his hair, and I realised that I was sounding a bit too much like a school bully.

I softened my tone. "Somewhere near here there's a Batibat. A nocturnal tree spirit."

"Fat naked woman," added in Aubrey, unhelpfully.

"Yeah, whatever." I gave the mage a serious look. "Can you find where she is?"

He nodded. "I can try."

"Great. Be aware that there are dryads around here as well.

They're pretty shy and probably wouldn't take too kindly to you mistaking them for an evil daemon."

It was his turn to look irritated. "I can tell the difference between a dryad and a Batibat."

Did everyone know what a bloody Batibat was apart from apparently Alex and me?

"You know what a Batibat is?" asked Aubrey, arching a surprised eyebrow.

Okay, me and Alex and Aubrey then. I felt slightly mollified, but still made myself a promise to do some proper research into some of the more obscure Otherworld nasties when I got home. I didn't enjoy feeling stupid. I supposed at least I was on a par with a hippy mage and a self-obsessed ex-bloodsucker, if nothing else.

Larkin gave Aubrey a scathing look. "Nice hat. I suppose you're the vampire, then?"

"What of it, wiz?" he snarled in return.

I stepped in before things got out of hand. "Chill, boys. Aubrey, you need to look after Lucy. Make sure she's okay."

His lip curled. "She's a shifter."

"Well done."

"I'm fine," Lucy gasped from behind.

I glanced over my shoulder at her. Her skin still had a remarkably green tinge to it. "Okay. But stay here with Aubrey anyway."

"How come you're so nice to her and so nasty to me?" whined the ex-vamp.

"Because I like her."

Aubrey's bottom lip started to quiver, and his eyes became glassy. A loud sob escaped him. Both the mages and Lucy stared at him in abject astonishment.

I shrugged, trying not to feel too guilty. "Hey, you asked. And I told you not to cry."

"I'm not crying," he gulped. At least I thought that was what

he said; to be honest, it was difficult to tell through his current
wave of unhappy emotion. I decided the best thing would be to
leave him alone.

"Here," I said, passing him over my plastic bag. "I'm trusting
you to look after this, Aubrey. "

He blinked, one hand lifting up the brim of his ridiculous
purple affront to the art of millinery so he could peer at me.
"Why?"

"Because I think you'll do a great job of taking care of it and I
need to go and make sure there's nothing else lurking in these
woods."

Almost to a man, my motley crew of unwelcome companions
stiffened. "You are not going anywhere on your own," huffed
Max. Larkin nodded vigorously in agreement.

"You have no idea what's out there, Mack," agreed Lucy. "I
can't let you do this."

I growled at them and, just for a moment, opened myself up
to my bloodfire, allowing the Draco Wyr spirit to flood through
me. I couldn't do it for too long – I was too afraid about what
might happen if I did – but there was no way I was going to stand
here arguing about what I was or wasn't going to do. A dulled
roaring filled my ears and I felt my heart pound, once, twice.
Then, almost as soon as it had happened, I yanked the feeling
away, and looked round at them all.

There was a deafening silence that was finally broken by
Aubrey. "I'm starting to think that maybe I was lucky that you
were on drugs on Hampstead Heath, even if it did this to me." He
motioned down at his human body.

The others flicked startled glances at him.

"Are we all agreed then?"

They nodded.

"Fanfuckingtastic," I said, tiredly, and turned away from the
group.

I could feel their wary eyes on me the entire time I was
walking away. It occurred to me that whatever they'd seen when

I'd let the bloodfire take me over had terrified the bejesus out of them. It terrified the bejesus out of me. There was no way I was going to let them know that though.

I wended my way across the path and into the trees. Everything appeared somehow different now it was daylight. The entire area was still unnaturally silent, with only the very odd call of a bird breaking the air, but everything felt less ominous than it had the night before. The power of sunlight, I figured. It was a shame that Aubrey hadn't yet come round to the joy of being out in the daytime. I wondered idly if he ever would.

Something caught my attention on a nearby tree. There was a branch that had clearly been slightly disturbed and looked out of place, as if someone had grabbed onto it. Heart in my mouth, I carefully picked my way over to it, trying to stay as quiet as I possibly could. I realised as soon as I reached it, however, that it was the tree I'd thought to conceal myself in the night before. There was nothing else there.

Cursing to myself, I moved deeper into the undergrowth. There were simply no signs of any other disturbance anywhere. The utter lack of any trace of anything was worrying. This was meant to be a popular tourist spot. The whole area, apart from the obviously scorched part with the dead dryad, seemed as if it had remained untouched for years. That did not compute. I considered briefly whether it would be worth tracking back and up, to see if I could find the clearing again and talk to the dryad from the night before. If this Batibat was living around here too, it seemed impossible that they wouldn't have bumped into each other. However, even given the entire race of dryads' apparent propensity for not telling the whole truth, it seemed ridiculous that she wouldn't have mentioned it already if she'd known. The Batibat was somehow tied up in the murder and Atlanteia had asked me here to essentially stop any more such murders from taking place. Withholding that potentially vital piece of information was pointless.

I continued forward, scanning the ground, the bushes, the

trees, everything, for any sign of anything. I was drawing a complete blank, however. A thought struck me, and I moved away from the trees and back towards the ward, heading for the area where Aubrey had been lying when the Batibat had apparently sat on him. Even before I got there, it was clear to see the evidence of his movements. The grass was flattened, indicating where he'd fallen over, not just once, but several times. I knelt down, focusing on what the ground was telling me. All around the barrier of the ward were the traces of his attempts to smash through it. All I needed to do was to find traces that didn't belong to him. It didn't take long.

To the left of where he'd fallen there were enough heavily bent stalks of grass, in a different formation to those already created by Aubrey himself, to indicate where the Batibat had been. I was no forensic environmentalist, but I'd spent enough time growing up around the woods of Cornwall to have some basic tracking techniques. And what they were telling me, beyond a shadow of a doubt, was the Batibat had come at Aubrey from within the ward. There was no sign of any tracks left within the burnt ground inside, but there was just enough on the outside to make it clear what had happened. He'd been attacking the barrier, and probably falling over idiotically as he did so, and the Batibat had emerged from the dead tree inside to teach him a lesson.

I shaded my eyes and stared at the dead grey branches. There was nothing to see other than the back of the forlorn figure of the dryad, visible through the twisted cluster of dead wood. That didn't mean there wasn't anything hiding there right now, camouflaged by some form of woody magic. If dryads could keep themselves hidden whenever they wanted to and from whomever they wanted to, I was pretty damned sure that a Batibat would be able to do the same. And that meant that the only thing left was to break the ward.

I looked across at the small group on the other side. Larkin and Max appeared to be doing what I'd asked, as Max was testing the edges of the ward to check whether there was any intrinsic magical alarm system built in and Larkin was trying – and failing – to cast an appropriate Divination spell. Every time he flicked his fingers forward, a puff of blue light appeared and then vanished. So much for tracking the Batibat by magic then. Aubrey was clutching my plastic bag for dear life, watching me carefully from across the expanse, and Lucy was on the ground, with her back to me, hugging her knees. I had my doubts as to whether I could protect any of them in the event that I managed to breach the ward and confront the tree daemon. I really had no idea about its capabilities. I was going to have to face it before night fell, however. I stared again at the dead tree. Perhaps there was a way to get inside without breaking the ward.

Casting around the ground for a few moments, I quickly found what I was looking for. There was a clump of pink shale half concealed by one of the tufts of grass, and I bent down to pick a piece up. I tested the edge, deciding that it would work, and then opened up my fingers and drew the stone across my palm, watching the thin red line of blood that sprang up in its place. Then I knelt down again and rubbed my hand on the ground.

I only had to wait a moment or two before the air started to crackle and shimmer purple and the figure of Solus appeared, an angry grimace marring his features.

He sprang towards me, pulling my body towards his, and hissing in my ear. "Where is it?"

I stayed calm. "Where's what, Solus?"

"The thing that attacked you. You're bleeding. Tell me where it is."

I was touched by the ire in his voice. "Sorry. Nothing attacked me. I just needed to talk to you."

He released me abruptly, spinning me round to face him. "Dragonlette, you are trying my patience. You could have just called." His violet eyes shot sparks at me, but I could tell from the way his muscles had immediately relaxed that it was more for show.

"Sorry," I said, although I wasn't really. "But I need you now, not in three days' time when you bother to answer me."

He clasped his heart in mock agony. "You wound me." He leaned in towards me. "I was busy annoying your brawny Brethren Lord."

Uh-oh. "Bloody hell, Solus, is that really necessary?"

"Not in the slightest," he grinned at me insouciantly. "But it's a hell of a lot of fun. The Furry One doesn't like me very much."

"I can't imagine why," I murmured, eyeing him unhappily.

The Fae arched an eyebrow and watched me carefully. "Have you read the translation yet?"

"Been kind of busy to be honest. It's back at home."

He grinned. There was an edge to it that both surprised and concerned me. "Interesting," he said, with a suspicious note of underlying glee, "be sure to let me know when you do."

I filed away his on-going interest in my reading of the translated Fae book for later. There were more pressing concerns to deal with right now. I gestured towards the centre of ward instead. "Can you transport me inside that?"

Solus turned and stared at it, his skin visibly paling as he did so. "That's a dryad."

I nodded. His fists clenched, and a ripple of fury shuddered through him. I swallowed involuntarily. I'd never seen him this upset before. He reached out and touched the ward, then drew it back again.

"You don't know what could be in there. Just because it looks empty, doesn't mean it is." His voice remained curiously emotionless and flat, which was almost more scary than if he'd allowed himself to show what he was really thinking.

"It's not empty." I outlined for him my theory about the Batibat.

He shook his head. "Except Batibats wouldn't attack dryads and certainly not like that. They prefer young men."

"Let me guess," I said drily, "you're an expert on Indonesian daemons along with everyone else."

He sent me a puzzled look. "It's common knowledge, dragonlette."

I rolled my eyes. Of course it was. "I don't need you to spell out the dangers for me, Solus, I just need you to get me inside."

"I'm not sure I can. Even if I managed it, it would drain me of all my energy and then I wouldn't be able to help you if things went wrong."

"I think I'm capable of looking after myself," I scoffed.

"You let a vampire get the better of you barely two days ago."

"It was one."

"Eh?"

"It was one vampire. And if you look closely, you'll see that he's not doing so well as a result."

Solus looked understandably confused. I gently pointed out Aubrey's figure to him. Even with the hat and trenchcoat, his features were obvious. The Fae's mouth dropped open. "Is that...?"

"Yup."

"He's a master vampire, dragonlette. One of the strongest. What in the hell..." Dawning realisation lit his features. "He drank your blood."

I nodded.

"And because your blood has the power to heal, it healed him. He's no longer a vampire."

"Yup."

"Bloody hell, dragonlette, do you realise that this makes you number one on the vamps' hitlist? They'll do anything either to control you or destroy you. That's unbelievable power. How many people has he told?"

I shrugged. "None. He's afraid of what the others'll do to him if they find out."

HELEN HARPER

Solus blinked slowly. "Of course. A cured vampire is the antithesis of everything they believe in." He smiled, and it wasn't very pleasant. "How very interesting."

"Solus?"

"Hmmm?" He was still watching Aubrey with a worryingly predatorial expression flickering through his eyes.

"You can't tell anyone."

"Mmm."

"Solus, I mean it. He was a horrible vampire. And right now he's a horrible human. But he has a chance to maybe turn things around and be a better person. You are not going to fuck that up."

"Dragonlette," he began.

I looked him in the eyes. "Don't."

"Okay."

"Give me your word, Solus."

"Okay."

I narrowed my eyes at him. He lifted his hands up in the air. "Fine! I give you my word."

"Excellent. Now, get me in there."

"It's not a good idea, dragonlette."

"Please."

"If I do this, then in return you need to do me a favour."

Of course. Why would I have expected anything less? "What?" I said, exasperated.

"I don't know yet. But," he held up one long elegant index finger, "you will owe me one favour of my choosing to be fulfilled when I require it."

I gritted my teeth. "Fine. But no giving away of my firstborn or secondborn or anything like that. No hurting of anyone, physically or emotionally. "

He winked at me. "What if it's an evil tree daemon?"

I gave him my death stare.

"Okay, okay, nothing that involves children or hurting things,

I promise." He gave me a cheeky boyish grin. "As if I would anyway, dragonlette."

I really hoped I wasn't going to regret this. Solus snapped his fingers and the air immediately began to flicker purple. "Give that bitch hell," he said, suddenly all serious again.

I nodded. I intended to.

CHAPTER FOURTEEN

THE MOLECULES IN THE AIR SNAPPED AND BIT. AS SOON AS I registered the purple shimmer, I stepped forward, not hesitating further. I was too nervous to delay further. Whatever had done that terrible thing to the dryad was not the kind of being that I should take lightly.

Transporting through felt different to how it usually did. Clearly the ward was going to make things as difficult as possible, and it created the effect of feeling as if my body was being rent asunder. The world outside the barrier pulled at me, as if, with a magnetic urge, it was demanding my physical presence remain there. I couldn't see what was happening to Solus, but I heard his cry of pain as I wrenched myself through, then collapsed panting, with pricks of tears forming in my eyes. My stomach lurched with devastating nausea, even worse than I normally experienced. I tried to force myself to face the tree, just in case my arrival had woken the Batibat from her sleep and she was already on her way to meet me, but the retching overtook me. My fingernails stabbed into the blackened ground, clawing in agony as my once pleasant breakfast deposited itself unceremoniously in front of me. I was dimly aware of the blur of frantic gestures from my little band of followers on the other side, but the effort to raise my head and acknowledge them to reassure them that I was alright was almost too much.

When the convulsions finally stopped, I collapsed, my cheek hot against the soot. I gasped for air several times, and had to force myself to take in deep heaving breaths to calm myself down. Eventually I was able to scramble back to my feet, where I stood trembling. I looked behind and saw Solus down on the ground. Lucy had managed to get round and was by his side, her hand on his arm. She mouthed something to me, but I couldn't work out what it was.

"Is he okay?" I shouted over.

She looked puzzled and mouthed something again. Shit. Clearly the ward blocked out sound too. I pointed down at Solus to highlight my worry and concern. She blinked in sudden understanding, and nodded back, this time enunciating her words more obviously, stating what appeared to be 'he's fine'. I watched him carefully, relief flooding through me when he stirred and slowly sat back up. He pushed his hair away from his face and grinned boyishly. I rolled my eyes. Idiot. Then, however, his gaze fixed on something behind me and his pupils narrowed to tiny sharp pinpricks of glass. Lucy too was now frozen and staring beyond me. I guessed the Batibat was finally awake.

I concentrated on my hands, allowing my now familiar green fire to light up and flicker, then I slowly turned, every sinew of my body ready to launch myself at the she-daemon.

Aubrey had been right. The Batibat, standing heavily in front of the dead tree, and thankfully blocking the dryad from my sight, was indeed hideous. She was morbidly obese, virtually the width of a small car, with folds of greyish fat and loose skin hanging down from every rounded corner of her body. Her breasts were drooping enough to hit the centre of her stomach, and her dirty blonde hair was scraggly and limp. My mouth dried, but I forced myself to lift my eyes up to hers.

She looked down at my hands then back up to my face, with a

complete lack of expression. For once in my life, I had absolutely no idea what my opponent was about to do.

I tilted my chin up. "Hello."

The Batibat stared back at me, without so much as blinking.

I tried smiling. It didn't reach my eyes, and I was well aware that I had the habit of looking like a maniacal psychopath when that happened, but I wasn't quite sure what else to do. She still just stared at me.

Okaaaaay. I took a step forward. She didn't move. I kept my arms by my sides, trying to show that I wasn't going to attack her unless she struck out at me first, but I didn't extinguish my flames, making sure that she knew that I was also more than ready to take her on if I had to. It occurred to me that maybe I should have thought this whole operation through in a little more depth first.

Just when I was starting to wonder if the Batibat was completely immobile, she suddenly let out a huge shuddering sigh, and turned her back on me, lumbering back to the tree that was just a few feet away.

"Hey!" I shouted out towards her, suddenly alarmed. The last thing I needed was for her to get back within the branches and completely conceal herself again. At least right now I knew where she was. "Where the fuck do you think you're going? I want to talk to you!"

She completely ignored me, continuing her shambling return to the tree. I so wasn't in the mood for this. I outstretched my arm and extended my index finger to just beyond her body, zapping the ground with a line of green fire. Thanks to the already heavily burnt earth, however, my efforts immediately sizzled away into nothing. The Batibat didn't even react, hooking one hand into one of the lower branches, and swinging herself up with a dexterity that astonished me. She clearly possessed some kind of affinity with trees, not least because the branches that looked dead enough to snap the second so much as a whisper of a breeze gusted by them, easily held her weight. Before I could so much as blink, she had completely vanished.

I remained standing in the same spot for a moment, utterly dumbfounded. I flicked a glance over to the mages and Aubrey who were still on the other side of the barrier, all their mouths gaping open, and gave an expressive shrug. So much for big old scary me, then. The seeming apathy of the tree daemon had me baffled. The entire point of forcing both Solus and myself to the point of physical pain to transport through the ward had been to confront her. And yet she just seemed as if she couldn't care less.

I considered my options. I could of course climb the tree as she had done. But I was no tree spirit. I'd end up flat on my arse with a bunch of broken sticks around me. The Batibat's very essence had been absorbed by the wood. The only thing that would be absorbed if I tried to do the same would be everyone's recognition of my own stupidity. I kicked irritably at the ground, sending a cloud of black dust into the air.

Sighing deeply, I figured that the least I could do now that I was here was to disentangle the dead dryad from her dishonourable position. It wasn't just that releasing her body from the hold of the tree might re-ignite the Batibat's interest and encourage her to reappear, but also that the dryad bloody well deserved to be taken down and properly cared for. I'd promised both her and myself that I would do that. The thought of having to touch her dead skin and feel the weight of her against me, without anyone nearby who would be able to help and provide companionship through the horror, made me sick to my stomach. I had no right to that emotion though. What Mereia had gone through to end up in that position in the first place was far worse than anything I could experience by cutting her down. Once her body was safely removed then I was going to torch that fucking tree with the Batibat inside it.

With a heavy heart, I walked round to the other side and looked upwards, avoiding spending too long gazing at the dryad's sunken skin and dead eyes. Instead I focused on her hands, trying to work out how she was being held up. Aubrey had been right before: her wrists were somehow twisted into the very branches of the tree itself. I'd already surmised that I wouldn't be able to climb up and reach her, so there seemed nothing else for it but to use shots of my green fire to bring her down. I'd have to do this carefully if I was going to give her the dignity she deserved.

Taking three steps backwards, I squinted up, trying to select the best place to aim. It was vital to be gentle. I closed one eye and pointed out towards one of the curving twigs and, oh so very carefully, sent out a soft small stream of fire.

When it hit the tree, the twig unravelled with a sharp hiss, loosening its grip on the dryad's arm. Emboldened, I tried again, this time with slightly more power. My shot rang true, and yet another dead branch was loosened. It was difficult to tell from where I was, but it appeared that Mereia's wrist was starting to pull away from the tree's unhappy knot.

"He won't be happy if you do that," stated a raspy voice, with an air of unerring calm.

I was so surprised that I lost my footing and half stumbled, sending up more clouds of black dirt as I did so. I looked upwards and saw the face of the Batibat peering down at me implacably.

Forcing my heart to return to a normal rhythm, I injected a flat air into my tone. "Who are you referring to?"

Her expression looked puzzled. "Him of course."

Seriously? I gritted my teeth. "I don't know who you mean. Can you tell me?"

"He won't like it."

My fingertips tingled with dangerous embers of heat. "Yes, you already said that. Who?"

She blinked languorously down at me. "He left her like that for a reason. He'll know if you take her down."

Nope. I couldn't do calm after all. I lifted my right hand

towards her, green flames still flickering round. "Fucking tell me who you mean or I'll destroy you now," I snarled.

"He has no name. He is all there is."

She began to draw back into the tree again, but I was determined this time not to let her disappear. I shot up one stream of fire, avoiding her face by millimetres. The Batibat hissed.

"Did he do this?" I shouted up at her. "Did he kill her?"

There was a loud creaking sound from the dead tree as she shrugged, shaking even the trunk into shuddering vibrations. The body of the dryad quivered in response. Screw this.

I turned back to the remaining snake-like branches that were clinging to the tree nymph's arm and sent out a streak of fire once again. Having snagged exactly the right section, her arm swung free, and her entire body fell heavily down to the side, now just hanging to the tree by her one remaining wrist. Her head dropped down to her collarbone, tendrils of dark green hair falling limply forward like a sad shroud, and her left foot dragged along the burnt ground.

"Not long now," I muttered, moving over to the other side to complete the process.

"He'll come," the Batibat stated obdurately down at me, although when I flicked a quick glance up at her there was a definite expression of fear across her heavy features.

"Let him," I grunted, eyeing up the remaining branches that were holding the rest of Mereia's corpse in place, in order to try and work out which point would be best to target. I had no time for mysterious evil-doers who couldn't even be bothered to have names.

The Batibat moved again, the tree groaning as she did so, and her whole body emerged from within the grey branches as she clambered back down and planted her bare heavy feet onto the dark ground.

"You don't understand," she rasped, "you cannot beat him. "

I half-turned towards her. "Do you work for him?"

She laughed. At least I assumed it was a laugh; it sounded like much more of a grating shriek than a hearty chortle. "You make it sound as if I have a choice." She leaned in towards me, a cloud of her foul breath wafting towards my face. "He has bound the trees that we live in. We either do his bidding or," she cast a quick look at the sagging dryad's body, "we suffer a similar fate to that poor creature."

I squinted up at her. "So when you say 'we', who do you mean?" I wasn't prepared yet to let her know that I was aware that there was another of her species in London causing problems, if not for the general population, then for the profits of a certain troll anyway.

"There are others like me."

"And where are they?"

"All over." Her voice was suddenly so quiet I had to strain to catch her words. I abandoned that avenue of questioning for now and switched tactics.

"Did he tell you to attack my, er," I paused for a moment. Aubrey wasn't my friend. "Companion?"

She half-cocked her head. "You mean the brown haired emotional boy? He's a bit weak that one."

I wondered what she'd say if she knew that until very recently he'd been a merciless master vampire. My eyes turned hard. "Answer the question."

She allowed herself a small smile. "That one was just for me." She licked her lips in a manner that turned my stomach. "I like young men."

He wasn't really all that young, I thought sardonically. I changed the subject. "So what does he want?" There was no doubt as to which 'he' I was referring to.

"What do all men want? Power. Control." She shrugged. "The usual."

"Most men don't go around slaughtering innocent tree nymphs," I commented, trying to keep my swirling bloodfire under control. I needed to keep it from consuming me so that I could get as much information out of the Batibat as possible. It was fucking hard not to give in to the temptation to blast her into a pile of smouldering cinders, however.

"Most men are not like him." She looked me up and down. "You have power of your own. I can sense it. It won't be enough though. He uses the old ways and dark, dark magic. He cannot be defeated."

I seemed to remember being told something vaguely similar about wraiths and look how that had turned out. Still, know thy enemy. "What does he look like?"

"Not as handsome as that one." The Batibat jerked her head behind me. Assuming she was talking about either Larkin or Max and not wanting to take my eyes away from her, I didn't bother turning around. "I might even keep that one alive for a while as a little toy. It can be rather dull waiting around here."

I ignored her pointless threats. "What exactly are you waiting for? What's he planning to do?"

Her lips turned down at the edges, fat heavy creases appearing in the folds of her cheeks. "How do I know? He wants the power of the land and will do what he can to get it. Many of these trees have been around for hundreds of years. He knows ways to take their life-force and use it. For what I have no idea. But you should be afraid."

I ignored the implied threat. "So he's behind the planned demolition? He's going to cut down the trees to drain them of their natural power? Why bother pretending to build something in their place?"

"I would imagine he needs some kind of cover story for the humans. They can be annoying when they get involved."

I thought about what Atlanteia had told me. "Has he done something to stop protestors from coming here? The humans who would stop the trees from being cut down?"

"Wards do many things," the Batibat grunted cryptically.

I chewed my lip. "So break the ward here and break whatever

magic he is using and that will stop preventing people from coming?"

She made her unpleasant version of a laugh again. "You can't break the ward. He's too powerful. You need to understand," she said, leaning forward, "you cannot beat him. He knows too much and can do too much. And if you free her body, then he will come here and destroy you all."

Bring it fucking on. Whoever this guy was, he wasn't going to know what had hit him. And when I broke his ward, he was going to get a tiny taste of exactly what I was capable of. I turned back to the dryad.

"If you're going to continue with this foolhardiness, then let me have a little taste of your friend first," the Batibat called. "The one who seems fixated on you. He looks angry. I'll probably be doing you a favour." Her voice deepened. "I like the strong ones. It's more fun when they struggle."

This time curiosity got the better of me and I flicked a glance over my shoulder. Oh. Corrigan was standing there, in a dark grey suit that looked completely out of place in the middle of a wood. His arms were crossed against his broad chest and he looked mightily pissed off. Even from this distance I could see the emerald green of his eyes flashing sparks at me.

Hey Corrigan. My Voice bounced against something that felt a bit like cotton wool. Corrigan's expression didn't change. Interesting. That meant that the barrier was blocking the usual shifter telepathy, which indicated why he'd not bothered announcing his arrival. It also meant that it was a fucking strong ward. I gave him a little grin and a wave instead. His frown deepened.

"Is he your husband?" inquired the Batibat.

I let out a bark of laughter. "As if."

She exhaled loudly and happily. "Then I can take him off your hands for you."

"That won't be necessary." I watched as Solus, clearly completely recovered now, made his way towards the Lord

Alpha. Whereas the mages were carefully keeping their distance from him, and Aubrey seemed to be hiding behind a tree, the Fae felt no such compunction. He reached Corrigan and punched him lightly on the shoulder as if to say 'hey, buddy', before turning to me and blowing a melodramatic kiss. Then he joined his index fingers and his thumbs together to form the shape of a heart and held it out in my direction. Corrigan's arms dropped to his sides, his fists clenching. It was time for me to wrap things up before either of them created some other kind of stupid inter-species war.

I turned back to the Batibat. "I'm going to finish bringing her body down. Then I'm going to destroy your tree and break your nameless dude's ward. It's up to you if you stick around or not."

She stared at me. "You can't break the ward."

"Watch me," I growled.

I flicked out a jet of fire towards the remaining branches that were holding Mereia in place. This time practice clearly made perfect as I hit the right ones first time around, and her body immediately began to fall to the ground. I ran towards her, catching her corpse before it thudded down, and then carried her gently away from the tree and laid her down at a safe distance at the edge of the ward. I didn't look at Corrigan or the others again.

"He's going to be angry," shouted the Batibat, her previously calm tones, now sounding panicked. "He'll..."

Her shout drifted away as I returned back to my previous spot, lifted up both hands and sent out twin spikes of fire towards the tree, this time not caring what I hit. I was dimly aware of her jumping backwards and hissing, but I completely ignored her, concentrating instead on the total destruction of the scene of the dryad's death. This, at least, I could do properly.

The dry branches, under the onslaught of all the fire I could muster, didn't take long before they lit up and caught. The flames gnawed their way along the dead wood, turning it as black as the surrounding ground. Burning twigs and branches began to fall to the ground as if in slow motion. The heat coming off the now skeleton-like silhouette was extraordinary, and my eyes began to water from the smoke. I didn't stop, however. The tree became a pyre, crackling and sending out sparks that made the Batibat yelp and back away further. I upped my fiery voltage and pelted out everything that I had. In the absence of the fucking embodiment of evil that had done this, I was going to take out my vengeance on the already dead tree. Let the wanker come and see what I'd done. I wasn't afraid of him.

When I was satisfied that I'd done enough to completely destroy the corpse of what had probably once been a magnificent example of nature's goodness, I left it burning and looked over at the Batibat, satisfied. She was slumped some distance away, the heavy crooks of her arms folded over and around her body, hugging herself. I didn't know whether the tree had originally been home to her or home to Mereia and I didn't really care. The dryad no longer needed it, and I couldn't give a flying fuck whether the Batibat was now homeless or not.

I called out to her. "If your lord and master comes calling, tell him that Mackenzie Smith did this. I'll be more than happy to deal with his complaints." I stared at her, hard. "Did you get that?"

She sent me a sullen look, filled with hate.

"Mackenzie Smith." I repeated. "And you can let him know that I'm not done, not by a long shot."

I walked over to the edge of the ward, briefly examining the wound on my palm for a moment. I dug my fingernails into it, wincing slightly at the pain, but smiling grimly as fresh blood oozed out. Then I scooped up Mereia's body, trying to ignore the cold feel of her dead skin, and gently cradled her almost weightless form against me, holding her in place with my free hand while I reached out against the ward with the other, smearing my blood against it. I was confident, given my past experience, that my Draco Wyr genes would be enough to break through it. There was a tiny part of me that doubted, considering the Batibat's assertions regarding the strength of the ward, but I needn't have bothered. As my blood came into contact with the barrier, the entire perimeter appeared to glow. Then there was a loud bang as it snapped open.

I stepped through, savouring the return of fresh, untainted air. Casting a quick glance behind me, it was clear that the Batibat had chosen to vanish to somewhere else. Suited me.

Lucy was standing by Corrigan's side, staring. "I thought you didn't want to break it in case it set off some kind of alarm? Is it not going to trigger something off?"

I felt all of the group's eyes on me. I shrugged, my mouth set into a grim line. "Oh, it'll have triggered something off. In fact, I hope it'll have triggered a screaming alert to the fucker that did this so that he comes running. Because I'm going to fucking destroy him."

CHAPTER FIFTEEN

IF I'D BEEN EXPECTING SOME KIND OF DRAMATIC DRUM-ROLL AT MY emphatic statement regarding what I was going to do to the Batibat's apparent boss, then I didn't get one. The not-so-merry band in front just watched me as if expecting the architect of the ward to immediately materialise so that I could make good on my promise. There was the rumble of a small plane overhead but, other than that, the entire area remained as silent and still as it had before the magical barrier had been destroyed.

Corrigan's eyes were narrowed at me, flecks of hot angry gold visibly displayed across their green depths. He broke the atmosphere by walking forward to take the dryad's body from my arms, but I side-stepped away from him. My movements clearly didn't do much to improve his mood.

"I need to take her to her kin," I said, by way of explanation. "I doubt they'll show up if you do it."

He snarled at me. "What exactly is going on here?"

I looked at him calmly. "Walk up with me and I'll explain. I assume you couldn't hear anything that went on inside the ward?"

He shook his head, not taking his snapping green eyes off me for even a second.

"Great!" exclaimed Solus, brightly. He stepped over and planted a wet noisy kiss on my cheek. Unfortunately, with Mereia's weight somewhat hindering me, I wasn't able to move away in time. A muscle throbbed in Corrigan's cheek.

The two mages frowned in unison. Max spoke up. "You can't just wander off with those two. If you're telling the shifters and the faeries what happened, then you have to tell us what happened also."

I sighed in exasperation. Lord, give me help.

Aubrey's plaintive voice called out from behind a nearby tree. "Don't forget about me! Where did that woman go? She's after me, you know. She almost killed me! You can't leave me here because she'll come back and hurt me."

Corrigan's brow creased in puzzlement "Who is that?"

"I'll explain later," I said dismissively, then looked from one member of the group to the other. "The Batibat didn't kill the dryad. It was some guy who is theoretically masterful and strong, and too self-important to even deign to give himself a name. He wants to cut down all the trees because they give him some kind of natural power boost. We need to stop him."

"Why does he want the power?" asked Lucy.

I thought about the Batibat's answer to that question and decided somewhat sensibly that repeating it wouldn't go down well with this rather testosterone heavy group. "Fuck knows. Because he's a vicious bastard who wants to screw the world as far as I can tell." I turned my attention to Solus. "You need to find out what's going on with Beltran. He needs to get those environmentalists here double quick to help stop the tree felling."

The Fae quirked an eyebrow at me. "But, darling, I'm not sure I want to leave your side. I find it so very hard when we are separated, and I know you do too." He winked at Corrigan.

I avoided looking at the Lord Alpha. If I didn't know what his reaction was, then I wouldn't have to worry about having to do anything about it. "Solus," I said, warningly.

He grinned disarmingly and bowed. "But, as always, your

wish is my command." The air shimmered and he vanished. I heaved an inward sigh of relief.

"You two," I said to Max and Larkin, "need to do something about that." I jerked my head to the blackened area, and the still smouldering tree. "It needs to be completely concealed before anyone else less…otherworldly…shows up."

They didn't look happy, but nodded in agreement anyway.

"Stay with them," growled Corrigan at Lucy, who bobbed her head instantly. At least when he gave an order, his people fucking jumped to it, I thought irritably.

"Hey," spat out Max, solidifying my thoughts, "we don't need babysitting by a bloody shifter!"

I stared at him coldly, trying to borrow some of Corrigan's immovably authoritative air. Somehow it worked, because he subsided into grumbles of acquiescence.

"Well, you can't order me around," shouted Aubrey, still from behind the tree.

Actually, out of everyone at this little assembly, he was about the only one I knew for sure that I could tell what to do and be sure that he'd do it. "Stay there," I snapped, then began walking up the hill, back towards the clearing I'd visited barely twelve hours before.

"Mack!" he shouted after me. "Don't leave me!"

I ignored him, shifting the dryad's body into a slightly more comfortable position as Corrigan fell into step beside me. I could almost feel the simmering waves of rage emanating in my direction. Once we were out of earshot, I spoke up, quietly.

"So, I get that you're a bit pissed off," I began.

"A bit pissed off?"

"Okay," I conceded, "a lot pissed off. I'm sorry I ran off from the Brethren's headquarters like that."

"You climbed out the window and scaled down the wall, Mackenzie. You could have broken your neck! You were not a prisoner. Do you really think I wouldn't have let you leave?"

I exhaled deeply and gestured behind myself. "Have you seen

what my life is like lately? I can't move without being followed around by a representative from virtually every major Otherworld group! The whole lot of you seem to think that I belong to you. If I'd tried to leave by conventional means, it would have taken me hours to persuade everyone to let me go."

"Because you were just bloody well attacked! What would have happened if that vampire decided to try again? There is not a single scrap of self-preservation anywhere inside you. How do you know that bloodsucker isn't somewhere near here now just waiting for the opportunity to pounce? And don't you dare tell me that you can look after yourself, because if that was true then you wouldn't have needed me to come and find you on the Heath! Do you have any idea how long it took to locate you?"

"I'm sorry, Corrigan, okay?" I shouted back at him. "But some things are more important than my safety! The dryads asked me for help and I had to give it to them. You can see from what just happened down there how bad things are. This guy might be targeting the tree nymphs now, but it doesn't mean he's not going to move on to someone else later. And, besides, I told you the vampire wasn't going to be a problem any more."

"You don't know that!"

"Yes, I fucking well do! That bloke, the one hiding behind the tree? That's Aubrey. He's the one who attacked me. And, believe me, he is not in any position to start draining me of my blood again."

Corrigan started. "That's not Aubrey. I know what he smells like."

"You know what he smells like when he's a vamp, you mean."

"Huh?"

"When he drank from me my blood did something to him. Healed him."

"Healed him? You mean he's cured of being a vampire?"

"That's exactly what I mean."

Corrigan turned on his heel, and began striding back down again.

159

"Hey!" I shouted after him. "Where are you going?"

"I'm going to rip his fucking head off," he muttered.

"Stop!" I tried to run after him but carrying Mereia's body made it difficult for me to move with any speed. I laid her gently down on the ground, and then jogged to catch up, moving in front of Corrigan to block his path. "You can't kill him!"

He looked me directly in the eyes. It was virtually impossible for me to look away. "Why the hell not, Mack? He almost killed you."

"But he didn't! I'm here and I'm fine. And he's human, you can't just go hurting him now. It wouldn't be fair!"

"Fair?" He grabbed me by the shoulders and leaned in towards me. I inhaled deeply, drinking in his spicy aftershave and my stomach tripped with little butterflies. "Was what he did to you fair?"

"You need to calm down," I said, doing my very best to ignore the tumult that was going on inside me.

His eyes narrowed. "Is there something going on between you and him? Is that why you're protecting him?"

For fuck's sake. "No! I just feel sorry for him that's all. He's not doing any harm, he's just a bit annoyingly pathetic. There's no reason to hurt him. Believe me, Corrigan, what my blood did to him is punishment enough."

His eyes bored into me and his grip tightened. "And the faerie?"

"You can't kill him either."

Corrigan's voice deepened to a rumble. "You know that's not what I mean."

I sighed. "No, there's nothing going on between me and Solus. He's just trying to irritate you."

"He's doing a good job."

"Only because you let him. You need to relax, my Lord."

"Somehow the last thing I can do where you're concerned is relax." He stared at me searchingly. "I don't like it when you call me that."

"Okay," I said, conceding. "I won't call you that. Only if you stop calling me kitten though."

He blinked in lazy agreement and his hands loosened.

"Why did you come here anyway?" I asked. "I thought you were busy somewhere else."

He shrugged, the muscles in his broad shoulders rippling as he did so. "It's being taken care of."

"Can I help?"

"It's just a group of rogue shifters that have been flexing their power a bit too much lately. I think we're bringing them into the fold, however."

"The mighty Brethren strikes again," I commented drily.

Something flashed in Corrigan's eyes, but he didn't rise to the bait. Instead he moved one of his hands from my shoulder to my hair, smoothing it down gently and tucking it behind my ear. My stomach flip-flopped. "I hope you'll wear it down like that for our date tonight."

Date? Oh, shit. How had it gotten to be Saturday already? "That's tonight?"

He nodded, a predatorial gleam in his eyes.

"Corrigan, I have to deal with this stuff first. I can't just go off gallivanting with you for dinner."

"You promised." He bent his head down, until his face was scant inches from mine and I could feel his hot breath on my skin. Warm tendrils of bloodfire uncoiled themselves and began zipping through my veins with anticipation. I swallowed.

"I know. But this guy, the one the Batibat told me about, sounds like he's dangerous. I can't just leave."

A touch of icy cold lit the edges of his eyes and he drew back. I tried to ignore the pings of disappointment. Remember, I told myself sternly, getting involved with the Lord Alpha is only going to end in tears. Get a grip. Unfortunately, that didn't stop me feeling irritatingly bereft at his sudden withdrawal.

"Fine," he shrugged, and his face shut down.

Goddamnit. He turned and continued off down the hill with

a lithe elegant stride. Alarmed, I called out after him. "Where are you going? You promised you wouldn't hurt Aubrey."

"I didn't technically promise. Besides, you promised me a date tonight and I believe you've reneged. " His voice was even but he didn't bother to either stop or turn around.

"Corrigan!" I shouted.

Relax, kitten. My word is good, even if yours isn't. I won't harm a hair on his head.

Streaks of hot annoyance ran through me. It wasn't as if I'd fucking planned for all this to happen just so that I could have an excuse to avoid having dinner with him.

Fine, my Lord, I shot at him.

Silence rebounded back at me. Well, sod you then, I thought uncharitably. I stomped back up to where I'd left Mereia and stood for a moment staring down at her corpse, all the anger abruptly flooding out of me. What right did I have to be enraged at something petty like a stupid argument with Corrigan when she was lying there dead? I might not have known her personally, but that didn't mean her death didn't deserve more attention. I had to stop worrying about the petty shit and start focusing on the matter in hand. Squaring my shoulders, I bent down and carefully picked her back up, unbidden and unexpected tears springing to my eyes.

"I'm sorry," I murmured, not entirely sure at that point whether I was apologising to her, to the now absent Corrigan, or to myself. I sighed heavily, and then plodded upwards, carrying my unhappy burden as gently as I could.

When I reached the clearing, I squatted down, laying her body softly on the ground. I adjusted her limbs slightly and looked at her sadly. A sudden breeze gusted through the trees, ruffling her hair. Free of the terrible crucified pose, and with her eyes closed and arms by her side, she suddenly looked at peace. The lines of pain that I'd avoided focusing on before had smoothed out, and she almost appeared to be merely sleeping. Almost. I wiped the tears away from my cheeks and glanced upwards.

"Here is Mereia," I called out softly, unsure whether I'd get any reply. "I think that now she's been taken down and the ward concealing her body has been destroyed, things might start returning more to normal. But you have to be careful. There's a Batibat around here. I don't think she's any danger to you – she seems more fixated on men - but she might cause some problems. And the person behind what happened to your friend might show up. If he does, you need to stay hidden. I'm not going to leave until he's dealt with, I promise you that."

I ignored the irritating nudge I felt deep inside that my promises weren't worth quite what they might once have been, and took a step backwards, bowing my head and closing my eyes. When I opened them again, a mere moment later, Mereia's body had gone. I nodded to myself.

A quiet voice drifted down from somewhere amongst the higher edges of the trees. "Thank you."

"You're welcome," I whispered back. Then I left.

CHAPTER SIXTEEN

ARMED WITH THE NEW, ALBEIT SCANTY, INFORMATION REGARDING the person behind the dryad's violent demise, it seemed important to get in touch with Alex again. When I made it back to the others, I noted with a touch of satisfaction that Max and Larkin had, between them, managed to cast some kind of Illusion spell to hide the remaining burnt evidence from any prying eyes. They were sitting down on a small grassy hillock with Lucy some distance away. There was no sign of Corrigan. I told myself that I didn't care and looked instead for Aubrey who, proving that the compulsion was still in play, remained in his previous position behind the tree.

Ignoring the others' curious gazes, I stalked over to him. He was curled up unhappily on the ground, hugging his knees to himself and singing softly. He seemed to have given up on his 'disguise', as his trenchcoat, hat and gloves were in a neatly folded pile next to his feet. I knelt down and poked him.

"Hey."

He didn't respond. I poked him again, harder this time. "Give me your phone, Aubrey."

The ex-vamp didn't even bother to look up; he just squeezed a hand into his pocket, pulled out his mobile and held it out.

"Thanks."

I turned it on and began to jab in Alex's number.

Aubrey cleared his throat. I ceased what I was doing for a moment and looked at him.

"You're really mean to me, Mack," he whined.

"Not too long ago you told me I was really nice," I commented.

He ignored my words and just glared up at me. "You left me here with those others. They won't even talk to me. It's like I don't even exist."

I tried not to give the ember of sympathy that stirred inside me any notice. "Yeah, well, maybe if you hadn't acted like such a prick when you were a vampire, then maybe they'd be nicer to you now."

"It's not my fault. That's like blaming a wasp for stinging or a mosquito for biting. It was in my nature to do those things. "

"You mean like now it's in your nature to hang around on the ground and complain a lot?" I inquired.

He screwed up his face. "See! You're just mean."

I gave up and returned my attention to the phone.

"Mack?"

"What?"

"I'm hungry."

"Then go and eat something."

The phone began to ring.

"There's nothing to eat." He pouted at me, unhappily. I ignored him.

The ringing stopped and Alex's voice filled the line. "Hey, Mack Attack."

"Hey, Alex. What's going on?"

"It's been as dead as a grave here, dude. Not much happens around this place during the day. Not seen that fat naked woman again though at least."

I was idly curious as to what relation Alex's Batibat was to mine, but it was barely relevant to my needs. Batibats were entirely the wrong gender. Instead I turned to asking about the only thing that could potentially be of any use. "Have you seen any men go into the shop?"

"One or two."

I chewed frustratedly on my bottom lip. "Can you describe them to me?"

"I can do better than that. I've got photos of them all so I'll text them over. I don't think any of them are your guy though. Most of them just looked like pretty ordinary customers."

A strange sound reached my ears.

"What the hell is that?" asked Alex.

I glanced over at Aubrey. He was gnawing loudly on a twig, ripping parts off with his teeth and masticating wetly in a manner that any cow would be proud of. When he caught me staring, he gave me a look as if to say 'what the fuck is your problem?' and carried on.

"Never mind," I said dismissively into the receiver. "I just need to be more careful about what I say, that's all."

"Don't we all, dude," drawled Alex. "So, as not much is going on here, can I leave now?"

I thought about it. I had to admit that it didn't sound as if he was going to have much success with his venture any longer. However, I needed to know who this mysterious man was, and not just because of my promise to Balud. There was no doubt in my mind that the dryad-killer and the shop owner were one and the same. I couldn't quite work out what the connection between the two could be: what did selling some hardware and destroying trees to get a burst of extra power have to do with each other? It stood to reason that whatever the point behind the weapons shop was, it was something nefarious and nasty. I couldn't believe the fucker who had crucified Mereia side-lined in selling sharp and pointy silverware as a mere day job. There had to be more to it.

"Stick around for another few hours," I advised him. There was an audible sigh. He was going to like my next request even less. "If nothing suspicious shows up and if those photos offer no clues, then you're going to need to go in and talk to the Batibat."

"The naked she-monster?" he screeched. "No way, Mack Attack, no way. She'll eat me alive. You know I'm no good at confrontation stuff."

"Alex," I said patiently, "I'm not asking you to attack her or anything. Just see if you can get some information out of her. You'll be good at it. I would just bulldoze in and piss her off and she'd clam up. You'll go softly softly and be much more successful. I wouldn't ask you if I didn't have faith in you."

"Aw, Mack Attack, I appreciate the vote of confidence but I'm just not sure…"

"You'll be fine. And once you've done that then you can go back home."

There was a moment of silence. Come on, Alex, I pleaded to myself. I need you to do this.

Eventually, he answered. "Okay, then." There was a distinct lack of enthusiasm in his answer, but it would have to do.

"Thank you. I really do appreciate it." There was a snap of a twig in front of me and I looked up to see Solus a few feet away. "I have to go, Alex, but I know you'll do brilliantly. You're more capable than you think."

"A'right. I'll text you those photos. Bye." He hung up.

I hoped he'd be okay. I had no doubts that Alex could charm the Batibat into revealing at least something useful. His cheeky surfer boy grin was probably exactly what her species was looking for. I just needed him to believe that he could do it. Unfortunately I was worried that he'd spend the next couple of hours not building up the confidence that he needed, but instead working himself up into a nervous lather that would lead him to babble inanely when he went inside.

"Boosting up your little hippy mage, dragonlette?" inquired Solus with a hint of humour. "I can help you instead, you know."

"I think this needs a more gentle touch than you can offer," I answered. "Besides, I have a feeling I'm going to need you around here. Did you find Beltran?"

"That I did."

Exasperated, I rolled my eyes at him. "And?"

He shrugged. "The tree huggers were proving rather difficult for him to manage. You would think that a Fae could merely glamour them into decamping here, but there was some kind of block. They all seemed completely incapable of believing that there was a problem here that they might be able to solve. They were determined to hang around Wales and lie in the middle of a few roads to apparently stop the inevitable." Amusement lit his violet eyes. "Humans really can be intractable creatures sometimes."

My heart sank. Atlanteia had seemed convinced that getting the environmentalists on side would help to stop the demolition. I certainly didn't have the faintest idea how to go about it. "So they're not coming?"

He waggled a finger in front of me. "That's not what I said. Somehow, round about the time that you busted the ward, whatever was preventing them from listening to Beltran completely evaporated."

"I was right. The ward wasn't just a physical barrier," I breathed in relief.

"Indeed. Whoever created it was a clever bastard because it was a psychological ward too. They're not easy to manage, you know."

"You sound like you admire him," I said, faintly disgusted.

"Just his work, my little dragonlette. Not him." He dusted off an imaginary speck from his shoulder. "Anyway, to cut a long story short, hey presto and supercalifragilisticexpialidocious, they are on their way. Should be no more than a couple of hours."

Thank fuck. I beamed gratefully at him.

He bobbed his head in arrogant acknowledgement and

opened up his palms, gesturing expansively. "Bring on the accolades."

Aubrey took that moment to spit noisily on the ground. Solus' lip curled in revulsion. I couldn't help snorting out a giggle.

"Can I have my phone back now?" There was a high pitched plaintive note to his voice.

"He's different," commented Solus, eyeing the ex-vamp with detached curiosity.

"He's not fucking undead anymore."

"You know what I mean." Solus frowned. "The Aubrey I knew might have been unlikeable, even as far as vampires go, but he possessed considerable inner strength. This one," he pointed at him with his toe, "is a pathetic excuse for a human. Why is he even with us?"

"I don't really know," I answered, honestly.

Aubrey scrambled to his feet, throwing away his half chewed stick behind him with an angry flourish. "I am here, you know!" he shouted. "It's rude to talk about people as if they're not there when they are! I didn't ask to be turned into a human. She did it to me." His voice continued to rise, and his right foot began stamping the ground several times in quick succession. "Now give me back my phone! It's mine!"

As if on cue, the phone in my hands beeped. I looked over at Solus and raised my eyebrows slightly. "He's having some adjustment issues."

"I'll say," murmured the Fae, with a slightly impressed expression.

"Just let me use it for a few more minutes, Aubrey. Then I'll give it back to you, I promise."

He folded his arms and wrinkled his nose, then sat back down and huffed loudly. I opened Alex's text. There were three images. I opened up the first one, with Solus peering over my shoulder.

"Who's that?"

"I'm hoping it's the prick that's behind all of this," I said, staring down at the hulking figure that Alex had managed to capture.

"Looks pretty strong. No match for our dragon though."

I gave the Fae a warning glance. Aubrey was by now no doubt starting to put the pieces together as to what I really was but that didn't mean that Solus had to hand the information to him on a plate. Fortunately for me he was still sitting glumly on the ground and muttering away to himself, paying us very little attention. Solus was right however: whoever this was that Alex had managed to snap, he looked as if he was built for one thing and one thing only. And that was fighting. This one was definitely a contender. I opened up the next one. It was a young looking guy wearing a hoodie. Alex had only just managed to catch him in profile, but he still looked remarkably babyish to be carrying out a reign of terror. Still, appearances could be deceiving.

I flicked my thumb over to the final image. This one was rather blurry, but it was still possible to make out the features of a somewhat nondescript looking man, wearing glasses and a suit. I frowned down at the phone. There was something about him that was vaguely familiar.

"He looks like that actor," commented Solus, "the one in that Hollywood film about a man murdering his wife and it all going terribly wrong."

I stared up at the Fae in surprise. "You watch movies?"

He actually blushed. "What's wrong with that?"

"Nothing, I guess," I said, still somewhat nonplussed. "Just, I guess I thought that you faeries would be above all that."

"Well, maybe you could come with me sometime." There was a sudden mischievous gleam in his eyes. "We could sit in the back row, share some popcorn, let our hands accidentally touch and then..."

I punched him in the arm. "Sod off."

Solus just laughed musically. I tutted at him and closed down the text. The Batibat's man could realistically be any of them or none of them. Looking at pictures was pretty much a waste of time.

I sighed. I knew I should probably call Mrs. Alcoon and tell her that I might not make it back to London for the bookshop's grand opening, but I didn't want to let her down. Despite the fact that it was clearly foolish optimism to think that I would be there, I decided to wait. I still had the image of Corrigan's frozen eyes in my head when I'd told him I wouldn't keep our date. I wasn't looking forward to doing the same to Mrs. Alcoon. I ignored the little voice whispering coward at me and decided I'd call her tomorrow, then threw the phone into Aubrey's lap. He stopped his incessant muttering and his expression brightened immediately. I watched him carefully for a moment, trying to work out if he was up to something. He had been avoiding all of his vamp pals up till now, but I couldn't help wondering if his sudden attachment to his phone was because he'd finally been in contact with them. Hadn't he said something about knowing a few who could turn him back to a creature of the undead?

"Have you done something stupid, Aubrey?"

"Like what?" he asked, his face a picture of wide-eyed innocence.

"Oh, I don't know," I said, slowly, "like contact some vampires to come here and wreak havoc on the now approaching humans?"

He evinced melodramatic hurt. "No! If I called them it would be to help me out so I can go back to being what I'm supposed to be!"

"An evil night stalker?"

"Someone who gets the respect they deserve! Someone who isn't ignored!" His voice faltered slightly. "Someone who doesn't feel all this inner turmoil all the time."

Oh, the existential problems of a cured vampire. I realised that I still didn't really have an answer to why he was suddenly concerned about where his phone might be though. I stared at him, hard, and put my hands on my hips.

"Okay, so you've not been calling the bloodsuckers. But you've definitely been phoning someone. What's going on?"

Aubrey looked guiltily away. A wash of concern filtered through me. I'd bloody kill him if he had done something to mess up my plans just as things were starting to look up. Why in the hell had I let him tag along? I should have left his sorry arse back in London on the streets where he belonged.

"I could compel you to tell me, you know."

He sniffed. "Go on, then."

At that very moment the phone in his hands beeped. Aubrey glanced down at it and his face lit up. My muscles tensed. Whatever he'd done and whatever he'd summoned, I'd dispatch it pretty damn fucking quickly. Bloodfire lit up inside my belly and there was a shout from behind me.

"Mack! Someone's coming up the hill!"

Giving Aubrey the dirtiest look I could muster, I motioned to Solus to stay and watch him, then turned round to face who – or what – was coming. I squinted downwards. The trees were masking the majority of their approach, but there were flashes of bright red and blue emerging from between the gaps in the leaves. I frowned. They clearly weren't trying to camouflage themselves in any way. I took several steps forward to get a better look. Were they carrying something?

The mages were both on their feet, flicking anxious glances between me and the moving figure. Lucy jogged over in my direction, then took up position next to me, shoulder to shoulder.

"What is it?" she asked quietly, equal measures of concern and menace in her voice.

I shook my head to indicate that I didn't know, and just watched, ready to defend our position if need be. It could be only one of two things: the Batibat's master or a buddy of Aubrey's. Both would be dangerous. Then a face appeared.

Human. I cocked my head, still trying to work out what he was carrying.

Lucy sniffed. "Hold on," she said. "I can smell that. Tomato, meat, some kind of herb…"

Her voice drifted off as a shout reached our ears. "Hey! Which one of you guys ordered pizza?"

I looked at Lucy and she looked at me. Then I turned back round to Aubrey.

He avoided my gaze. "I told you I was hungry," he huffed.

I rolled my eyes and stomped irritably off to get things ready before the campaigners started arriving.

CHAPTER SEVENTEEN

I CALLED MY MERRY BAND OF RAGTAG OTHERWORLDERS TOGETHER, leaving Aubrey in peace to eat his stupid pizza.

"So, the humans will be here soon and we need to be prepared," I said, trying to sound as serious as I possibly could. It wasn't easy with both the mages and Lucy casting occasional hungry glances towards Aubrey and his cheesy meal, with the constant sound of his smacking lips and delighted murmurs interrupting.

"Why do we need to bother with them?" drawled Solus.

I pursed my lips. "I'm here because the dryads asked me to come, and the dryads believe that the environmentalists will be able to stop the demolition that's due to take place on Monday. Therefore, they want them here. They've got the most experience at this kind of thing. Besides, I doubt any of us want to hang around for weeks until the planning permission manages to get blocked."

They all nodded fervently.

Corrigan joined us. I gave him a quick glance, wondering where in the hell he'd been, and tried to ignore the sudden weak sensation that seemed to be attacking my knees. I pushed my shoulders back and stood up a bit straighter instead. He still looked ridiculously out of place in his well tailored suit. It was important not to focus too closely on the way the first few buttons on his white shirt were undone, revealing his smooth, tanned, and oh so very inviting, skin. Get a grip, Mack, I told myself firmly.

"And what happens when the architect of the ward shows up to find out what's happened?" he asked, green eyes fixed on me unblinkingly.

"Then we kill him," I replied matter-of-factly.

"In front of the humans? Don't you think they might have something to say about that?"

Shit. "Well, we make sure none of them are around," I snapped.

He raised a dark eyebrow. "Because that will be easy to manage in a small wooded area."

Larkin looked concerned. "The Lord Alpha is right. We don't want them involved. What if one of them ends up getting hurt? Or killed? What the hell do we do then?"

"That's why we need to be prepared and ready to effectively manage the situation," I stated, calmly, not feeling very managerial or effective in the slightest. I thought quickly. "Look, we know that whoever created the ward is going to head here to find out why it's no longer working. We just need to make sure that the humans stay away from here. This whole area is effectively one big circuit. There are criss-crossing paths, but it's really just a circle. If we can direct them to camp on the other side, then we'll be fine." I glanced over at Max. "Can you maybe set up a couple of light wards to keep them away from here?"

He bobbed his head in agreement.

"Lucy, if you find a suitable campsite area, somewhere with running water nearby, then we can direct them to that place and keep them there."

She turned towards Corrigan, annoyingly seeking his approval. He gave her a curt nod. Great.

"It stands to reason that when they are actually protesting, they're going to be away down at the entrance where the car-park is because that's where the equipment and the builders will be," I continued. "Solus and Larkin can stay down there and keep an eye on things. That way, if anything happens, Solus can transport himself to tell us what's going on, while Larkin can use his magic to contain things."

"Beltran will be here too," Solus added.

"Even better. He already knows the humans so he can stay with Max and Lucy to keep an eye on them. Corrigan, uh, the Lord Alpha, and I are the ones most geared up for a fight. We'll stay here and make sure this bastard doesn't hurt anyone else ever again." There was rage-tinged steel in my voice, but I still looked over at Corrigan to make sure that was okay with him. He nodded in lazy acknowledgement and I sighed inwardly in relief.

Max cleared his throat. "Uh, one thing?"

I looked at him. "Yes?"

"We aren't here to stop some trees from being cut down. We are here to make sure that you are safe."

I bit down my annoyance. "I'll be safe if you can keep the humans away from the big bad guy so that I don't have to worry about them getting in the way or getting hurt. Besides, you might think this is none of your concern, but you saw what happened to that dryad. This isn't some two-bit Otherworlder making a nuisance of himself. We need to work together to stop him."

Fortunately, Max seemed to accept that.

"And who is the big bad guy? Do we know what he looks like?" interjected Lucy.

"Erm, no," I reluctantly confirmed. "I'm sure he'll make himself known pretty fucking quickly though."

"If he looks human then how will we be able to tell the difference between him and the tree-huggers?"

"He'll be the one trying to kill you," Corrigan said, his arms folded and his eyes still trained on me.

Larkin swallowed. "So shouldn't we, um, get some reinforcements in? It'd take no time at all to get more mages here. The Arch-Mage will be happy to help."

"That'll just complicate matters and put more people in harm's way," I stated emphatically. "And give the humans more reason to become suspicious." I could deal with this fucker on my own; there was no way I was going to create a situation where I'd end up with even more blood on my hands than there already was.

"The Welsh pack is sending some help," Corrigan said unhelpfully.

"Well, fucking tell them to go back home again then. The environmentalists are a tight group and will be wary of even more strangers hanging around. You and I can deal with this guy ourselves." I couldn't resist flicking a look at him and adding, "unless you really want someone else to do your dirty work for you that is, my Lord."

His eyes flashed in anger towards me. I felt an answering surge of fear at the menace in his gaze, but did my best to quash it and look him directly in the eyes. He might be the all mighty leader of the Brethren and be more powerful than I ever would be but he didn't scare me. Honest. My knees shook ever so slightly. Damn it.

Solus stepped in. "Our dragonlette here," he drew out every syllable in a long and deliberately affectionate purr, "is a woman of strength as well as unquestionable beauty."

Corrigan's muscles tightened visibly. I cast an annoyed look at the Fae, who grinned unconcernedly back at me.

'Aren't we forgetting something?" asked Lucy, clearly wanting to change the subject very, very quickly.

Everyone turned to face her.

"There's that Batibat thing as well. She's still got to be hanging around here somewhere. How do we deal with her too?"

There was a small cough from behind. Aubrey was standing

up, empty pizza box next to him and a smear of tomato sauce on his face that was unfortunately reminiscent of blood.

"I'll keep an eye for her and sort her out if she gets involved," he said.

I started. "Er, what?"

"I said, I'll worry about her." When he caught sight of the look on my face, his bottom lip pushed out stubbornly. "I used to be a master vampire, you know."

"Yeah, but…"

"She likes men. I can get her to focus on me so you can focus on her boss." He snapped his fingers. "Easy as pie."

Wonders would never cease. Perhaps pizza had some miraculous curative properties of its own and Aubrey was beginning to get over his emotional issues and man up, as Mrs Alcoon might have tried to say. I gave him a small look of approval and his cheeks reddened slightly. Corrigan was staring at him as if he might squash him like he would a flea.

I turned the group's attention back to me. "Excellent. So everyone knows what to do and where to go. Let's get cracking."

* * *

An hour later, I was getting impatient. There was still no sign of Beltran or any of the environmentalists, no word from Alex about the Batibat in London, and, in fact, no anything anywhere. The group had split up, each venturing off to their respective areas. Aubrey had settled back down, pulling out one of the vampire encyclopaedias that I'd brought along with me to pour over. His finger tracked through the words and he occasionally clucked in irritation to himself as he read something that displeased him. Corrigan, clearly still pissed off at the idiotic comment I'd made questioning his courage, had stalked off somewhere on his own, leaving me to sweep the area around where the ward had once stood. There were already signs that things were starting to return to normal. Birds were chirping above in the sky, and there was the occasional rustle in the undergrowth indicating some natural creature or other poking its way round to investigate. That, at least, was pleasing to hear, even if there was nothing to suggest there were any potentially endangered bats sleeping off the last few hours of daylight. So much for that idea for encouraging a bit of heated green campaigning then.

I was on my fifth tour of the area when, looking up, I noticed something caught in the upper branches of one of the trees that gave me pause. It looked like a piece of paper with some writing on it but, on the ground as I was, it was difficult to be sure. My eyes scanned the area. Everything remained quiet and peaceful and there was little else to do other than wait, so I decided that it was worth investigating further. Even if it was only a piece of rubbish that had been blown up by the wind I reckoned I'd be doing some good by freeing it from the tree's branches.

It was a sturdy contribution to the wonder of nature. My knowledge of trees didn't go much beyond recognising the more obvious varieties of oak and conifer, but that didn't mean I couldn't appreciate their beauty nonetheless. At this point of the year, the beginning of the summer months, it was displaying itself in full glory, wide veined leaves creating a cloud of emerald hues that rustled gently in the late afternoon breeze. Fortunately for me, there were also some low lying branches that I could easily swing myself up onto. The bark was rough under my skin, and I had to take care to avoid leaving traces of blood from the small wound on my hand, so I made my way up slowly and gingerly, yanking myself from one branch to another until I was close to the top and just a few feet away from the scrap of paper that was irritatingly out towards the edge of one of the outer branches. I couldn't go much further out than I already was without the more slender parts of the tree giving way under my weight so instead I wrapped one arm around the thinner part of the trunk and tried to reach out.

My fingertips barely scraped the sharp border. Cursing

softly, I tried to push myself out further to use the edges of my fingers to pincer the corner of the paper and drag it in. The bough I was standing on creaked complainingly under my weight, but I inched forward just enough to be able to pinch the paper and start to pull it. The far corner was caught on a twig and, as I snagged the nearer side and yanked it, there was a ripping sound. One white scrap danced away, caught by the light breeze. I leaned again, pushing myself to my absolute limits, and finally managed to free the rest of it, clutching it in my now sweaty palm and moving back against the safety of the trunk.

I lifted it up and tried to smooth out the creases to read what it said. The missing words didn't actually hamper my understanding. As I scanned through what was left, it was clear that this was a notice regarding the upcoming development. Legalese proclaimed that all the right channels had been utilised and the demolition and the building would be going ahead as planned. I frowned grimly. Not if I had anything to do about it.

At the bottom of the paper, there was a website link and a small logo that appeared to be some kind of circle, with five straight lines drawn inside it, three reaching upwards and two down, all in heavy black ink. The website proclaimed itself as a company called Endorium, who appeared to be behind the so-called holiday homes development. I'd never heard of it before, but at the very least it was another lead to use. Satisfied that my efforts hadn't been fruitless, I carefully folded the paper and shoved it into my back pocket.

I was just about to start clambering back down when I heard a twig snap below me. Peering down through the leafy branches, I could just make out the top of Corrigan's head. It would have been nice to have hoped that from this vantage point I'd have been able to make out a bald patch to prove that he wasn't quite as perfect as he appeared, but sadly his black as night hair curled silkily around his entire head. I opened my mouth to call down to him when there was another shout from somewhere to my left.

"My Lord Alpha!"

It was Lucy. My eyes narrowed as I watched her jog up. She was supposed to be with Max, making sure that there was a suitable camping ground for the campaigners, well away from any potential danger spots.

Corrigan turned to her. "What is it? Aren't you supposed to be with the mage sorting out the area for the tents?"

I smiled smugly.

"I just wanted to let you know that we've found the perfect spot. It's a bit secluded and difficult to find, but it's well away from here. There's a stream nearby and there's plenty of flat ground to pitch tents on so we shouldn't have any trouble persuading the humans to set up there."

"Good."

"Are the Welsh pack coming?"

Corrigan grunted. "They're going to wait in Shrewsbury so they can get here quickly if we need them."

I scowled down at him. We weren't going to need them though.

"And Mack? Where is she?"

"Off somewhere checking the area. I'm looking for her now. She shouldn't be hard to spot with that red hair of hers."

That's what you think. I resisted the urge to call down 'cooeee'.

Lucy jerked her head in acknowledgment. There was a moment of silence before she spoke again. "Uh, my Lord?"

"Yes?"

"I don't want to speak out of turn..."

"But?"

"But, well, I wondered why you bother about her so much."

I immediately froze. Uh oh. I wasn't sure I wanted to hear this. And what the bloody hell was Lucy doing talking to her lord and master in that prying manner anyway? He was definitely going to castigate her for being so incredibly presumptuous as to question him.

Corrigan gave a short laugh. "You mean why am I so determined to follow her around the countryside even though she seems to hate me?"

I blinked. Was that what he thought? I didn't hate him. Far from it, unfortunately. He just annoyed the arse off me sometimes.

Lucy nodded. "I know it's got nothing to do with the mages and the faeries. Why do we care what they do?"

His voice was a deep rumble. "She's got a lot of strength, Lucy. We don't want her to side with them against us."

My heart sank. I'd been right. His interest in me was all just about a power play between the lot of them. A painful lump rose in my throat. As much as I'd secretly been hoping otherwise, it was clear that the only thing he was concerned about was a game of Otherworld one-upmanship.

"Yeah, but we don't really care about them, do we?" she persisted. "I like Mack, I do, but she's so...aggressive sometimes. And when she gets angry she's bloody scary. She's also not very nice to you."

I frowned. Didn't she know that I wasn't actually very nice to anyone?

"I didn't realise quite how inquisitive honey badgers were."

Lucy was immediately apologetic. "I'm sorry, my Lord, I don't mean to step out of line."

"That's okay. You're potentially risking your life to be here, Lucy, you have the right to ask."

I was stunned. Why wasn't he biting her head off for daring to question his authority?

"My Lord, I'm here because whoever did that to the dryad deserves to be brought down. I know you wouldn't put me in danger needlessly."

Oh, here we go, I thought sardonically, back to blind devotion.

"But you're here in the first place because I asked you to watch Mack and you want to know why," commented Corrrigan.

Lucy didn't answer. He ran a hand through his hair and sighed. "You should talk to Staines. He and I had a very similar conversation recently as well, because he seems to think that I should leave her well alone. It's just that Mack has a habit of getting herself into dangerous situations and I needed to know that she wasn't going to do anything stupid like get killed. I couldn't be here at the time because Leah needed me."

Who the fuck was Leah? My eyes narrowed. Was that the dark haired shifter I'd seen him with at Alcazon?

"The first time I saw her – Mack, I mean – she was on the beach with Tom, teaching him how to improve his fighting skills. I'd never seen anything like it before. She's got a grace and poise that's extraordinary."

I swallowed hard. The adulatory words and his tone of voice were almost overwhelming.

"I couldn't understand afterwards when I got to know her why she was so prickly. But I do now."

"Because she was pretending to be a shifter when she's actually not?"

"That's part of it," Corrigan answered. "She was with them, but she wasn't really a part of them. She was still on the outside. That alpha that's in place now?"

"Anton?"

"That's the one. He really hates her. Not only that, but she was a kid when her mother dumped her with that pack in the first place. She's been abandoned by people her entire life. It's no wonder that she pushes them away now. It's a self-preservation thing."

"I'd not thought about it like that before."

Neither had I.

"She's got a lot of strength. Not just physically. You saw how she managed to bring everyone in line out there. She's got shifters, faeries, mages, and even a vampire, all working in harmony towards the same goal. I couldn't do that. People gravitate towards her. All sorts of people. Then she gets under their skin until all they can do is think about her virtually every moment of the day. Where they can't sleep because she's in their dreams, where they can't concentrate because she might do something stupid like snap at the wrong person and end up getting hurt. Where even though she might growl and hiss and bite like an angry kitten, the only time they feel any peace is when they're near her."

My mouth dropped open. My heart was thudding deep within my chest and my bloodfire was swirling around inside me in warm scared confusion.

Corrigan laughed humourlessly. "Sorry, I shouldn't have told you all that."

"No, I, er, no, it's fine," stuttered Lucy. "I won't tell anyone else."

"I know you won't." Corrigan's voice was back to normal now, the calm measured tones of the absolutely-in-charge-no-matter-what Lord Alpha.

"Just…?"

"Yes?"

"Why don't you tell her all that?"

"Because she's not ready to hear it. She's still fighting for her independence and for her own identity. Sooner or later, however, Mack will come around."

There was a moment of silence.

"You think like Staines," commented Corrigan expressionlessly. "You don't think she'll ever come around."

Again, Lucy didn't answer. My throat felt clogged up and my breath was coming in short gasps. I screwed my eyes shut tightly, trying to calm myself down. I couldn't let them know that I'd overheard such a personal soul-bearing conversation so I had to stay quiet. My fingers were digging painfully into the bark of the tree trunk, but I barely noticed. All my thoughts and feelings were in a messy whirl of confusion and agony. How had I not seen this before? How I had not noticed that I was like that? Or that Corrigan felt that way?

He cocked his head to one side, as if listening, and I thought for one heart-stopping moment that he'd heard some tiny movement I'd made up above in the branches. Instead, however, he gestured off into the distance.

"The humans are here. You should get back, Lucy."

"Yes, my Lord." She reached out and touched him gently on the arm, just for a moment, and then jogged off.

Corrigan remained there standing, his head bowed, then he let out one deep sigh and walked off himself, leaving me completely alone.

CHAPTER EIGHTEEN

WHAT I WANTED TO DO, WHAT I REALLY, REALLY WANTED TO DO, was to stay up in the trees and never ever come back down. I had absolutely no idea how to deal with what I'd just heard. They say that eavesdroppers never hear anything good about themselves. Well, they were fucking wrong. What they should say is that eavesdroppers never know how to cope with what they hear about themselves. What the fuck was I going to say to Corrigan when I saw him again? My cheeks felt hot and feverish, and there was a curious burning sensation along the tips of my ears. The environmentalists were here and I had to get back in case the dryad's murderer was also showing his face, but my thoughts were completely consumed by Corrigan's revelations.

My bloodfire skipped through my system, zinging its way along with happy little twists and flips. He wasn't just interested in me because I was a Draco Wyr and I might prove useful to him. He wasn't pretending to like me because he didn't want me to sidle up to either the Faes or the mages and get cosy with them instead. Neither was he just after a quick roll in the hay and another notch on his bedpost. It was me he liked. Really me. Mackenzie Smith me.

I chewed on my lip. Maybe when I got to him, I should just

go right up and tell him that I fancied the pants off of him and that it was time we stopped wasting time playing around. He'd probably think I was joking. No, I should tell him that I really admired the way he'd taken on the role of Lord Alpha and that he was doing an amazing job. Then he'd realise that I liked him too and...no. If I said that then he'd think that I was being sarcastic. Maybe I could comment on how good he looked in that suit as some kind of opener? I rolled my eyes at myself. That was completely inane. Butterflies scooted nervously round my belly. I had to say something to him.

I stopped dead in my tracks. Actually, I didn't have to speak. I could just grab him by the lapels and kiss him. For a very long time. I gave myself a little grin and an inner high five. He'd know how I felt and there wouldn't be the pesky problem of having to articulate any words. Perfect. I started to jog towards the area where the ward had been. The faster I got there, then the less chance there would be that I'd lose my nerve.

I was so focused on my destination and what I was going to do when I got there, that I didn't even notice Aubrey coming up on my right to join me.

"Hey, Mack."

I barely paid him any attention, just lifted up a hand in brief acknowledgement and continued on my path.

"So, there's no sign of the Batibat."

I grunted.

Aubrey peered at me. "Are you okay? You look a bit pale."

"Not now, Aubrey, please. Go find something to do and make yourself useful."

He stopped jogging alongside me, falling back as I continued on.

"Fuck off then! Just fuck off! I don't have to do this you know! I'm risking my now, thanks to you, considerably shortened and less charmed life to help you, and all you can do is dismiss me out of hand!" He shouted with a high pitched and angry voice.

Damn it. If the pizza had induced any sense of well-being and calm into him, then clearly the effects had now worn off. He was right, however: he deserved better than that. At least now, anyway. I stopped and turned back towards him.

"I'm sorry, Aubrey. The humans are here and I need to talk to Corrigan." Now. I licked my lips nervously. "I'm not trying to dismiss you, I'm just busy."

"I'm trying, Mack!" he shouted again. "I know I was a prick before and I did horrible things, but I am trying to be a better person. A better human. Why can't you see that?"

My stomach lurched as he said that. Was I so constantly self-absorbed and inward looking that I could never see what was happening in front of my face? I walked over to him.

"I'm sorry," I repeated. I reached out towards him to put my hand on his shoulder, but drew back when he visibly flinched. I sighed.

"Aubrey, I do see how you're trying. I really do. In fact, I'm so impressed at the turn around you've made. It's really brave of you to volunteer to keep the Batibat in check as well."

"I just want to feel needed," he sniffed.

I stared at him for a moment, emotions conflicting inside of me. Then I had an idea. "You know what you could do to really help me out right now? Because it was such a good idea of yours in the first place?"

His unhappy eyes looked up at me with hope lighting them from deep within. "What?"

"Pizza."

He looked confused.

"Pizza," I repeated. "Order me some pizza. You'll need to go down to the road to collect it, because I don't want any of the humans seeing where we are and getting too curious, but if you could get that guy from before to deliver a large pizza, you have no idea how much you'll be helping me out."

He nodded several times. "Pizza, yes, I can do that. What kind do you want?"

"You know what? I trust your judgment. You choose."

"Really? You'd trust me that much?"

To choose toppings for a fucking pizza? "Yes," I said soothingly.

"Okay, okay, I'll do it right now."

"Don't tell Corrigan though, okay? It'll be our secret."

"Whatever you say, Mack."

I patted him on the back.

"Should I go now?" he asked anxiously.

I smiled at him. "That would be perfect."

He saluted me with a puppy dog grin and ran off. I watched him go and then, when he'd vanished from sight, squared my shoulders and returned to the matter in hand. Kissing Corrigan to show him that I had indeed 'come around'.

When I rounded the bend, the Lord Alpha was there, waiting in front of where I knew the concealed area with the dead – and now destroyed – tree to be. He had taken off his suit jacket and laid it on the ground, and his sleeves were rolled up, displaying strong tanned forearms. My mouth went dry. You can do this, I told myself. You've killed an unkillable wraith, you've gone up against a demi-goddess, you've climbed fifteen stories down the outside of a building. This is easy in comparison. Unfortunately, my nerves didn't seem to be getting the same message. Tendrils of heated anticipation were sneaking their way along every vein and every artery. I could have sworn that I could hear my heart beating. When I got closer, Corrigan looked up, his emerald green eyes tracking my progress. I took a deep breath and walked up to him. Should I hold him by the shoulders? Or cup his face? Maybe it would better not to touch him at all, and just dive straight in. Come on, Mack.

I went right up in front of his lean, muscular body and he straightened, looking at me quizzically. It was now or never. I leaned in and...Corrigan immediately tensed and his head whipped round away from me. Aaargh.

"There you are. All the humans are down at the campsite area." It was Beltran.

Fuck off, I screamed at him in my head. It didn't work.

He nodded at Corrigan and bowed. "Lord Alpha, I am Beltran of the Seelie Fae."

Corrigan gave a bow back. Despite myself, I was rather impressed by the cool show of cordiality. Beltran turned to me.

"Lord Sol Apollinarius told me that you have some photos of potential suspects."

Corrigan frowned at me. "You didn't tell me that."

Irritated at the turn of events, I scowled slightly, then realised the way I was acting would just make me appear 'prickly' so I tried to smooth my features back into a smile. It was a struggle. "They're just customers who've been visiting a weapons shop in London. It's run by a Batibat called Wold and we think the two might be linked somehow."

"We?" Corrigan's eyes narrowed dangerously and a streak of gold flashed across them.

"Okay, me, I guess."

"If you give me the photos," said Beltran, "then I can check them against the humans who are here. Just in case."

It was a sound idea. I nodded, before suddenly stopping and frowning. Oops. "Actually the photos are on Aubrey's phone."

"So find Aubrey and get it from him," said Corrigan.

"I can't," I responded. "He's, er, he's...not here."

Beltran shrugged. "That's okay. You saw the photos and I assume you can remember what they looked like."

I murmured in affirmation.

"Then come with me and you can check through all the humans yourself."

I looked at Corrigan. He had a vaguely bored expression on his face.

"But..."

"What?"

"Well, Solus saw them too. Can't he go instead?"

"You told him to stay by the entrance," Corrigan reminded me. "Given that's where your big bad dryad killer will arrive."

Oh yeah.

"But if he's already here, then he'll come to check out his ward, and if Corrigan's on his own, then..."

"I think, kitten, I can look after myself." He was throwing the argument that I was always making to him back in my face. Fuckity fuck fuck.

I squared my shoulders. Okay. It would be better to get this done and out of the way as quickly as possible so I could get back to my original plan. I nodded at Beltran.

"Alright then," I sighed, "lead the way."

Beltran began gracefully gliding back in the direction that he'd arrived. I sneaked a quick peek at Corrigan. He was watching me with a bemused expression on his face.

"Are you okay?" he inquired.

No. "I'm fine," I snapped, then immediately regretted it. "I'll be back as soon as I can."

"I'll be waiting here with bated breath," he commented, with just the tiniest hint of sarcasm.

Perhaps not, but I will be, I thought sourly, then stomped frustratedly after the Fae.

* * *

FORCING myself to put Corrigan out of my head, and focus on the matter in hand, I stared with some degree of astonishment at the encampment. There must have been over forty people, and all of them were already busy putting up tents and getting little fires going. One man, who appeared quite a bit older than all the others, was striding around, shouting out orders.

"Don't you dare cut down any branches!" He called out with an imperious tone. "Just use what is already on the ground and what nature has provided."

A dread-locked girl wearing a tie-dyed skirt went past, hissing under teeth. "Idiot."

I grinned, then sniffed the air. "What is that?"

"A most interesting mixture of patchouli, hemp and the unwashed," stated Max from behind my shoulder. "Unpleasant, isn't it?"

He moved on before I could answer, ostensibly to help a girl begin to hammer in pegs for her rather threadbare looking tent. It seemed to me that he was hovering around her more so that he could check out her bottom when she bent over than help. I had to bite my tongue to avoid snapping at him and drawing undue attention to us, and instead began casting around, trying to glimpse the features of all the male protestors.

There were more women than men, so it wasn't hard to pick each one out. The vast majority had the same long dreadlocked hair, as if they were buying into some kind of pack uniform all of their own. I watched them thoughtfully. That was what it was all about, really. Feeling like you belonged somewhere and being part of a group or a family. It might be a coven of vampires, or the Ministry of Mages, or a shifter pack or even a band of hippy protestors. But what mattered was feeling connected. And I didn't have that. Sure, there was Mrs. Alcoon, but I didn't think that two people necessarily counted. Maybe the reason that I was always so bad-tempered wasn't anything to do with my freaky genetics, maybe it was, as Corrigan had essentially intimated, that I was just fucking lonely. I had the weirdest sensation that the clouds in the sky were parting and a dawning ray of light was shining down on me in acknowledgement of my sudden epiphany.

The moment was somewhat ruined when a bloke went past me and farted, loudly. He looked over at Beltran and myself standing there and gave us a half-grin.

"Sorry about that," he drawled. "It's those damn beans we're always eating."

He stuck out a grubby hand. "Good to meet you. I'm Bo."

I could feel Beltran's superior Fae instincts recoiling from the idea of having to sully his pure Fae skin by touching this back-to-mother-nature-imbued human, so I reached out myself and shook his hand.

"Mack," I said, by way of introduction.

"You here for the protest?"

I nodded.

"Brill," he said. "A lot of people don't like bats, but it's important that every one of God's creatures is allowed to live in peace. They do a lot of good in maintaining the balance, you know."

I tried not to let my surprise show that the bat idea had caught on. "Yes, bats are hugely important to the eco-system," I replied solemnly. "As are all these great trees."

He smiled and patted me on the arm. "A fellow freedom fighter! We won't let those council wankers bulldoze their way through here. They simply have no sense or understanding that we need to preserve these places for everyone's futures, not just our own." He snorted. "Holiday homes! Ridiculous!"

Naturally, I didn't point out that it had nothing to do with the local council, and instead everything to do with some nefariously evil man hiding in the shadows. I just tried to look as serious and environmentally fighting friendly as I possibly could.

Beltran cleared his throat pointedly, in case I'd forgotten that we weren't here simply to shoot the breeze. I tried to avoid scowling at him. I couldn't just open every conversation with 'did you or anyone you know crucify a tree nymph near here in order to boost your evil Machiavellian power plans?' now, could I?

"I'm pretty new here," I said to the guy. I gave a little laugh. "Well, very new."

"I know!" he grinned back. "I'd have noticed you around here before otherwise."

I ignored the opportunity for a little flirtation. I didn't have time to mess around to get the information that I needed. Let's face it, all I really wanted to do was to get back to Corrigan as quickly as possible. I went for the more direct route instead. "Are there any other newcomers around? Maybe we could band together."

It stood to reason that my dryad-killer-slash-weapons-dealer hadn't spent any time up till now hanging around with the protestors. With his ward in place, he'd have had no reason to worry about them. That meant that if he was here now, hiding in amongst the other humans, then he had to be new. And I reckoned that, like me, any newbies would stick out like sore thumbs.

"Nah. Just Tran here, and yourself. Other than that, everyone else has been with us for months."

I immediately stiffened at the mention of some guy named Tran, then relaxed when I realised that Bo was gesturing towards Beltran with his thumb. Oh, of course.

"It's Beltran," glowered the Fae.

I tried not to smirk in amused understanding at his annoyance.

A girl came up and joined us, offering me a quick smile, before focusing her attention on Bo.

"We have a problem," she said, her features set.

He raised his eyebrows questioningly.

"We need some tree trunks for the tripods, Bo."

"And?"

"There aren't any."

I was utterly confused. We were in the middle of a forest. Trees were not in short supply.

Bo, however, sighed heavily. ""We've been through this."

"Yeah, but…"

"We kill a few to save a lot. You know that."

I was even more baffled now. And I definitely didn't like this talk of killing. "Uh, what's going on?" I inquired, doing my very best to keep my tone light.

Bo turned back towards me. "We need to stop the bulldozers

from getting here. It's the best way to prevent any demolition from taking place. So we build tripods across the roads preventing any gas-guzzling vehicles from getting here. We send two or three people to sit on top of the tripods meaning that the bulldozers can't pass through without knocking them down and potentially killing them. Murder for holiday homes is not a headline that these corporate soul-sellers enjoy."

I must have still looked puzzled, because he explained further. "We need materials to build the tripods from."

Realisation hit me. "You need to cut down trees."

Bo's face looked pained. "Yes. But only the young slender ones. And it's for the greater good."

"I told you we should have taken scaffolding from that builder's yard," the girl snapped.

"Well, we didn't," he shot back at her. "Just pick the smaller trees on the edges of the woods. We don't have a choice."

"I am not a tree-killer!"

"If you don't do this," he said, evenly, "then all these trees will be slaughtered!"

I nudged Beltran's arm. This didn't seem like an argument that we ought to get ourselves involved in. Besides, we had the information we needed. Our murderer wasn't here. The Fae nodded at me, and we both quietly slipped away, leaving Bo and the girl continuing to argue and bicker. As much as I understood her position, Bo was making sense. If these tripod things stopped vehicles from getting here, and the only thing that the tripods could be built from were trees, then the 'greater good' would indeed have to prevail. I'd just have to hope that the dryads saw it that way too. At least I knew their habitats were much larger and older than any of the trees the protestors would end up using. I shrugged. As he'd said, you kill a few to save a lot.

It was just a shame that thought would come back to haunt me so much later.

CHAPTER NINETEEN

A<small>FTER LEAVING</small> B<small>ELTRAN AT THE EDGE OF THE ENCAMPMENT, WITH</small> strict instructions to be alert for any strangers trying to approach and inveigle their way in, I picked my way back towards Corrigan. As far as I was concerned, things were looking good. The protestors were all set up and clearly deeply involved in the business of stopping any development from even starting to get going. The evil bastard that had killed Mereia was, at least according to the Batibat, going to show up soon – and he had no reason to venture near the humans before he checked out his now defunct ward, meaning that I could kill him before he ended up hurting anyone innocent. And the Lord Alpha of the Brethren really liked me.

I gave a little skip. I just couldn't help myself. It was amazing the way that life could turn around and give you a great big sloppy kiss on the chops right when you were least expecting it. And speaking of kisses…

"Pssst! Mack!"

I twisted my head to the left, registering the figure of Aubrey hovering at the fringes of the trees and holding aloft a large pizza box. I grinned to myself. This was just getting better and better. I jogged over to him and smiled.

"I got you the Meat Feast," he said anxiously. "I hope it's alright?"

I gave the ex-vamp a reassuring nod. "It'll be perfect, Aubrey, thank you."

The pleasure on his face was evident. Perhaps he wasn't so bad, after all. I made myself a promise to do everything I could to be nicer to him from now on. He was trying his best to adjust to his new existence. The least I could do was to be more patient with him.

"Can you do me a favour now?" I asked, not wanting to compel him, but rather to treat him like an equal.

His eyes lit up. "Of course. What?"

"Aubrey," I tutted, "don't agree to anything unless you know what it's going to be first."

"Yeah, yeah," he said dismissively, and with an unnerving trust in me. Still, it was probably better than hysterics and tears. "What do you need?"

"Can you make sure that no-one disturbs either me or Corrigan unless it's important? You know, unless the prick who killed the dryad shows up or there's something dangerous around?" I wasn't about to be interrupted again this time. I had a plan.

"I will do that, Mack, no problem. I'll make sure that fat woman doesn't appear either."

Somehow I had the inkling that, thanks to the fear I'd seen on the Batibat's face when I'd broken the ward, she was going to make sure she was as far away as she could possibly get. But I nodded my thanks at Aubrey anyway, and took the pizza box from him. The heavy scent of cheese and garlic floated up to me. I hoped Corrigan enjoyed fast food.

With a meaningful look at Aubrey, hoping that he realised that the figurative 'Do Not Disturb' sign was also for him, I turned away and headed back out towards where I knew the Lord Alpha was.

The sky was starting to darken, the sun dipping below the

tree line and streaks of burnt orange and gold signalling the close of the day. My stomach was squirming with nervousness, but I pushed down the feelings as best I could. As sure as I was that it wouldn't be long before we'd be interrupted by the arrival of my current nemesis, I needed to do this first. Nothing in my life had ever seemed this important – or this scary – before. Still under the cover of the few remaining trees, I stopped a few feet away from the small clearing where I knew Corrigan to be and swallowed hard, closing my eyes and clenching my teeth together. Then I forced myself to relax and stepped out.

Whatever I'd been expecting, it wasn't that. Corrigan was sitting down on the ground, his long muscular legs spread out in front of him. Next to him was a chequered cloth, laden with gleaming silverware, two long-stemmed glasses, and a picnic basket. There was even an ice-bucket with a bottle of champagne nestled inside. When he saw me approach, he sprang lithely to his feet.

His green eyes, with hints of warm gold flickering within their depths, watched me carefully. I stared at him, my mouth dropping slightly.

"Hello, kitten."

My tongue seemed to be clawed to the roof of my mouth. Corrigan sighed and raked a hand through his hair. "Look," he said, "I know this isn't ideal. I'm not trying to make light of the terrible things that happened here and this isn't a celebration. But, in view of the fact that we have to stay for now, and that you promised me dinner, I thought that maybe we could at least manage some food."

His eyes drifted down to the pizza box in my hands, and I gave him a shy half-smile. "You beat me to it," I said softly.

A slow lazy grin, tinged with just a hint of surprise, spread across his face. "Where did you get pizza from?"

"I had a little help from Aubrey," I admitted. "Where did you get the posh picnic?"

"I arranged it earlier when you went off to talk to the dryads."

We both remained standing there, just looking at each other. I bit my lip. Corrigan's eyes moved to my mouth, then back up to my eyes again. Without looking away from him, I knelt down, and placed the pizza box carefully on the cloth, then stood back up again. A look of mutually surprised understanding passed between us. My heart thudded.

"Last chance to back out, kitten," he said quietly. There was a hopeful wariness on his face.

"I told you not to call me that, my Lord."

A predatorial smile curved its way across his mouth. I smiled back. Then we sprang at each other.

Corrigan's lips were hot against mine as I pressed against him with an insatiable, insistent need. He tasted warm and masculine, with just a hint of toothpaste mintiness hovering in the background. He raised up one hand, twisting his fingers through my hair, while the other curved tightly round my back. I wrapped my arms around him, luxuriating in the feel of his tight trembling muscles under my skin.

His hand moved down to my bottom, squeezing it and pulling my body even closer against his, then his lips left mine and began moving down my throat, nibbling and nipping downwards. I moaned and clutched him tighter, all semblance of rational thought completely leaving me. His breath was scorching hot against my skin and, deep inside, my bloodfire matched it, swirling around with heated seductive need. Corrigan shifted his weight ever so slightly, causing both of us to stumble and fall backwards, me on top of him, with an answering crash of breaking glass as one of our feet connected with the ice-bucket and sent it flying into the champagne flutes. I laughed and half-sat up, straddling him with my legs, my hands gripping his broad shoulders. Leaning over him, I smiled down.

"Looks like you've found yourself in a rather compromising position, my Lord."

He half-growled back at me, hands on my waist, and flipped me round in a movement so swift that it took my breath away, completely reversing our positions, his body hot and heavy against mine. Then he curved his head down and whispered in my ear, "Not for long, kitten."

His mouth found mine again, stifling whatever response I could possibly have managed to muster. One of his hands was snaking its way under my t-shirt, searing against my skin. Sod this. I pushed him back slightly, forcing him to half sit up, then I peeled off my t-shirt and flung it away to the side. He grinned down at me then gestured to himself, so I reached out and undid the first button on his crisp white shirt, then the second and the third. When I fumbled on the fourth, I cursed and gave up, pulling at the fabric and ripping the remaining buttons off. Corrigan just raised his eyebrows at me in amusement, then shrugged out of the rest of his shirt, throwing it to the side so that it sailed through the air and joined my t-shirt in a messy heap on the ground.

I stared up at him for a moment, his broad tanned chest with smooth skin and erect nipples, then I reached up and ran my hands over him, revelling in the feel of his body. He groaned and leaned downwards again, crushing my body and kissing me hard before moving down my chest, his hand cupping one breast while his mouth attended to the other, sucking at it through the soft satiny fabric. The barrier of my bra annoyed me, and I felt the faintest flicker of embarrassment that my underwear was considerably more functional than pretty. I needed to feel his lips on my skin, not teasing like this.

"Corrigan," I groaned.

He understood and half lifted me up, undoing the clasp at the back with a deft movement that any well-advertised Latin lover would be proud of, and pulling it away, until it remained caught around just one of my arms. Then he returned his mouth to my breast, gently nipping and pulling with his tongue and his teeth until I could barely breathe. His hand moved up to my shoulder, caressing the deep marks of my Draco Wyr scar, and making me shiver.

The weight and length of Corrigan's erection was obvious and I tugged at the button on his trousers, trying to undo them. A sharp stone was digging uncomfortably into the small of my back so I reached underneath and pulled it out, flinging it to the side, then returned my attention to much, much more important things. My fingers scrabbled away, until I finally achieved success, unfastening the button. He pulled away and stood up, looking down at me. My eyes travelled down the expanse of his chest and stomach, admiring the clearly defined muscles and the trail of dark hair that led downwards.

"Are you sure about this?"

His voice was gruff and I was forced to pull my attention away from the tight bulge in his now unbuttoned trousers. The doubt that was reflected in his face made my heart ache, and I suddenly wished that I'd not been so stupid as to waste so much time in getting to this point. Instead of answering him, however, I undid the fastening on my own jeans and wriggled out of them. Hot molten gold lit Corrigan's eyes, and he did the same, then looked down at me.

"Mack, you've got no idea what it is you do to me," he groaned.

I drank in the sight of him, towering over me. There were innumerable scars over his body, most of them faint lines carved into his skin. They didn't detract from his immutable sex appeal, however, they just added to it. I didn't think I'd ever seen a man who was such a testament to virile masculinity. I actually had a pretty good idea of what it was that I did to him, because he was doing the same to me. I reached up and curved my hands round his hips and tugged him back down. He smiled, baring his white teeth, pushed my panties down, pulled them off and then with one swift movement moved inside me with a possessive roar. I cried out as he filled me, my hips rising to meet his.

Twisting round, I forced him beneath me so I could be more in control. Then I leaned back slightly, enjoying the sensation of having him deep inside me, and we found a rhythm. My breath was coming fast and sharp, and Corrigan groaned as his hands reached up to my waist then slammed me down onto him, again and again. I moaned as the need and desire overwhelmed me, building to a crescendo of feeling.

"Mack…"

My eyes met his. "Now," I half-sobbed.

He jerked his head in acknowledgment and thrust upwards. I screamed as my body shuddered in ecstasy. Corrigan quaked beneath me, then I collapsed on top of him, sweaty and panting. His arms wrapped round my back, hugging me to him, and we both lay there, exhausted, with our ragged gasps as the only sound filling the entire area. I could feel his heart throb against my ribcage and I closed my eyes, peace and happiness flooding through me. Corrigan's hand moved up to my head, and softly stroked my hair, smoothing it down.

"I have to admit, our date has somewhat exceeded my expectations," he said with a low purr.

I smiled into his chest. "I'm sorry."

His body stiffened beneath me. "For what?"

"For being so pig-headed, Corrigan. I shouldn't have pushed you away before. I was an idiot." In oh so many ways.

He relaxed. "Yes, you were. Why the sudden change of heart?"

I really didn't want to tell him that I'd overheard his conversation with Lucy. It seemed sneaky, eavesdropping on him like that. But I didn't want to lie to him either. I took a deep breath. "Well…"

He jerked suddenly. "Someone's coming," he breathed into my ear.

Alarmed, I sprang up. The last thing I needed was to deal with anyone happening upon us in such a state of in flagrante delicto. Not that I was ashamed of course, but the never-ending innuendo that I'd have to deal with afterwards wasn't worth it. I scrabbled for my clothes, yanking my pants and jeans back on. Corrigan did the same, albeit at a more leisurely pace. I was just hooking myself back into my bra when I heard Aubrey's raised voice. I couldn't work out who he was talking to, but it was nice to see that he'd taken my instructions seriously.

Corrigan raised his eyebrows slightly.

"I told him to make sure we weren't disturbed," I explained.

His mouth quirked up at the side. "So you had this all planned then, did you?"

I pulled my t-shirt over my head and shook out my hair. "Not exactly."

Corrigan chuckled. "Clearly, I had no chance."

I scowled at him. "Hey, you weren't exactly complaining."

He licked his lips, and my stomach flipped. I was prevented from saying anything further, however, as the figure of Solus appeared, rounding the corner. Aubrey was hanging onto his ankles and shouting something along the lines of 'stop it, they're eating pizza!'. Well, that was a euphemism if ever I heard one. Solus shook him off, and wandered casually up to the pair of us. Corrigan was still shirt-less and it was all I could do not to slap the leery grinning Fae in the face.

"Well, well, well," he smirked.

Corrigan moved in front of me, and my mouth dropped open. Oh, he so wasn't going to go all caveman on me now, was he?

"You're interrupting," he growled. "We're busy." The emphasis that he placed on the word 'we' left very little to the imagination.

"I can see that," murmured Solus, no end of amusement audibly visible in his voice.

I stepped out from behind Corrigan, irritated. "What do you want?"

"Dragonlette, you don't have to worry," he said, "I'm not the jealous type. I don't demand monogamy in my partners."

Corrigan's entire body rose up in angry tension. Before he could say or do anything that all three of us would regret, however, I cleared my throat and repeated my words. "Solus, what is it?"

His violet eyes flicked smoothly over to me. I could see the warring emotion within him, but fortunately the need to tell us his news won out over the temptation to cause more aggravated mischief.

"Someone's approaching," he finally said. "The mage set up a small ward down by the main road after the humans arrived. It was intended to deter anyone else from deciding they wanted a quiet evening walk, but wouldn't really stop anyone with any power."

"And?"

"And it was broken about fifteen minutes ago. " He glanced from Corrigan to me. "Not the only thing that was broken through apparently."

Corrigan snarled. I put a calming hand on his forearm, ignoring the sudden flare of my bloodfire.

"So he's finally coming then," I stated in satisfaction.

"Whoever he is."

I nodded distractedly. "Okay. Solus, you need to get back down to Larkin and make sure the two of you get out of sight. It's up to you to make sure he doesn't get hurt. Let Mereia's killer get up here so that the two of us," I motioned to Corrigan, "can deal with it."

He clasped a hand to his heart. "Aw, dragonlette. So what you're really saying is that you don't want me to get hurt, but you don't mind if the furry one here ends up as collateral damage?"

"Solus..." I said warningly.

He grinned. "Yes, yes, okay. I will do as you ask. I'm sure I'd be more use to you in a fight than protecting a wizard though."

For a half second, my mind flicked back to that terrible scene back at the mages' academy when both Thomas and Brock had wound up so very dead. I steeled myself. I was not going to let anything like that happen again. Ever.

"Just do it, please," I said quietly.

Solus bowed and clicked his fingers, vanishing in an airy shimmer of purple. I realised belatedly that the reason he'd not arrived that way was he'd known what was going on with Corrigan and me in the first place. The Fae wasn't all bad. One quick look at Corrigan's face made me think that there was fat chance I'd persuade him of that, however.

"I couldn't stop him!" howled Aubrey, still lying prone on the path ahead of us, his arms outstretched. "I tried, Mack! It's not my fault!"

"I know," I called over. "It's okay, Aubrey. I need you to go and join the humans with Max and Beltran now. Stay there until we come and find you."

"You're protecting that bastard now too?" muttered Corrigan.

I shrugged, unwilling to admit that, despite myself, I was now kind of starting to like the ex-bloodsucker, as well as merely feeling sorry for him. He wore all his emotions on his sleeve, without trying to mute them in order to appear more normal. That made him occasionally annoying, but not dislikable.

"We can deal with this guy on our own," I replied, as Aubrey scrambled to his feet and vanished into the trees.

"He killed a dryad."

"You don't need to remind me of that," I snapped. "But they're easy prey. You're the Lord Alpha of the fucking Brethren, and I'm a dragon. Let's see how scary he is when he's got us to deal with."

"Well, then," remarked Corrigan, "let's rock and roll, kitten."

I used my Voice to blow a raspberry at him then injected as much sarcasm into my thought as possible. *Sure thing, my Lord.*

Corrigan chuckled, then swung me to him and planted a swift hard kiss on my lips. "Before I forget," he said.

"Mmm?" I asked distractedly, my senses still reeling.

He bent over and opened up the picnic box. I admired his bum, much in the same manner that Max had been doing earlier with the protestor. This is different, I told myself, the Lord Alpha is a willing participant. I smirked. Very willing.

He stretched back up, a smallish box in his hands. I looked at him quizzically.

He raised up a shoulder. "Sorry, I can't open it myself." He grinned disarmingly. "Silver and I don't really mix."

Astonished, I took the box from him and lifted the lid, registering the contents, then stared up at Corrigan. "You brought my daggers? Both of them? But I only left one at the keep."

"We found the other one not far from where you were lying unconscious on Hampstead Heath. The mages helped us pick it up and keep it safely covered."

I took both of Balud's weapons out, hefting each in my hands, before shooting him a grateful glance. "Thank you, Corrigan."

His eyes crinkled down at me. "Just make sure you don't mistake me for him. Whoever he is."

"We're about to find out," I said grimly, then tossed the box to the side, and gripped the daggers in my hands.

The pair of us turned to face the path, ready for whatever was coming. The familiar surge of angry bloodfire hit my veins. This wasn't the warmth of heated passion that I'd felt minutes earlier. This was full-blown angry revenge mode.

"Bring it on," I whispered.

At my side, Corrigan nodded.

CHAPTER TWENTY

THE WAIT WAS AGONISING. THIS BASTARD HAD DONE THINGS TO that dryad that showed a callous heartlessness. He completely deserved the full ire that my Draco Wyr blood could offer. I was itching to show him that he should learn to pick on someone his own size. Or at least someone who didn't belong to the quiet and entirely non-violent world of tree nymphs anyway. The longer it took for him to show up, the more my bloodfire boiled.

My simmering anger must have been getting remarkably obvious because Corrigan eventually turned to me. "Cool it."

I snarled at him. "I can't."

"Of course you can. Weren't you just trying to calm me down a few moments ago?"

"That was different."

"Right."

"Corrigan," I grated, "I am a Draco Wyr. That means that sometimes, usually when I'm entirely justified to do so, I get angry. Well, it's not so much anger as full-blown red-hot rage. It's in my nature and I can't help it." I was uncomfortably reminded for a moment that Aubrey had made the same argument regarding his vampiredom behaviour, before I pushed that thought away.

"Bullshit."

I started.

He reached out and gripped my shoulder, taking great pains to avoid the silver daggers that I was still clutching in my hands. "Think, Mack. When was the last time you were angry? You know, blood boiling out of control angry?"

I considered. Then my cheeks irritatingly heated up. It was when I'd seen Corrigan with that dark-haired shifter and had downed the stupid bottle of TemperSoothe. I didn't really want to go there.

"A while ago," I muttered to myself.

"It was when you shifted into a dragon, right?"

"Um…"

"That was months ago. You know you're in control of yourself now. Bloody hell, that vampire over there almost killed you and he's walking around as happy as a lark now."

"He's not a vampire anymore," I pointed out, stubbornly. "And I wouldn't say he's particularly happy either."

"That's a moot point and you know it. You're not that out of control person any more."

"You know why?" I said softly. "Because when that happened before, when I turned into a dragon, I stopped being me. I would have killed anything that got in my way. There wasn't a single rational thought in my head. Do you have any idea how terrifying that is?"

"You lived with a pack of shifters for most of your natural life! You know that's what it's like at the start, especially when you shift for the first time."

I stared at him. "How would I know? I didn't shift, remember?"

"Nobody talked to you about what it was like?"

I thought about it. They might have tried to. I was so pissed off at not being able to become a shifter myself that I was pretty sure I'd stone-walled the lot of them until they'd stopped trying to speak to me about it. But the fact that they found it hard to control their impulses when they first shifted didn't mean that my circumstances were the same.

"Look, it's all very well saying that it's normal to feel that way when you shift at first. But I'm not a fucking were-hamster! I'm a dragon. If I shift there's no telling what I could end up doing."

"Have you not once transformed since that day?"

"No." I folded my arms. "And I'm not going to."

"You're more in control than you think, Mack. You just need to believe that you're in control."

I was saved from replying further because Corrigan stiffened suddenly, his head cocked to the side. "He's here."

The flames inside me roared in delight. I thought about what Corrigan had said. Then I thought about what Thomas would have said. He had known better than anyone what it was like to lose control. And he'd believed that I had a handle on my inner rage. I took a deep breath and the fire inside me banked back down. Okay then. I was still going to destroy this fucker though, even if I remained relatively calm when I did it.

I glanced over at Corrigan. He was stepping neatly out of his suit trousers, and placing them to the side. I tried not to gawk. I failed. Abruptly, his skin exploded into sleek black fur, and there was a snapping and cracking of bones. His were-panther form snarled with the brief agony of the shift, then he was on all fours, the muscles of his huge forelegs bunching, poised for attack. At least he was in the same frame of mind as me. This wasn't going to be a peace treaty or a negotiation; it was going to be a take down.

Finally, from around the corner of the small curving path, a figure appeared. Whatever I'd been expecting, it wasn't the slight suited man that appeared. For one bizarre moment, I thought that Solus had been wrong or that Larkin's ward hadn't worked, and this was merely a guy out for an evening stroll. But when I took a closer look, I realised that wasn't true. Because I'd seen him before, and not just in the photos that Alex had texted over. It was the vaguely bookish bloke who'd stood next to me on the street in London, commenting on the antics of Lucy, the mage and the Fae when they'd been tailing me. And he didn't seem in the slightest bit surprised to see us.

Pushing his glasses up the bridge of his nose, he lifted one hand and waved in greeting. Corrigan growled.

"A little Otherworld welcoming committee," he called out. "How perfectly charming."

My eyes narrowed, spitting hatred. "Who the fuck are you?"

"Well, Ms. Smith, that is a complicated question."

Corrigan's Voice filled my head. *How in the hell does he know your name?*

I shrugged tensely in response. I had no bloody idea.

"Why don't you try to answer it?" I was impressed with the fact that I managed to keep my tone even and calm.

"I think not. You and your Lord Corrigan will just have to suffer without that knowledge. I am pleased, however, that you are here. I could feel your power in London and I was curious to find out more. Now I will get my own answers, it seems."

He started to move towards us, with a slow almost leisurely pace, then stopped and flicked his wrist towards the old warded area. The concealment spell evaporated, revealing yet again the blackened earth and now equally scorched stump of a tree. For a half-second his features twisted, before smoothing back over into studied blandness. "I really wish you hadn't done that."

"Yeah?" I said, tauntingly. "Well, then you're going to fucking hate this."

I raised up my left hand and let the dagger fly. At the same moment Corrigan sprang forward, sprinting towards him with claws and teeth flashing. This time I knew my aim was true. It didn't matter, however. In the half heartbeat that it took the blade to reach him, he lifted up an arm and the dagger fell uselessly to the earth. I blinked. Okay, so maybe he had a few nifty tricks then.

Corrigan leapt in the air, launching himself forward with unbridled power, but our opponent merely lifted up another arm, and he landed with a heavy thud onto the ground, in much the same manner as the dagger.

Corrigan! I screamed with my Voice.

He twitched. *I'm fine, just fucking kill him.* He was already starting to stagger back onto his large paws.

I ran towards my right, in order to make sure that the fucker's attention was on me and me alone. This time I kept hold of my second dagger, and instead began to send out streams of fire. He'd built up some kind of protective ward around himself, however, and the flames bounced harmlessly off.

"Interesting," he remarked calmly. "You are not a mage, and yet you have magical power. Tell me what you are."

"You first," I grunted, then changed tactics and directed my flames at the ground, creating a wall of fire between him and me. If defeating this bastard was going to mean getting up close and personal, then that was what I was going to do. I zigzagged towards him, spraying more green fire as I went. He remained standing, and unblinking, watching my progress impassively.

His right arm started to rise up again, but I was getting wise to his actions, and this time threw myself at the ground in a roll, not losing my forward momentum but still avoiding whatever weird magic he was managing to zap out. Then I straightened and halted. There were less than two feet between us, and a wall of my fire was trapping him. He smirked, crooking one finger as if to beckon me closer. I just laughed. How stupid did he think I was?

Using my one remaining dagger, I slid its point across my index finger, not taking my eyes off Mr. Freaky Mage Man. I didn't need to look down to know that blood was already welling up. Then I flicked my finger out towards him and watched the drops curve into the air and splash against his own personal invisible ward. As soon as they hit the space about two inches from his actual body, there was a hissing sound and a puff of red steam ejected into the air. The brief flash in his eyes told me that my plan had worked – and he didn't like it. Goody.

I sprang forward, through my own fiery barrier, and lashed out, my fist connecting satisfyingly with his face. His head smacked to the side with a snap, and there was the tinkle of glass breaking as his spectacles fell off, landing in a twisted heap onto the ground. Then Corrigan's black shape barrelled into him, knocking him down onto the ground. He hissed out one inaudible word and, from behind, there was a sudden thunderous crack. I half turned, and gaped as, from out of nowhere, a huge monstrous shape appeared. I kicked the figure on the ground, pissed off that I'd given him the opportunity to speak and summon whatever that thing was, and he collapsed with an ooph, then lay unmoving. For good measure, and to ensure that he was down forever, I stabbed his chest in one swift motion with my remaining dagger, letting the blade slide all the way through and come out the other side. It pierced the ground, holding him in place like a staple. Satisfied, I pivoted round to face the new threat.

The thing in front of us was massive: at least eight foot tall and with a body as broad as a bull elephant. The most striking thing about it, however, was its head: a large misshapen bulge with two bright red saucer shaped eyes that, for a moment, put me in mind of Aubrey. Though the smell reeking off in stifling waves was far worse than even that of a vamp's. It was like some horrifying mixture of skunk and wet dog. Not that I'd ever smelt a skunk before, but it was how I imagined it would be. Despite the thing's size, it was eerily silent, not making so much as a single sound.

It lunged forward with surprising speed, and I only just managed to leap out of the way in time. Corrigan's were-panther snapped forward, his huge jaws latching onto its hairy leg, embedding themselves deeply through its skin. Dark, almost black, blood seeped out. It lifted up its leg, trying to shake Corrigan off, but he clung on with sheer shifter tenacity. I smiled grimly, before attacking it myself, reaching out to grab its arm and force it backwards, almost as if in some kind of childish playground type stunt. Except I was trying to break the thing's arm, not get it to call out pax.

I pulled backwards, straining with every ounce of strength and energy that I could muster, grimacing as it resisted against me. Just as I finally heard the dull snap of breaking bone, its other arm came twisting round, knocking me on the side of my head and sending me flying backwards. Hot fiery adrenaline coursed through every vein. I jumped back up to my feet, ignoring the painful throbbing across the entire right side of my face, and saw Corrigan release the creature's leg and spring up against its chest instead, knocking it over onto the ground. The pair of them were locked together in some kind of deadly embrace, rolling and spinning this way and that. I hopped from one side to the other, trying to get an opening whereby I could finally end this. They were moving too quickly, however, and I didn't want to miss and end up striking out at the Brethren Lord instead. Still, the only sound I could hear was Corrigan's breath and snapping teeth. I couldn't believe that, even with the agony the red-eyed monster must be feeling, it wasn't so much as panting heavily in pain. It was as if someone had pressed the mute button.

Corrigan's sharp claws were swiping at its face, etching out deep scratches and virtually ripping its skin to shreds. And yet it didn't quit, writhing to its left, then to its right, in a bid to break free. Its unbroken arm scrabbled to gain purchase on Corrigan's fur, succeeding in pulling out tufts here and there, although not quite managing to connect with his actual flesh. I watched it carefully, waiting for my chance.

This thing smells worse than Staines' laundry basket, hissed Corrigan's Voice.

Well, let's hope it doesn't rub off on you, I shot back sardonically.

With one great heaving movement he rolled to his side, trapping the monster's arm underneath itself.

Are you just going to stand there and watch?

Do you mean that you need some help defeating the smelly nastie, my Lord?

Corrigan growled aloud. I half-cocked my head, pondering the situation, then calmly walked over to the beast's head, grabbed both its ears and pulled, exposing its thick neck.

Will that do you?

He gave a feline snort, then his massive head arched upwards and his mouth opened, exposing gleaming white fangs.

It'll have to.

Then he snapped his jaws closed onto the monster's jugular. Dark blood sprayed out, splattering my clothes and landing on my face. Corrigan immediately sprang backwards, planting his paws by my feet. The thing choked and gurgled, the only sound it had made this entire time, before jerking once and falling still.

His green eyes slid up to me. I could have sworn there was amusement lurking in their depths as he watched me wipe off the gloopy blood from my cheek.

Was that entirely necessary?

He bared his teeth at me in what I assumed passed for a panther's version of a cheeky grin. I rolled my eyes at him. Idiot.

"Job done," I said aloud.

I turned back towards our besuited foe's body. Oh, shit. My stomach dropped as I took in the scene. My dagger remained exactly where I had left it, and there was a dark stain around it indicating where it had slammed through the dryad-killer's heart. But of the killer's body itself, there was no sign.

CHAPTER TWENTY-ONE

It didn't make any sense. I stood there, staring in utter bafflement at the now apparently vacated spot. I leaned forward and touched the dagger gingerly with my toe, just in case his corpse was somehow now only merely invisible rather than completely vanished. Unsurprisingly, there was no camouflaged body blocking the path of my boot. He had definitely gone. What the fuck was going on?

Corrigan padded up beside me and sniffed, then looked at me with troubled eyes.

Can you smell anything?

He shook his head. *I can't get the stench of that thing out of my nostrils. It's blocking virtually everything else.*

I twisted round, raising one hand, and shot out fire towards the red-eyed beast's body, lighting it up. Unfortunately the smell of its burning flesh only appeared to compound the problem, rather than solve it. Giving up, I turned back.

What in the hell happened, Corrigan? He couldn't have just gotten up and walked away. I fucking killed him! The bloody dagger is still there!

He sat back heavily on his haunches. *He wasn't a ghost. He wasn't even undead. I could smell death around him, but it wasn't of him per se. It was more like...a perfume.*

I wrinkled my nose in disgust. Great. A guy without a name who enjoys making art out of dead bodies, has the ability not only to recuperate from being dead himself, and who wears eau de corpse. Why me? Then I stopped in mid-thought, dread flooding through me. Because it wasn't me he was interested in. It had never been me he was interested in.

"The dryads," I whispered.

I looked down at Corrigan in horror. His feline green eyes met mine and a single moment of mutual understanding passed between us. I moved forward, yanking my dagger out of the dark ground in one swift movement, gripping it tightly in my hand. Then we both turned and started to run.

The clearing where I'd met Mereia's friend previously was a good twenty minutes walk up the hill. Neither of us were strolling now, however. I pelted up the slope, mustering every single ounce of energy and speed that I possibly could. Corrigan, in his were-panther form as he was, far outstripped me. He bounded up at almost twice my speed and, even as fast as I was going, was soon almost out of sight.

I put my head down and gritted my teeth. How could I have been so stupid? Why had I taken my eyes away from that bastard? I should have known that it couldn't have been this easy to defeat someone as intent on pure evil as he had been. He was clearly drawing on forces that were far beyond my comprehension. I swore under my breath and forced my legs to pump faster, scree and small twigs flying up into the air around my wake. The trees and dark shadows around me began to blur into the background as I whizzed past, heart pumping. I could feel every facet of my body tingling with fiery heat. I was going to destroy him. I'd rip every limb from his fucking body and bury them at the four corners of the earth so that there was no way in hell he'd rise again. Whoever he was, he wasn't going to fool me again.

It wasn't long before I realised that up ahead of me a harsh glow was emanating from the clearing. Suspicions unhappily confirmed, my resolve hardened even deeper. I continued to sprint the last couple of hundred yards, finally zipping away from the beaten path and into the trees themselves, until I came to a grounding halt at the edge of the small open area. Corrigan was already there, a dark sleek ball of growling tension. I stared ahead.

Our nasty death-defying sorcerer had planted himself smack bang in the middle. It wasn't clear exactly where the light was coming from, but it seemed to centre itself somehow around his body. It wasn't that which caught my attention, however. Rather it was the two dryads, suspended about two feet in the air on either side of him that drew my eyes. The one on his right was the shy nymph I'd already met. Both her and her friend were writhing and twisting in the air, obvious agony on their faces. I snarled.

"Let them go."

Their captor blinked slowly at me. "Dear me, why on earth would I do that? You have to understand, Ms Smith, that I require their energy. The thing is, I was only going to start with the trees. I had plans, you know. You and your little furry Lord Alpha have rather disrupted them." He shrugged. "But I can adapt. I had intended to be more merciful, and to permit the remaining dryads to continue with their rather dull and pitiful existence." He smiled unpleasantly. "Well, most of them, anyway. Unfortunately for their species, your interference has changed all that. By bringing the humans here and interrupting my schedule, I have no choice but to fast forward my plans. You shall have to live with the results."

I laughed coldly. "I do believe your over-confidence is going to be your undoing. I am going to fucking pulverise you."

"Goodness, such language. Someone really ought to wash your mouth out with soap. I will admit that I hadn't expected you to display the power that you did. Believe me, it hasn't gone

HELEN HARPER

unnoticed. I don't suppose you are willing to tell me now what you are?"

"Fuck you."

A pained cry rang out from the dryad to his left, and he raised his eyebrows. "I would watch what you say. Your words and your actions have consequences."

Corrigan snapped forward at the same moment as I used my one free hand to jet out green fire. Both dryads immediately shrieked and blood began to blossom in the centre of each their chests, a dark flower staining their skin. I withdrew my hand, and Corrigan adjusted his attack, sailing over the threesome instead of slamming into them, and landed on the other side, twisting around to face their backs and flank them. The fire that had already reached the bastard ate away at the edges of his suit but did little other damage. Both the dryads' screams subsided into quiet sobs, although blood continued to drip from their bodies, turning the dark ground even darker as it fell.

His mouth quirked up at one side. "I did warn you."

"You're not going to get away with this."

"Oh, how terribly comic book of you. I think you'll find, Ms Smith, that I will get away with it. With this and with, oh, so much more."

Rage was beginning to scorch its way through me. My lungs were filling with fire, and I knew I was close to shifting, whether I wanted to or not. This time I chose not to bank down the flames. Becoming a dragon again might fucking terrify me, but if that was what it was going to take, then that was what I was prepared to do.

He cocked his head towards me. "You are turning a most peculiar shade of red. Interesting."

We need a plan, Corrigan.

I know. His Voice was grim. *Are you going to shift?*

I might not have a choice.

"The pair of you are communicating telepathically." He gestured backwards towards Corrigan in a flippant manner that

218

raised my hackles even further, if that were possible. "So that would make you some kind of shifter then. Except I've never seen a shifter who can use magic as well. Ms. Smith, you are a charming conundrum."

If you attacked from behind, knocking him over, and I used the dagger on him again, we might be able to get the dryads released before he hurts them anymore. I don't think he's put a ward in place.

It'll need to be fast. With what he's shown us so far, it won't take him more than a second to kill the pair of them.

"I tell you what," he murmured. "You wanted to know my name. I'll give you it if you tell me what you really are."

If I transform, it'll distract him.

It might also give him enough time to slaughter both of them too.

I spoke aloud. "Sure. You first."

"Somehow I don't think I trust you, Ms Smith." He sighed. "I am also starting to rather tire of these antics."

"So stop then."

"Do you know why I chose the dryads over the Batibats? Certainly I imagine that you would be less inclined to be getting in my way right now if I had opted for that direction. And both are linked to the earth, granting me the power that I need to draw."

Hmm. I kept a mental note of that comment, trying not to let the fact that he'd piqued my interest with his sudden clue to his motives show on my face. "Enlighten me," I grunted.

He snapped his fingers together, and a dark shimmering shape appeared in front of him. I peered at it. A fucking portal. It looked different somehow to normal ones; usually even in darkness they were identified by streaks of light purple. This one just looked black. If it wasn't for the light that he was already casting, I doubted I'd have managed to make out even a single flicker of the gateway he'd opened.

We can't let him escape.

I growled back. *I know.*

"You see," he stated calmly, "every dryad is connected."

Where is he going with this?

Corrigan sounded as baffled as I felt. *No clue, but keep him talking.*

"To their trees? So what?"

He waved a hand dismissively in the air. Mereia's friend moaned and my muscles tightened in anger. "Yes, yes, to the trees. More than that, however, they are connected to each other. An invisible web, if you like. It's entirely unique to their species."

Suddenly, I saw an opening. It was risky but it might work. *Corrigan, I think I have it. I know how I can take the dryads out of the equation. His only leverage will be gone and you will be free to attack him. You just need to keep him away from that portal.*

But you can't get both dryads at the same time, Mack. They're stuck fast and he's in control. He's using magic to keep them in place. How are you going to snap his spell?

"I'm afraid I still don't quite see your point," I said aloud, trying to keep my opponent relaxed and chatting so we could plan out our move.

Do you see where both their feet are pointing?

Their toes are focused on...I see it.

It was subtle, but glaringly obvious once you knew it was there. Freaky Mage Man had already given it away in fact with his words. He was using the tree nymphs to leech power from the earth. And in order to keep the nymphs suspended where they were, he was using the earth back at them, forcing them into position through the one point that both their feet were demonstrably aiming towards. It was too much of a coincidence to not be important that there was one single patch of ground that all twenty of their toes were being drawn to, as if by some invisible magnetic force. Add in the fact that there was an oddly shaped patch of black-as-death shadow in that very spot and, hey presto, there was our way out. Break that connection and break the dryads' prison. If I could fling all of my power at that one spot – blood and fire together – then

Corrigan would be free to destroy this prick without fear of the consequences.

"You are thinking narrow-mindedly, Ms Smith."

Actually, no I wasn't. There was no way I was going to tell him that though, of course.

"The thing is," he continued, "if I slant things just right, if everything aligns in the way that I want it to, then what I take from one, I can take from all."

I had absolutely no idea what he was on about. I didn't really care either. I didn't want to let on that we had discovered the chink in his armour, however, so I kept talking. "Why not do that before now then? You already slaughtered one of them. Why not take everything you needed then?"

"As I said, I wanted to be merciful. But," he motioned towards me, "things change. Besides, power is a funny thing. Overload everything all at once and you risk creating a shortage."

"And you're not worried about that now?"

Are we good to go?

"Since my first visit here, I have been building and growing my capacity. I wasn't in a position to take everything before." He smiled toothlessly, in a manner that sent an icy cold trickle of hatred through me to join the angry swirl of bloodfire in my veins. "I am confident now, however, that I can manage to draw it all in. You can be content in the knowledge that your actions are responsible for the extinction of the dryad race."

Uh, what? This guy wasn't just a power hungry murderer, he was a wannabe genocidal maniac making absolutely no sense whatsoever.

"So whatever you and the kitty cat are planning in those little heads of yours, you can abandon it now. I will grant you one boon, however."

"Oh yes?" I said, distractedly.

On a count of three. Three...

"My name."

Two...

"So you can spend the rest of your pathetic life with something tangible to curse."

One...

"It's Endor."

Now!

Several things happened at once. Both dryads let out abrupt piercing shrieks as Endor outstretched both his arms towards them. Corrigan launched himself from behind, claws flashing in the air as he aimed his great rippling panther body at the sorcerer. I threw my one remaining dagger down and leapt towards the dark point on the ground, fire shooting out from my fingertips and intermingling with the drops of blood that were still welling up at the surface of my skin. The fire and blood mix hit the spot with an angry hiss, sending up a plume of dark steam but, just when Corrigan was scant inches from Endor's body, he took one swift step towards the portal. I could have sworn there was merry amusement twinkling in his eyes as his entire figure vanished. Corrigan and the dryads thumped virtually simultaneously onto the hard ground, and all four of us let out individual exclamations of pain, anger and frustration. The light that had been surrounding the area winked out, and we were plunged into darkness.

Without thinking, I threw myself at the strange blackened shimmers of the gateway in a desperate bid to follow him, but, for some reason, my passage was blocked and instead I also slammed down to the ground. I smashed my fist in thwarted anguish against the earth, and instead crawled over to Mereia's friend.

She was muttering something to herself. Literally, as I watched, the colour was draining from her shadowed skin. She reached one hand out to me, and I clutched it, panicking.

'What's happening?" I shouted. "What can I do?"

She moaned, her fingers tightening around mine. "He's taking it all," she gasped.

With an inarticulate snarl and snap, Corrigan shifted back into his naked human form, and crouched over the other dryad.

"She's fading, Mack, I don't know what to do."

I wrenched my hand away and ran the few steps to the portal, trying to smear my blood on it to close it and stop whatever Endor was doing to the dryads. He had to still be linking to them from wherever he was. If I could force the magical doorway shut then I could break his connection. The wound on my finger had nothing left to give, however. I cast around quickly, my eyes landing on the gleam of the silver dagger gleaming in the weak moonlight that still lit the area. Scooping it back up, I pressed it again into my hand, creating yet another wound. The pain didn't even register. Then I sprang back to the portal of darkness and shoved my bleeding palm towards it. The shimmers reacted, almost as if they were angry, flickering faster and colliding with each other. The gateway, however, remained open. I cursed and tried again.

"Mack," said the dryad weakly.

I barely heard her, using the dagger to open up my wound even more. I must just need more blood. Again, I thrust towards the shadowy shimmers. Again, the portal refused to close.

"Come on, come on," I muttered desperately.

"Mack," she said again. "You need to do it now."

"I'm trying!"

"No, you don't understand. You need to end it now. Kill us."

Her words slowly sank in as I looked first at her and then at Corrigan. His face was pale under his tan as we both stared at each other. What the fuck?

"He was right," she gasped, the pain in her voice obvious. "I can feel it."

"Feel what? I don't understand."

The colour in her eyes was already starting to dim and leak out. "Through us he's linked to everyone."

I still didn't get it. The fog of confused desperation was almost overwhelming.

"He..." she paused for a moment as a wave of agony overtook her, before swallowing hard and continuing on. "He's using us to get to them all. He was right that we're all inter-connected. By taking our life-force he's taking it from every single dryad in the country. He's used the power he already took from Mereia to somehow force us all together as one and tap into the system that binds us. If you don't end it for us, then they will all die. Kill us now, Mack. You have to. You can't let him destroy all of us. And you can't let him take that much power."

Her companion joined in, chiming weakly. "I can feel them all fading away. Do it now. You must."

Atlanteia's invisible roots. An icy hand of frozen anguish gripped its way round my heart, squeezing tightly. "No," I whispered. "There must be another way."

"There's not. Do it, Mack, do it before it's too late."

"No! My blood. If you take my blood then it will heal you."

I began thrusting out my hand towards her. How much would she need? I'd need to make sure there was enough for both of them. The dryad, however, was shaking her head.

"You can't. I can't. It will heal us, but it won't break the link. The others will still die, Mack. All the others. You need to kill us to save them." Her eyes pleaded with me.

The realisation of what Endor had meant when he'd said that Corrigan and I would have to live with consequences of our actions hit me. All that stupid power inside my blood and not one single iota of it could help. Dully, I stared down at her, then back towards Corrigan. He watched me grimly, then nodded. Barely able to draw breath, I nodded back. Tears filled my eyes, blurring my vision as I knelt down beside her. Her hand grasped up towards me.

"It's the right thing," she whispered.

No, it fucking wasn't. I took her hand in mine, then reached out with my other one and smoothed down her tangled green hair. Corrigan was beside the other dryad, cradling her head in his hands.

I clenched my teeth. "I'm so so sorry."

She lifted her eyes to mine, stubborn denial at my words lighting their depths. "Do it. We will have our revenge through you in another life."

Kill a few to save a lot. To save them all. It wasn't fucking right. I took a deep breath, moving my hands round the sides of her head. Then I twisted it sharply right and broke her neck.

CHAPTER 22

"I brought your clothes, my Lord." Lucy's voice wafted over to me. I ignored it and pulled my knees closer to my chest. When both dryads had died, so did the portal, winking out of existence as if it had never been there in the first place. Now there was nothing left to do. I buried my face into the soft fabric of my jeans and tried to block her out.

"Thank you."

"What happened?"

"It's a very long story. Gather the others together down by the carpark. What happened here is now over."

Her footsteps crunched on the ground as she apparently ran off. I still didn't bother looking up. There was a faint rustle as Corrigan apparently dressed himself. I sniffed, not even bothering to try to stem the silent tears that were creating a damp patch on my clothes.

"Mack." Corrigan laid a hand on my shoulder.

I remained where I was. His grip tightened and he shook me, gently. "Mack, you should get up."

I lifted my face up to his and stared at him searchingly. "What did we just do?"

He sighed heavily and crouched down beside me, his fingers tracing the tracks of my tears across my cheeks, then tucking a loose strand of hair behind my ear. "What we had to."

"We fucking killed them, Corrigan! They'd done nothing and we just did away with them as if they were nothing!"

"He hadn't given us a choice. You know that." His voice remained quiet and calm. I didn't have the faintest idea how he managed it.

Another tear rolled down. I didn't bother brushing it off. I looked away from him and down at the broken bodies of the dryads. Yet again I'd screwed everything up and there was a pile of corpses left in my wake.

"Don't you dare do that!" He took hold of both my shoulders and leaned in. "This is not your fault, do you hear me?"

"If I'd shifted then maybe I could have stopped him."

"How? What could you have done differently? He gave us no choice, Mack."

"There's always a choice," I answered dully, finally pulling away from him and standing up. "What do we do now?"

"We go back home and find out everything we can about this bastard so we can put him down once and for all. At least we now know his name."

"Know his name? Know his fucking name? Big freaking deal! And what if he comes back here again, Corrigan? How do we stop him? What if he goes after other dryads in other places?"

"Which is exactly why we need to get back to London and get a proper plan of action in place in order to make sure that doesn't happen. I've called in the Welsh pack. They'll be here in fifteen minutes and will make sure he doesn't show up again."

I scoffed. "As if they could stop him if he did."

"Mack," Corrigan sighed, looking me in the eyes, "he's done here. You know he is. He has what he wanted, which is more of the dryads' power. He's gone off to goodness knows where. He's certainly not on this plane anyway. We need to get back and work out what we are going to do next. Staying here is not going to stop anything. Not anymore."

I knew he was right. The stubborn streak inside of me just didn't want to admit it. I still couldn't believe that we had been so resoundly hammered into submission. Bloodfire welled up inside me yet again, seething its way into an angry boil. I took a deep breath and forced it back down. I had to stay calm. Getting pissed off and letting my emotions rule me yet again was not going to help this situation. I blinked in acknowledgement and Corrigan's grip loosened.

"Okay," I said, finally relenting. "Just give me a minute, alright? I'll meet you back down at the car-park soon."

Corrigan watched me warily. "I'm not sure…" he began.

I reached over and pressed my finger against his lips. "Please. I won't be a long."

A muscle tensed in his cheek, but eventually he nodded, and turned away, striding out of the clearing. I waited until he had gone, then I knelt back down again, beside the first dryad's body.

"I'm so sorry," I whispered, reaching over and gently closing her eyes. "I promise you that I will get your revenge. I won't let this go unpunished. Not if it's the last thing I do."

I moved back over to the other dryad and did the same, repeating my promise to her. Then I stood back up. A branch to my right creaked and every muscle in my body tensed. When I saw who it was, I relaxed again. A tree nymph hung there, sadly watching me. Even in the darkness, I could still see there was an unhealthy pallor to her skin. Anger re-lit inside me.

"We will take care of them," she said softly.

"Are you alright?"

She nodded. "We will be." She looked off into the direction that Corrigan had disappeared in. "He is right. There was no choice. We thank you for your efforts."

"Yeah, they weren't good enough though, were they?" I said bitterly.

"They will be." Her eyes turned downwards. "The humans are here now. They will prevent the development from moving further forward."

"It was only ever just a ruse to hide what he was really planning."

She inclined her head in acknowledgement. "Still, I believe we are now safe. Again, we thank you."

I didn't think I had ever felt less deserving of those words. With nothing further to say, however, I raised my hand to her in dejected farewell then gave the two dryads one final glance, before turning and heading after Corrigan.

* * *

I was halfway to the carpark, when Max caught up to me. "The humans are all good," he said, "safe and sound in their little encampment. I think they are planning to start building their tripod thingies at first light."

"Great," I responded, not massively caring.

"Your weird bloodsucker friend won't leave though."

"Huh?"

"He refuses to leave. Says he can't until you come and find him."

I cursed inwardly. Part of me was tempted just to leave Aubrey where he was. Did I really care what happened to him now? I felt the responsibility of the compulsion I'd laid on him, however, and nodded briskly to the mage. "I'll sort him out."

I changed direction, heading cross country back towards the protestors instead. Even before I got there, the sound of their singing was clear, drifting through the trees. It was vaguely familiar. As I got closer, I realised that it was a remarkably tuneless version of Big Yellow Taxi. The words 'they took all the trees and put'em in a tree museum' made me wince. I supposed that at least the protestors' cloud of ignorance about what had really happened this night would mean that they would indeed happily stay to put a spanner in the works of the ridiculous campaign for holiday homes. I thought of the piece of paper that I'd found tangled up in the branches of the trees; the company behind the development was called Endorium. No prizes for guessing where that name came from then. I supposed that if I'd not shown up then what would have happened would have essentially been the same. Endor would have used the development as an easy cover to cut down the trees and smoke out more dryads so he could leech more power from them. It would probably have just ended up being a longer and more drawn out process, that was all. I fervently hoped that somewhere he was having a painful power surge that was causing an overload and a shortage, as he'd so casually phrased it. Unfortunately, I doubted that was really true.

Before too long, the tents came into view. There were small clusters of people sitting around, still humming that bloody Joni Mitchell song as I approached. Aubrey was at least easy to spot thanks to his isolation. He was sitting to one side, carefully watching the trees. My battered plastic bag with my few belongings encased within was propped up carefully against his side. When he saw me coming, he sprang to his feet and beamed.

"I told them! I told them you'd come for me!" He peered at my face and his smile faltered. "What happened? You look upset."

"You don't want to know," I said tiredly.

Aubrey looked hurt, but I couldn't summon the energy to worry about his feelings. He painted on a sullen pout, and handed out his phone to me. I stared at it for a moment, uncomprehendingly.

He waved it in my face. "Your friend has been calling. Over and over again. He really wants to talk to you."

It took a moment to work out who on earth Aubrey was referring to. Then realisation dawned. Alex. It was a bit late now for whatever information he had to give. I supposed I should at least be glad that he was alive and hadn't gotten himself

into any trouble for asking questions about Endor on my behalf.
As confident as I'd been before that it would have been no
problem, I was now starting to realise that the last thing I should
be placing any faith in was my own confidence. I muttered a
thanks at Aubrey and took the phone from him.

"Come on. We're leaving."

He beamed at me, although there was still an edge of concern
to his features. I ignored it and instead turned the phone on,
hitting the button to return Alex's last call, and started walking
back through the woods.

"What do you want, Vlad?"

I was somewhat taken aback at the vehemence in Alex's voice.
"Er...Alex?"

"Mack Attack! It's you! Where the hell have you been, dude?"

I couldn't face telling him the sad story right now. Instead I
prevaricated. "I'll explain later. I need you to stay away from
that shop now though, Alex. Do you hear me? Don't go
anywhere near it. Go home and stay home."

"Eh?" he sounded surprised. "I've been in already. You were
right, there was absolutely nothing to be afraid of in the slightest.
In fact," his voice took on a confidential tone, "I also take it back
about the Batibat being hideous and scary. She's actually rather
charming."

"Um, okay. Still, go home now and don't go back there again."

"If that's what you want. You want to hear what I found about
the shop owner or not though?"

Pain glanced through me. "Yeah, Alex, I guess so."

"Well, you could sound a bit more enthusiastic, Mack Attack.
This is a dude we need to be scared of. Apparently his name is
Endor. Even without the info from the Batibat, you know what
that means."

"Not really," I said, suddenly pausing. Was this really more
Otherworld general knowledge that I was completely ignorant
of? Would knowing whatever Alex was about to reveal have
meant that this night's terrible events could have been avoided?

"Oh," he said, somewhat deflated. "I guess you didn't go to Sunday school then. The witch of Endor is in the bible. She's a medium who King Saul calls up to contact the ghost of Samuel. Needless to say, bad things happen as a result."

I shook my head frustratedly. The bible? That was hardly up to date, of the minute information. "I don't see what this has to do with our Endor. He's not a woman."

"You're missing the point, Mack Attack. The witch of Endor could call upon ghosts because she had the power of the dead. The Endor here and now is using her name because he's using the same power. He's a necromancer. It's serious black magic, dude. He's a nasty nasty guy."

No shit. That explained why he had been so keen to kill the dryads, I supposed though. The more dead dryads, the more dark power he could glean.

"That's useful information." Sort of. Not really. It wasn't exactly surprising.

"Wait, there's more!"

My heart sank and fingers of dread clutched at my heart. How much worse was this likely to get? "Go on."

"The Batibat came across some stuff in the back of the shop. She doesn't like her boss very much. Apparently he's using her to look after things there so he can make some money and keep his other operations going. She's not very happy about it. I think he's using various Batibats to do his evil bidding, or else."

Yeah, I thought, or else he'll suck the life out of them.

"Anyway," Alex continued, "she found this thing that was ripped out of some book. She reckons it's his plan to get more power. It seems that he's looking to harness the four elements in order to boost his own strength. That's…"

"Earth, air, fire and water," I filled in.

"Yes. Mack Attack, you have to understand, that's crazy. First of all I have no idea how you would even go about doing such a thing. Second of all, it makes no sense. Those elements don't have anything to do with necromancy. Thirdly, can you imagine how powerful someone would be if they really pulled that off?"

I stopped walking and closed my eyes, resting a hand on a nearby tree. Fuck. "Did she mention whether she knew if he'd been successful at all?"

"Nah, Mack Attack. She reckons he's pretty much delusional. I'd say the same as well to be honest. I don't see how anyone could do it."

There was a moment of silence as I absorbed all of Alex's intelligence.

Eventually he filled the void. "So? Did I do good? I gotta tell you, I'm really proud of myself. I mean, I don't believe much of what she said. It's a lot of pie in the sky stuff, but maybe I actually have a bit of a calling for this, you know?" He deepened his voice dramatically. "Alex Florides, the super spy."

"Yeah, Alex, you did great." I could almost hear his smile from across the phone. "Look, I have to go now. Thanks for the info. I mean it though – stay away from that shop from now on. It's too dangerous to go back."

"What, really? Dangerous how? Wait, do I need to hide myself? Is that Endor dude going to come after me because of what I found out?"

I reckoned he probably had bigger plans than bothering with a surf loving mage. "No. But still, it wouldn't hurt to stay out of sight for a little while."

"Sure, sure. Okay, I'm going to go now then. Maybe I should go abroad? Not, that's too obvious. Um, perhaps up north somewhere?"

"Bye, Alex."

"Yeah, bye, Mack Attack," he responded distractedly.

I hung up and passed the phone back to Aubrey. He was watching me carefully. "There are bad things afoot, aren't there?"

"Yes, there are."

"Worse than vampires?"

"Much much worse than vampires."

Aubrey nodded. "Okay, then. What do you need?"

"I need to get back to London as soon as possible. Can you run?"

His eyes widened. "To London? Isn't that kind of far?"

I patted him on the shoulder, trying to avoid appearing patronising. It was hard. "No, you prat. The car park. Come on."

CHAPTER 23

Twelve hours later, I was at least feeling physically refreshed. I'd had what was probably the longest shower of my life, eight hours' sleep, and a good breakfast with lots and lots of coffee. If you could call a meal at three o'clock in the afternoon 'breakfast'. There was a hard numbed shell around both my heart and my thoughts whenever I even began to consider the terrible events on Haughmond Hill, but I kept pushing that oh so very recent memory away, knowing that I needed to start feeling more prepared to deal with all this necromancy bullshit. At least for once in my life I'd really appreciated being able to travel halfway across the country via a portal. It meant that there was far less faffing around, and far more time to really get down to business.

I'd known when I'd entered the now shiny red door to my little flat in the wee hours of Sunday morning, with all the others outside watching me as I'd entered, that Corrigan had been hoping that I'd invite him in. I had desperately needed the hours of solitude to get my head into gear, however. It had nothing to do with pushing him away, and everything to do with just wanting to sort myself out. As much as I wanted to feel his arms around me, I had decided that some real undisturbed sleep was more important at this point. I wasn't completely convinced as to whether he had understood that or not, but I was damned sure that I'd make him realise it.

Leaving a note for Mrs. Alcoon to explain (although how I could possibly appropriately convey that there was an ex-vampire sleeping in her shop on a scribbled bit of paper, I really had no idea) I'd installed Aubrey in a campbed at the back of Clava Books. I'd pointed out to him in no uncertain terms that it was a very temporary measure. He had been pathetically grateful. Out of all of us, I was pretty sure that he was the one least happy to be back within the steel and cement arms of the nation's capital. I had been debating whether to invite him along to the formal meeting of the Otherworld's great and the good that had been called for later that day, but had eventually decided that as an ex-member of the undead himself, he might have some insights that he could shed on necromancy. Vamps weren't exactly the same as necromancers, but I reckoned they probably lived in the same metaphorical neighbourhood.

Considering what on earth the future could possibly hold for Aubrey, I lifted up my half-empty coffee cup and stared down at my hands cupping its still warm exterior. My mind flitted immediately back to when they'd been in the same position around the dryad's delicate skull. I winced in the pain of the memory and dropped the cup abruptly. Then I picked it up again and threw it with all my might against the bare wall facing me. The china smashed into shards, and I watched as the remaining coffee dribbled down the wall. I reached out for the vase containing Corrigan's now very dead flowers and did exactly the same. The decaying stems mingled with the dark caffeine infusion in a messy heap on my floor. I didn't feel any better.

I flexed my fingers and held them out in front of my eyes. They didn't look any differently to how they had before I'd used them to kill the dryad. They didn't really feel any different. But the knowledge of what they'd done was gnawing away at me. Atlanteia had asked me to help save her extended family. Instead I'd helped destroy them.

A sharp knock at the door broke me out of my self-absorbed reverie. Somehow the tinge of arrogance that lent itself to the sound made it clear who was there waiting. A wave of relief shuddered through me. Standing up I walked over and opened it.

Corrigan took one look at my face and pulled me towards him. For once I let him, allowing myself to lean towards his hard body. He rested his chin on top of my head, and I sucked in his familiar spicy citrus aftershave. Neither of us said anything for several moments. Finally he drew back and looked me in the eyes.

"How are you doing?" he asked softly.

I shook my head slightly, realising that if I tried to speak, I'd end up sobbing hysterically. He seemed to understand. I sank back into his broad chest again, and remained there for several moments, trying to re-compose myself. It occurred to me, in some dim recesses of my brain, just how happy I was that he was here. Despite what I'd overheard from his conversation with Lucy, there had been the chance he'd feel he'd gotten everything he wanted from me during our session in the woods. The fact that the Lord Alpha of the Brethren was right now standing in my little doorway, with his muscle steeled arms around me, meant that he still wanted to be with me.

"I'm sorry I didn't invite you in last night," I said, my words somewhat muffled as I spoke them into his chest. "I just needed the time to sort myself out. To get some sleep and get things straight in my head."

His voice rumbled above me. "I understand, kitten. You know I do. And you should also know that things haven't changed since yesterday, not with us and not with the reasons behind everything that happened and everything we did. There wasn't a choice to make. Endor forced our hand and we had to react."

I sighed deeply. "I know. But that doesn't make it any better."

I pulled back and looked into his warm eyes. "What's going to happen at this meeting? Is everyone going to be able to work together against him?"

Corrigan's expression was serious. "There's no other way this can go. If we can't find a way to work as one to bring him down then we really will have failed."

I nodded, trying to ignore the hard little nugget of worry in the pit of my stomach. We'd all managed to sort ourselves out and be a team at Haughmond Hill, even if the results of that collaboration hadn't gone our way. But that had only involved a small group of us, and the fact that neither the Arch-Mage nor the Summer Queen had been there had meant that there were less authoritative egos to have to manage. I knew as well as anyone that the clash of different Otherworld species and personalities could cause a lot of problems. I reckoned that it would just have to be down to Corrigan and me to try to encourage them all to keep the peace.

"Shall we?" Corrigan asked, motioning out towards the open door.

I blinked in assent. "I need to pick up Aubrey first though."

For a moment, Corrigan didn't answer. I could see that his muscles had tightened infinitesimally at the idea, however. I felt the need to elaborate.

"He's on our side," I said. "And he might be able to help. If anyone can provide some insight into what an evil fucker who deals with death might do, then it's got to be a vamp. Ex-vamp."

The tension in Corrigan's frame remained. I had to bite my tongue to stop from snapping at him that he was already letting his pre-conceived ideas about other members of the Otherworld get in his way. Thankfully, however, he finally nodded grimly. I let out an inward sigh of relief and already felt more optimistic. If Corrigan could put aside his antagonism towards Aubrey, then there was a good chance the rest of the Otherworld's leaders would be able to do the same with each other.

An expensive looking car was sitting outside, looking somewhat incongruous against its slightly shabbier surroundings. It seemed ridiculous to climb into it to drive a couple of blocks to the shop, so I gestured to Corrigan that I'd meet him outside Clava Books once I'd picked up Aubrey. Corrigan was having none of that, however, and flicked a hand towards the invisible driver to instruct him to follow us. Then he carefully manoeuvred himself between my body and the road, in some old-fashioned idea of chivalry. I shot him an irritated glance, but he chose to ignore it, and the pair of us walked down in silence. At one point, his hand brushed gently against mine. I didn't know whether it was by accident or by design, but it still made my heart skip a beat. Stop acting like a love-sick teenager, I told myself firmly, you're a grown woman. Then he shrugged off his jacket and folded it over his arm. His black t-shirt stretched across his body in a manner that made my mouth go dry. Damn it.

When we reached Clava Books, Corrigan waited outside, clearly not wanting to spend any more time in Aubrey's company than was strictly necessary. I entered, surprised that the door was already open, but that was nothing compared to my shock when I took in the scene beside the small till area. Slim was hovering in the air, a smile stretched across his face, and a cup of tea cupped in his small hands. He'd substituted Mrs. Alcoon's scarf round his waist for a pair of bizarre looking Bermuda shorts that were probably designed for toddlers. Mrs. Alcoon herself was propped up against the counter, her head cocked to one side as she listened intently to the stream of nonsense that was coming out of Aubrey's mouth.

"So, then Mack tells me to order a pizza, which is no mean feat in the middle of a forest. Giving directions without a postcode is hard, you know? She trusted me enough to choose it for her, and I thought that she was going to eat it herself, but then she took it and went to Corrigan and told me that they were not to be disturbed. At first I thought she was just hungry, but then I realised…"

I cleared my throat. All three of them suddenly sprang up to attention, with slightly guilty looks on their faces. Mrs. Alcoon was the first to recover.

"Mackenzie, dear, your friend was just telling us about your exploits. I thought you were going to have a proper rest and a bit of a holiday, not go gallivanting around the countryside."

I raised my eyebrows at her. It was interesting the way in which she could turn the fact that she'd clearly been involved in a deep gossip about what I'd been up to into apparent concern that I hadn't been sat on my sofa for four and a half days watching daytime television. She smiled at me innocently.

"So I suppose you won't be here for the fecking opening tomorrow then?" growled Slim.

"Don't you worry about that," I said, walking over and patting him on his little purple shoulder. "I'll be here. I just might have some other things to take care of too." Like working out a way to kill an apparently unkillable necromancer who had a penchant for slaughtering innocent creatures.

Mrs. Alcoon suddenly cast me a concerned look. She reached and touched me gently then drew back with troubled eyes. I guessed that her weak mage skills were springing to the fore.

"It wasn't your fault," she said softly. "You're too hard on yourself."

I watched her carefully. "What else do you see?"

She shook herself. "Just..." she lifted her blue eyes to mine. "Nothing, dear."

"Mrs. Alcoon..." I began, before stopping. Maybe it was better not to know. "I need Aubrey."

He snapped up, straightening his back. "I'm ready! Where are we going? Are we going to kick some nasty shit's butt?"

I shot him a look. He was definitely no longer the aloof and slightly scary master vampire that I'd first met. "We're going to a meeting. You're going to come along and only speak if you're spoken to. Okay?"

He nodded vigorously. "Okay, okay, yes, no problem."

I gave my old friend an apologetic look. "I'm sorry. I will be here tomorrow, I promise."

She smiled at me, although it was with a tinge of sadness that worried me. "I know you will, dear. You go and sort them all out. The council needs you."

I was momentarily confused. Council? Before I could ask her about it however, there was a rap on the glass. Corrigan was getting impatient.

"We should go."

Mrs. Alcoon nodded, and both she and Slim raised their hands in almost identical salutes of farewell. Weird. I left them to it, with Aubrey trotting happily at my heels.

By the time we were outside, Corrigan was already there at the car, holding the passenger door open. I bit back a retort about how I was perfectly capable of opening a car door by myself and instead slid myself in. He climbed in after me, leaving Aubrey to sort himself out. The ex-vamp rather clumsily stepped up, bumped his head on the edge of the car and winced in dramatic pain. Corrigan rolled his eyes and pulled him inside, then reached over and shut the door. Almost immediately the car rolled off.

Aubrey picked himself up off the floor and sat on the leather covered seats opposite Corrigan and myself. He fumbled for the seatbelt for several moments, then eventually managed to slot it into place and leaned back. He opened his mouth as if to speak, and then, as if remembering suddenly that I'd compelled him otherwise, snapped it shut again. His eyes drifted from myself to Corrigan and back again, as if he were watching a particularly engaging game of tennis. I gave up watching him and turned to Corrigan instead.

"So where is this meeting?"

He half turned to me, and smiled. I was so conscious of his proximity that it was almost difficult to breathe. "It's at a neutral location. Somewhere I believe you've been before?"

Oh. "Alcazon?"

He nodded. I cursed inwardly. Fuck. I still really wanted to ask him about the dark-haired shifter I'd seen him with before. There was no way I was going to do it in front of Aubrey, however. I could have used the Voice to ask him about it, but for some reason this was a conversation I wanted to conduct aloud. It seemed that it would be more honest that way. So, instead, I leaned back in my own seat, and stared silently out of the window. The edge of Corrigan's hand scraped gently against my thigh, seemingly as if by accident. I allowed my own hand to fall down against his. His skin was warm to the touch. A tiny smile lit the corners of my mouth. Not much more than twelve hours' earlier I'd done some terrible things, unspeakable things. And I was facing an opponent about whom I knew next to nothing, other than he had far more power than I could begin to imagine and shady plans afoot that were absolutely terrifying. However, with Corrigan by my side, it somehow felt as everything was going to be alright.

CHAPTER 24

When we finally reached the glass-fronted restaurant, we were quickly ushered inside and into the lift. Rather than heading for the public area where I'd previously dined with Solus, we were led into a back room. It was filled with a large walnut boardroom type oval table, and plush cream carpet covered the floor. Swanky. Everyone else was already sitting there waiting.

The magnitude of this meeting hit me. Sure, I knew that on occasion the Otherworld heads met up to try to avoid unnecessary conflict. In fact that had been how I'd come to meet Aubrey in the first place: when I'd sort of gate-crashed his vamp lair in order to steal back the Ancile and leave the Palladium in its place. But this was different. There was a sombre atmosphere, and the gravity of the situation was clearly not lost on anyone. At one end of the table were the Fae: the Summer Queen, Solus, Beltran, and two others, all of whose grace and elegance rather put me to shame. Opposite them were the mages. Alex, apparently not in hiding after all, was seated next to the Arch-Mage. Max and Larkin were both there, along with a couple of austere looking female mages who I vaguely recognised. In the far corner were Staines, Lucy, and Tom. There was an empty seat next to them that was clearly meant for Corrigan himself. More surprisingly, Balud the troll was also present.

I pulled out the chair next to Balud and sat myself down. At least this way I could not only ensure that I kept my promise to him, by detailing everything I knew about Endor's weapon shop, but also maintain some semblance of neutrality by not visibly aligning myself with any of the other groups. Aubrey sat next to me. The cushion on his chair let out a gentle farting sound as he rested himself upon it. He giggled to himself. Everybody else ignored him.

The Summer Queen tapped her long tapered fingernails impatiently on the table top. "Where's Atlanteia? She should be here as well."

My stomach dropped. I wasn't sure I was ready to face the dryad just yet. To do so would be to ultimately acknowledge not only my failure to keep her extended family safe, but also my culpability in their deaths.

"She is as yet too weak to leave her habitat," stated the Arch-Mage. "The attack took it out of her and she is not ready to supplant herself so far away from her tree."

The Summer Queen raised her perfectly manicured eyebrows. "You've been in contact with her? I seem to recall that it wasn't too long ago that you were using the dryads for silly teaching experiments."

He scowled in obvious annoyance. Before he could answer, however, Corrigan interrupted. "We're not going to get anywhere by starting off in conflict. We can talk to Atlanteia later. Let's focus on the matter in hand instead." He looked meaningfully at me.

I cleared my throat somewhat nervously and began, laying out the details of how I'd come to end up at Haughmond Hill, including both Balud's 'request' to discover the identity of his competitor, and what Atlanteia had asked of me.

"This is not something you should have undertaken alone," frowned the Arch-Mage.

"Well, I didn't think it was actually going to be that big of a deal. There was no reason to expect there to be a fucking all powerful necromancer behind everything," I explained, trying to remain patient and not point out that even having a string of shifters, mages and Fae along for the ride hadn't really helped all that much.

"He really is a big deal, dudes," added in Alex. The Summer Queen winced. "According to the Batibat I spoke to, he's trying to harness the four elements, earth, air, fire and water. His ultimate goal remains unclear, but you can bet it ain't anything fluffy and sweet."

"It's impossible, though. No necromancer can use death magic to gain leverage over the elements."

I turned to the Arch-Mage. "But I think he already has," I said quietly. "That's what killing the dryads was all about. They're tied to the trees and the trees are tied to the earth. He's already got that one in the bag." Several faces around the table paled.

"It doesn't make sense," stated Staines, firmly. "He killed that one dryad, Mereia, and then didn't go back until you blundered in and destroyed his ward."

I forced myself to stay calm. "Because initially he didn't want to take all the power at once. He described it as some kind of overload. That he'd short out if he did too much at once. When he came back the second time, he was strong enough to take more."

"So is he going to go back? Do we need to protect the dryads all over the country?"

"Even though he didn't manage to draw power from all of them, I get the feeling that he's done with them," I answered slowly. "He's going to move onto another element."

"Still," said the Summer Queen, "we can't be too careful. We should ensure that the tree nymphs are safe from further encroachment."

"Oh, yes?" inquired one of the female mages. "And how exactly are we going to do that?"

The Fae Queen turned cold eyes onto her. "I would rather think that the mages could manage that. After all, not only are you apparently versed in creating protective wards, you also owe the dryads in the first place for the torture you inflicted upon them."

"Torture? We didn't torture them! We didn't know that what we were doing was hurting them. As soon as we did know we stopped!" The mage's voice rose with each sentence. "You're the Fae. You're the ones meant to be at one with the Mother Earth. Maybe it should be you stepping up to the plate for once."

All of a sudden, a collection of raised voices filled the room. The tension was palpable, and I thought I could even hear the beginnings of a magic crackle in the air that didn't forbode well.

I slammed my palm down onto the table top with all my strength. Startled, everyone silenced and stared at me.

"Look," I said, annoyed, "there are enough mages around to create wards at the main dryad habitats. If the Fae and the shifters each post guards as well, say, just one each, then no-one will be too stretched. I don't believe that Endor is going to bother with them again though. He's going to move onto another element."

"So that means, water sprites perhaps?" asked Lucy. "They're an easy target."

"What if he goes for air instead? There are any number of creatures he could attempt to draw from. How on earth do we know which ones he'll go for?"

"What if he goes for fire?" Corrigan's voice was quiet, and his eyes were on me.

The others all turned in my direction, puzzlement in a few faces, comprehension in others. "We'll set up a bodyguard rotation," said the Arch-Mage firmly. "No-one is going near Miss Mackenzie without our say so."

"Or she could just come to Tir-na-Nog. Problem solved," hissed the Fae Queen.

"Stop it!" I yelled. "He doesn't know what I am. And I'm hardly the only Otherworld creature that uses fire. " I looked at the Arch-Mage. "Just set up a fucking Divination spell. Several Divination spells. We know he's not on this plane right now, but the spells will alert us when he is. Then we find out who he's aiming for."

There were several vigorous nods. Jeez, logic wasn't the natural setting for these guys.

"Except, when he does appear, how do we kill him?"

Everybody stilled. Staines continued. "The Lord Alpha, the strongest of all our shifters, couldn't even come close. Neither could our pet dragon for that matter." I scowled while Lucy blinked in surprise. I guessed that cat was out of the bag then. Thank you very much, Staines, you fuckwit.

"I'm just saying. It's all well and good being able to find him when he shows up, but if we don't have a plan for how to attack him, then all this is pointless."

I looked at Aubrey, sitting silent and wide eyed next to me. "Aubrey? He's a necromancer. He has the power of the undead. What do you think?"

Aubrey thought for a moment before answering. "Well, vampires are obviously different."

There was a snort from the other side of the room. "Obviously."

I ignored it. "Go on," I nudged.

"Fire works," he said, wrinkling his nose. "Stake through the heart too, although it has to be wooden…"

"Oh this is pointless," called out Beltran, "we're not dealing with a vampire. And even if we were, we all know how to kill one of them anyway."

Aubrey snarled. I was taken aback. There was a glimmer there, just for a second, of the old red-eyed master.

"You're not listening. Fire works because it destroys everything. Stakes work because they go through the heart. Now we know from Mack that silver is useless…"

"Yeah, it's only the weak arse shifters who can't cope with that," called out one of the mages.

Lucy growled. Corrigan laid a calming hand on her arm. She subsided, but her eyes were still spitting hatred.

"So we just need to find a weapon that does work," concluded Aubrey. "The heart is always key. No matter what you are."

I twisted left. "Balud?"

He nodded to himself. "I can do some research. Find materials that might be useful."

"Good. And as Staines has so helpfully pointed out, I'm also a dragon. Or Draco Wyr, anyway. I can work with the shifters," I said, deciding to focus in the determination filling me, rather than my annoyance at so many people now knowing my secret. "Maybe I can learn how to get control of the transformations. Then I can use my fire to destroy him too."

I received several approving looks.

"It'll take time," said Corrigan, concern etched across his face.

I kept my voice deliberately quiet. "What else do we have? We don't know when he'll return."

"But when he does, we'll be ready," stated the Arch-Mage firmly.

"Our dragonlette will win the day."

I looked over at Solus. There was an unhappy shadow visible within his expressive violet eyes. Not sure what was up, I flashed him a quick reassuring smile. He smiled tightly back. That wasn't good. It was unlike him even in times of such dramatic and tragic circumstances to lose his usual bouncy arrogant personality.

The Summer Queen spoke up again. "We need a formal task force."

"You're right," agreed the Arch-Mage. "With representatives from each of us. I recommend that the mages take the lead. I can nominate someone agreeable to everyone."

"And why should the mages be in charge?" asked Corrigan, his voice dangerously low.

"We're the best all rounders. The shifters can fight and the faeries have magic. We have both. It stands to reason that we should lead because we understand both worlds and we are in the best position to ensure Endor's defeat."

"You can't possibly compare our magic to yours," interrupted Beltran. "We have more knowledge and more power in our little fingers than you could possibly ever demonstrate."

"You don't even live on this plane," Lucy said to the Fae, scorn dripping from her voice. "The only Otherworld leader who had enough nouse to be where the real danger was to begin with was Lord Corrigan. It should obviously be a shifter in control."

The room descended into a cacophony of chaos. Two of the mages were on their feet, arguing loudly with Lucy and Staines. Alex was jabbing a finger at the faeries. Both the Summer Queen and the Arch-Mage looked about ready to boil over. I glanced at Corrigan.

This isn't helping. They're going to spend more time arguing than ever getting anything done.

Welcome to the machinations of the Otherworld, kitten.

I shook my head slightly in irritation. Then I stood up, pushing my chair back. Nobody took any notice. Rather than attempt make myself heard above the mayhem, I shot a single bolt of green fire at the centre of the table. It smoked and hissed, scorching the expensive sheen of the wood. Oh, well. The room went quiet again.

"Look, we're all agreed that we need a task force, right?"

"Let's call it a council," suggested one of the Fae.

I blinked at that, and thought of Mrs. Alcoon.'s words. "Okay, a council then. We also all know what we need to do to guard against Endor's next move."

There was more nodding.

Corrigan spoke up. "She's right. Let's leave the issue of who's in charge alone for now, and worry about the important matters instead."

There were some grumbled mutters.

"Lord Alpha, I don't think you appreciate that without a head, this entire operation will collapse before it begins," commented the Arch-Mage. "Someone needs to keep everyone in place."

"Let me guess," added in Beltran sarcastically, "you think that ought to be you."

The Summer Queen rose to her feet. She was tapping her mouth thoughtfully. "We'll choose a leader. We'll just wait awhile before we do so."

The Arch-Mage also stood up. "With all due respect..."

She stared at him, some kind of message in her eyes. I watched her carefully. What on earth was she up to?

"Let's get some food first, then reconvene in, say, an hour's time?"

Without waiting for an answer, she held her hand out to Beltran. He took it, and the pair of them swept imperiously out of the room.

I looked at Corrigan and shrugged. Everyone else began to file out, one by one. I nodded to Aubrey, and he left too.

"How on earth do you lot ever get anything done?" I asked, once the room was empty.

"That's easy," he answered distractedly, running a tired hand through his midnight black hair. "We never do."

"You're a bunch of power hungry maniacs," I said, annoyed at the childish truculent behaviour of almost every single Otherworld member.

He narrowed his eyes at me. "It's a dangerous world out there, Mack. You know that." Changing tack, he reached out and touched me lightly on the arm. "I'm sorry about Staines. He shouldn't have revealed that about you."

"How did he even know?" I didn't want to start getting pissed off at Corrigan, but I needed to be able to trust him.

A muscle throbbed in his cheek. "It was a mistake. He was going on at me to leave you alone. That things would never work out because you were a mage. It just kind of burst out."

I sighed. I figured that I couldn't really berate him for

snapping something out in anger, not given my own natural proclivity for letting rage rule my head anyway. "Whatever. I'm going to go and hit the bathroom. I'll see you in a few minutes."

* * *

I was washing my hands in the marble sink when the door to the bathroom swung open. My eyes widened slightly as I realised it was Solus.

"You do know this is the little girls' room right?"

He just blinked at me, then mouthed the words 'I'm sorry'. Confused, I gave him a puzzled frown. He shook his head slightly, as if warning me to be quiet. The bathroom door creaked as it opened again. It was the Summer Queen.

I looked from her to Solus, then back again.

Finally, I opened my mouth to speak. "Okay, what gives?"

"You're an intelligent woman," she said, "I'd have thought that was obvious."

I shook the droplets of water from my hands, then dried them on the back of my jeans. Her nose twitched slightly.

"Well," I drawled, "I guess you'll just have to enlighten me."

She took a step forward. I realised that she was at least a foot and a half taller than me. I tried not to feel small and insignificant by comparison.

"You are friends with Solus."

"Yeah."

"He's Fae."

"Yeah."

"You are also friends with that mage. Alex? The one with the appalling vocabulary?"

"Yeah."

"And with the Lord Alpha."

Well, I didn't know if I'd call him a friend, but okay. I shrugged. "Yeah. What's your point?"

"Nobody else has the ear of all three groups. You even have a vampire on your side."

"Ex-vampire." I had a horrible feeling I knew where she was going with all this. I really hoped I was wrong.

"You have strength. And magic. You have proven yourself worthy in a number of situations."

I had the faintest inkling that the dryads might beg to differ slightly on that point, but I kept my mouth shut.

She continued. "You are the obvious choice to lead our new little anti-necromancer council."

Fuck. "No. Absolutely not. I am the worst possible choice."

"Hear me out, Mackenzie. You saw how bad things were in there. How much everyone disagreed with each other. The only person who's ever had any real success in getting us to work together is you. You did it at Haughmond Hill and you did it to some extent in that room."

I felt slightly nauseous. "I have a terrible temper. I'd be as likely to bite someone's head off as to motivate them to work with others."

"It seems to me," she said, "that you have somewhat conquered those baser impulses. Besides, people need their heads bitten off on occasion."

I swallowed. "I like working alone. I'm an independent kind of person. There's no 'I' in team," I added for cheesy melodramatic effect.

"There's an "I" in council. And it needs someone independent to lead it. Someone who will get things done."

"I don't want to," I stated petulantly.

"We all have to do things we don't want to do from time to time. That's what responsibility is. You know as well as I do that if we can't work together then we'll never be able to overcome someone as powerful as this Endor is. He's a genuine threat to each and every one of us. You don't want more blood to spill, do you?"

I stared at her. I couldn't believe she was pulling that card.

"Fuck off," I said rudely. "Whenever I'm involved, that's exactly what happens." I leaned in towards her, bloodfire lighting up along the lines of my veins. "I get people killed. You need someone else."

"There is no-one else," she stated implacably, ignoring my aggressive stance. "You know there's no-one else whom everyone will be able to respect."

"She's right, dragonlette," Solus quietly said.

I looked away. Fuck the pair of them. I didn't want to be anyone's leader. I certainly didn't want to be the leader of these idiots who could barely agree on the fact that sky was sodding blue.

The Summer Queen was watching me carefully. "What alternatives are there, Mackenzie?"

Damn it. There were none and she knew it. The shifters would never accept a faerie or a mage. The faeries and the mages would be the same. There was Balud, but I was pretty sure that his main motive lay with his profit margin.

"What about Aubrey?"

They both just looked at me, unblinkingly.

I sighed. "Okay, fine. Whatever. I'll do it. But not for long, alright? Only until we get rid of Endor. And only if every single person in that room agrees."

The Summer Queen permitted herself a small smile. There was a tentative knock on the door, and the Arch-Mage's head curved round.

"Well?" he asked.

"She agreed."

He exhaled loudly. "Great. Did you...?"

The Summer Queen shook her head. "Not yet."

I stared at them suspiciously. "What?"

"You need to be impartial, Mackenzie."

Well, duh. "I think I can manage that."

"If you're not impartial," chimed in the Arch-Mage, "then the council will fall apart before it even starts."

"Okay. I'll be fair. I can't think why you'd believe I wouldn't be." As soon as the words were out of my mouth, I realised what they were getting at. My mouth dropped open. "No."

"You know that we need you to head the council if we're going to have any chance of beating Endor."

"You can't make me do this."

"You grew up with the shifters, Mackenzie. Even with your other alliances there will be concerns that your loyalties will lie with them."

"I left them," I said desperately. "Of my own free will. I don't have ties to them any more. Not like that. I'll be fair. I'll be impartial. You can't force me to do this."

"We're not forcing you. It's ultimately your decision."

"But unless you give him up, you can't be the unbiased leader of a mixed council."

"And without a mixed council, without that collaborative power, there's little chance we'll be able to beat Endor."

I could feel my whole body sagging in response to their tag-team approach.

"You can't be in a relationship with the Lord Alpha, dragonlette."

I stared at Solus, angry flickers of fire sparking up all over my body.

"You have to be seen to be above reproach," the Summer Queen stated simply.

The Arch-Mage's expression was pure stone. "And you need to rise up beyond such things and think rationally. You will have plenty of opportunity once this whole nasty business is done and dusted to make it up to him. But for now the split needs to be real. You have to have a purely business relationship with Corrigan from this point on."

"Let's face it," the Queen added, "it's not as if you're already in a long term relationship with him. It's been what, less than twenty-four hours since you both…"

I glared at her. She fell silent. I threw Solus a dirty look for passing on idle gossip. He was staring unhappily down at the tiled floor. Screw him then.

I kicked angrily at the wall. There was no choice. Yet again. What was the point in having free will if you were constantly being painted into a corner?

"Fuck!" I shouted aloud, my cry echoing around the room. "Fuck!"

"Thank you, Mackenzie." The Summer Queen bowed her head. She knew that inside I'd already agreed. "It's for the greater good."

"I'll call the others back in," said the Arch-Mage. "You're doing the right thing, you know."

Hot tears pricked at the back of my throat. How could this be the right thing when it felt so wrong?

Both the head of the mages and the ruler of the Seelie Fae turned and left. Solus and I were alone.

"I'm sorry, dragonlette," he said miserably. "I didn't..."

"Shut up. Just shut up." I brushed past him, my heart aching. Sorry just wasn't going to cut it.

CHAPTER 25

I wanted to talk to Corrigan on my own. He deserved to hear from me personally, without any of the others nearby. I needed to explain what was happening. By the time I'd exited from the bathroom, however, he was nowhere to be seen.

I pushed out my Voice. *Corrigan? Where are you?*

Back in the boardroom. Apparently we've been summoned to return. There was a touch of sardonic amusement in his reply. My heart sank.

I need to talk to you.

"Mackenzie, we need you inside now." The Summer Queen was holding open the door and gesturing me inside.

"I want to talk to Corrigan first."

"There's no time. We need to wrap this up now before things degenerate further."

I opened my mouth to refuse, but I was interrupted by the sounds of a scuffle from within Alcazon's private boardroom. Heart sinking, I walked inside. Beltran had cornered one of the other mages and the pair of them were shouting at each other. I yanked at the corner of his shirt and pulled him backwards.

"Get it together, you idiot," I hissed, despair that his petty altercation was preventing me from getting hold of Corrigan raging through me.

"Why don't you sit down, Mackenzie?" invited the Fae Queen, her tone all sweetness and light.

It took almost everything I had not to turn around and slap her but with the weight of everyone's eyes suddenly on me this wasn't the time to make my real feelings clear. Unfortunately it was neither appropriate to demand a little alone time with the Lord Alpha – not any longer. Instead, I took my seat. I could feel Corrigan looking at me, but somehow I couldn't turn round and meet his gaze. Everything was going all so very wrong.

Mack? What's wrong?

I swallowed. *Corrigan, I...*

"We've had a little meeting just now," declared the Arch-Mage. "And I'm pleased to say that I think we have a solution to our problems."

"Indeed," said the Summer Queen. "We are all agreed that we need to work together if we are to defeat Endor. He has already proven himself too powerful and, while we do not yet know what his end game really is, we must acknowledge that he is to be stopped before he even comes close."

There were mutterings of agreement. I was really rather hoping that Endor would take this very moment to appear and prevent her from saying anything more. No such luck, however.

She continued. "Therefore, we have decided that the most appropriate course of action is to appoint Mackenzie Smith as head of the council that will deal with his demise."

I could see Corrigan stiffening in the chair opposite me. I closed my eyes briefly as everyone swivelled back round to face me.

"As neither Fae nor mage nor shifter, she will be able to bring everyone together."

There was a moment of pure silence.

Mack? The wary doubt in Corrigan's Voice was clear.

"Hold on," said Beltran. "I don't deny that she's powerful. And that she has the makings of an effective leader, but isn't she kind of a shifter?"

"No. She's a Draco Wyr. It's different," stated Lucy firmly. "I think it's a brilliant idea."

What exactly is going here, Mack?

"Yeah, but, her and him," Larkin jerked his head towards Corrigan, "don't they kind of have a thing? She'll be looking out for his interests. Not ours."

Oh, Larkin, I thought sadly. Please shut up. Please, please, shut the hell up.

"I'll let Miss Mackenzie answer that one," said the Arch-Mage.

Don't make me do this here, I pleaded silently. It's not fair.

"Mackenzie?" The Summer Queen arched her eyebrows at me.

Blast it all. Surely there had to be another way? I looked round at all the faces turned expectantly towards me. Most were displaying open hope. Corrigan's expression was blank, his eyes cold chipped jade.

I'm sorry, Corrigan.

He didn't answer. I took a deep breath. "The Lord Alpha and I will maintain a purely platonic relationship. There is nothing more between us. Not any longer."

Lucy was staring at me, shock in her gaze, while Staines had a vaguely unsurprised expression. Corrigan didn't move a muscle.

"How do we know that's true?"

"Because I give you my word," I said quietly. I felt sick to my stomach.

"Excellent!" The Summer Queen clapped her hands. "Now can I suggest that we reconvene in, say, three days' time? You'll set up the Divination spells at the Ministry?" The Arch-Mage nodded. "And Balud, you'll begin research on a weapon." The troll grunted. "Miss Mackenzie, I'll leave to you to decide who to contact amongst the shifters to get some help with your transformations." She stood back up. "Ladies, gentlemen. I think that's what you call a success."

It had all happened so quickly. Clearly, the Seelie Queen could be lethal when she needed to be. I watched from my chair as she walked out, the other Faes trailing in her wake. Solus didn't look at me. The Arch- Mage and his minions followed, along with Balud and Aubrey, then Lucy and Staines both got up. They seemed reluctant to leave, but Corrigan flicked his wrist, and they both gave short bows and disappeared.

"Corrigan, I'm sorry. I didn't want to do things this way. You have to believe me."

I stared at him searchingly, waiting for him to give me something, anything in return. Eventually he lifted his eyes. The look in them was so cold and so hard that I recoiled.

"Corrigan…"

He stood up, pushing his chair backwards. It slammed hard against the wall, making me jump. "Who's the power hungry maniac now, kitten?"

I clenched my teeth, unhappiness seeping through every bone of my body. I opened my mouth to speak, but no words came out. What the fuck could I say?

"I don't ever want to see you again. Do you hear me?"

I nodded miserably.

"If you want help transforming then you can damn well contact Staines or Lucy or Tom. Leave me out of it." His tone was quiet and even, but the tension and anger he felt were visible. His hands shook as he gripped the edge of the table.

"Have you got that?"

I nodded again.

"I said have you fucking got that?" he snarled.

"Yes," I answered in a small voice. "I've got that."

"Good." He pivoted on his heel and stalked out without so much as a single backwards glance.

* * *

I got back home via the tube. Everyone else had already left. Even Aubrey seemed to have disappeared somewhere, realising that now was not the time to be getting in my way. My shiny red door gleamed as I approached, as if it were mocking me. I fumbled with my keys, finally managing to fit them into the lock and get it open. Then I carefully shut the door behind me and leaned my back against it. The pain in my chest was unbearable. Had it really only been a couple of hours since Corrigan and I had stood here holding each other? I'd hurt him so badly. I didn't blame him for never wanting to have anything to do with me again. I'd effectively just completely humiliated him in front of the mages, the Fae, and even his own shifters.

I walked into my little kitchen, shoulders sagging. The broken china, dribbles of coffee and collection of dead flowers still lay where I'd thrown them. I sighed and bent down to pick them all back up and dump them in the bin. Then I opened up the window to let in some fresh air and get rid of the faint smell of rotting garbage. A gust of wind sneaked in, ruffling my hair. A single tear dropped slowly down my cheek, and I wiped it angrily away. The papers on the table – the Fae translation of the story of my heritage - caught in the breeze, and several fluttered to the ground. With a heavy heart, I scooped them back up and attempted to put them into order.

As I did so, some words caught my attention. I stared at them unblinkingly. Of course. I let out a sharp humourless laugh that echoed sadly round the room.

Draco Wyr do not generally possess the ability that shifters do of being able to communicate telepathically with others. Occasionally they are able to receive such communications, but they are virtually never able to initiate them. However, it is generally acknowledged that when a Draco Wyr meets their soul mate, that is the one partner in the world with whom they are both physically and emotionally compatible, they are capable of not only receiving telepathic messages from that one person, but are also able to independently send them.

My legs gave out from under me and I sank down onto the cold floor. And I sobbed and sobbed and sobbed.

Thank you so much for reading Blood Politics! Bloodlust, the thrilling conclusion to Mack's tale is available now.

ABOUT THE AUTHOR

After teaching English literature in the UK, Japan and Malaysia, Helen Harper left behind the world of education following the worldwide success of her Blood Destiny series of books. She is a professional member of the Alliance of Independent Authors and writes full time, thanking her lucky stars every day that's she lucky enough to do so!

Helen has always been a book lover, devouring science fiction and fantasy tales when she was a child growing up in Scotland.

She currently lives in Edinburgh in the UK with far too many cats – not to mention the dragons, fairies, demons, wizards and vampires that seem to keep appearing from nowhere.

OTHER TITLES

The complete *FireBrand* series

A werewolf killer. A paranormal murder. How many times can Emma Bellamy cheat death?

I'm one placement away from becoming a fully fledged London detective. It's bad enough that my last assignment before I qualify is with Supernatural Squad. But that's nothing compared to what happens next.

Brutally murdered by an unknown assailant, I wake up twelve hours later in the morgue – and I'm very much alive. I don't know how or why it happened. I don't know who killed me. All I know is that they might try again.

Werewolves are disappearing right, left and centre.

A mysterious vampire seems intent on following me everywhere I go.

And I have to solve my own vicious killing. Preferably before death comes for me again.

* * *

A Charade of Magic complete series

The best way to live in the Mage ruled city of Glasgow is to keep your head down and your mouth closed.

That's not usually a problem for Mairi Wallace. By day she works at a small shop selling tartan and by night she studies to become an apothecary. She knows her place and her limitations. All that changes, however, when her old childhood friend sends her a desperate message seeking her help - and the Mages themselves cross Mairi's path. Suddenly, remaining unnoticed is no longer an option.

There's more to Mairi than she realises but, if she wants to fulfil her full potential, she's going to have to fight to stay alive - and only time will tell if she can beat the Mages at their own game.

From twisted wynds and tartan shops to a dangerous daemon and the magic infused City Chambers, the future of a nation might lie with one solitary woman.

Book One – Hummingbird

Book Two – Nightingale

Book Three – Red Hawk

* * *

The complete *Blood Destiny* series

"A spectacular and addictive series."

Mackenzie Smith has always known that she was different. Growing up as the only human in a pack of rural shapeshifters will do that to you, but then couple it with some mean fighting skills and a fiery temper and you end up with a woman that few will dare to cross. However, when the only father figure in her life is brutally murdered, and the dangerous Brethren with their predatory Lord Alpha come to investigate, Mack has to not only ensure the physical safety of her adopted family by hiding her apparent humanity, she also has to seek the blood-soaked vengeance that she craves.

Book One - Bloodfire

Book Two - Bloodmagic

Book Three - Bloodrage

Book Four - Blood Politics

Book Five - Bloodlust

Also

Corrigan Fire

Corrigan Magic

Corrigan Rage

Corrigan Politics

Corrigan Lust

* * *

The complete *Bo Blackman* series

A half-dead daemon, a massacre at her London based PI firm and evidence that suggests she's the main suspect for both ... Bo Blackman is having a very bad week.

She might be naive and inexperienced but she's determined to get to the bottom of the crimes, even if it means involving herself with one of London's most powerful vampire Families and their enigmatic leader.

It's pretty much going to be impossible for Bo to ever escape unscathed.

Book One - Dire Straits

Book Two - New Order

Book Three - High Stakes

Book Four - Red Angel

Book Five - Vigilante Vampire

Book Six - Dark Tomorrow

* * *

The complete *Highland Magic* series

Integrity Taylor walked away from the Sidhe when she was a child. Orphaned and bullied, she simply had no reason to stay, especially not when the sins of her father were going to remain on her shoulders. She found a new family - a group of thieves who proved that blood was less important than loyalty and love.

But the Sidhe aren't going to let Integrity stay away forever. They need her more than anyone realises - besides, there are prophecies to be fulfilled, people to be saved and hearts to be won over. If anyone can do it, Integrity can.

Book One - Gifted Thief

Book Two - Honour Bound

Book Three - Veiled Threat

Book Four - Last Wish

* * *

The complete *Dreamweaver* series

"I have special coping mechanisms for the times I need to open the front door. They're even often successful..."

Zoe Lydon knows there's often nothing logical or rational about fear. It doesn't change the fact that she's too terrified to step outside her own house, however.

What Zoe doesn't realise is that she's also a dreamweaver - able to access other people's subconscious minds. When she finds herself in the Dreamlands and up against its sinister Mayor, she'll need to use all of her wits - and overcome all of her fears - if she's ever going to come out alive.

Book One - Night Shade

Book Two - Night Terrors

Book Three - Night Lights

* * *

Stand alone novels

Eros

William Shakespeare once wrote that, "Cupid is a knavish lad, thus to make poor females mad." The trouble is that Cupid himself would probably agree…

As probably the last person in the world who'd appreciate hearts, flowers and romance, Coop is convinced that true love doesn't exist – which is rather unfortunate considering he's also known as Cupid, the God of Love. He'd rather spend his days drinking, womanising and generally having as much fun as he possible can. As far as he's concerned, shooting people with bolts of pure love is a waste of his time…but then his path crosses with that of shy and retiring Skye Sawyer and nothing will ever be quite the same again.

Wraith

Magic. Shadows. Adventure. Romance.

Saiya Buchanan is a wraith, able to detach her shadow from her body and send it off to do her bidding. But, unlike most of her kin, Saiya doesn't deal in death. Instead, she trades secrets - and in the goblin besieged city of Stirling in Scotland, they're a highly prized commodity. It might just be, however, that the goblins have been hiding the greatest secret of them all. When Gabriel de Florinville, a Dark Elf, is sent as royal envoy into Stirling and takes her prisoner, Saiya is not only going to uncover the sinister truth. She's also going to realise that sometimes the deepest secrets are the ones locked within your own heart.

* * *

The complete *Lazy Girl's Guide To Magic* series

Hard Work Will Pay Off Later. Laziness Pays Off Now.

Let's get one thing straight - Ivy Wilde is not a heroine. In fact, she's probably the last witch in the world who you'd call if you needed a magical helping hand. If it were down to Ivy, she'd spend all day every day on her sofa where she could watch TV, munch junk food and talk to her feline familiar to her heart's content.

However, when a bureaucratic disaster ends up with Ivy as the victim of a case of mistaken identity, she's yanked very unwillingly into Arcane Branch, the investigative department of the Hallowed Order of Magical Enlightenment. Her problems are quadrupled when a valuable object is stolen right from under the Order's noses.

It doesn't exactly help that she's been magically bound to Adeptus Exemptus Raphael Winter. He might have piercing sapphire eyes and a body which a cover model would be proud of but, as far as Ivy's concerned, he's a walking advertisement for the joyless perils of too much witch-work.

And if he makes her go to the gym again, she's definitely going to turn him into a frog.

Book One - Slouch Witch
Book Two - Star Witch
Book Three - Spirit Witch

Sparkle Witch (Christmas novella)

* * *

The complete *Fractured Faery* series

One corpse. Several bizarre looking attackers. Some very strange magical powers. And a severe bout of amnesia.

It's one thing to wake up outside in the middle of the night with a decapitated man for company. It's another to have no memory of how you got there - or who you are.

She might not know her own name but she knows that several people are out to get her. It could be because she has strange magical powers seemingly at her fingertips and is some kind of fabulous hero. But then why does she appear to inspire fear in so many? And who on earth is the sexy, green-eyed barman who apparently despises her? So many questions ... and so few answers.

At least one thing is for sure - the streets of Manchester have never met someone quite as mad as Madrona…

Book One - Box of Frogs

SHORTLISTED FOR THE KINDLE STORYTELLER AWARD 2018

Book Two - Quiver of Cobras

Book Three - Skulk of Foxes

* * *

The complete *City Of Magic* series

Charley is a cleaner by day and a professional gambler by night. She might be haunted by her tragic past but she's never thought of herself as anything or anyone special. Until, that is, things start to go terribly wrong all across the city of Manchester. Between plagues of rats, firestorms and the gleaming blue eyes of a sexy Scottish werewolf, she might just have landed herself in the middle of a magical apocalypse. She might also be the only person who has the ability to bring order to an utterly chaotic new world.

Book One - Shrill Dusk

Book Two - Brittle Midnight

Book Three - Furtive Dawn

Printed in Great Britain
by Amazon

45693447R00158